"You do *not* know what I feel," she accused.

Burke stared speechless at her until finally he spoke. "Every time we make love, we feel each other's need—each other's love! It's there in our touch, in our kiss. It cannot be denied, ignored or dismissed. You will have to face it eventually. I love you, Storm—and there's no changing it or denying it."

"Don't love me," she nearly shouted at him.

He laughed. "You can't command my love."

"It can never be," she said, shaking her head.

"It already is," he said, and reached out and drew her into his arms.

And she didn't have the strength to fight him any more . . .

Other **AVON ROMANCES**

DONNA FLETCHER

Taken By Storm

AVON BOOKS
An Imprint of HarperCollins*Publishers*

This is a work of fiction. Names, characters, places, and incidents are products of the author's imagination or are used fictitiously and are not to be construed as real. Any resemblance to actual events, locales, organizations, or persons, living or dead, is entirely coincidental.

AVON BOOKS
An Imprint of HarperCollins*Publishers*
10 East 53rd Street
New York, New York 10022-5299

Copyright © 2006 by Donna Fletcher
ISBN-13: 978-0-06-113625-2
ISBN-10: 0-06-113625-5
www.avonromance.com

First Avon Books paperback printing: October 2006

Printed in the U.S.A.

10 9 8 7 6 5 4 3 2 1

Chapter 1

Burke Longton grabbed hold of his chains and scrambled to his feet as soon as the motley crew of five stormed his prison cell. He didn't know for whom, out of the six in the cell, they had come, but he intended to make sure he left with them. Two weeks in this stinking hellhole had been enough. He wanted out and he wanted home.

"There's little time," the tallest of the men said. "Follow our orders and we'll get you out of here."

Burke had no problem with that. Whatever it took to be free, he was ready, and it looked like the other prisoners agreed. All had gotten to their feet, some with difficulty, and held out chained wrists, eager to be rid of the weighted metal cuffs that had rubbed their flesh raw.

Their jailer suddenly stumbled into the room, and Burke glared at him. He hated the sight of the

1

paunchy man. His entrance always heralded torture, and his enjoyment of his job was obvious from the constant smile he wore.

Only this time, the jailer looked fearful, his eyes wide, sweat pouring down his reddened cheeks.

"The keys!"

Burke blinked twice. Had a lad stepped from behind the jailer? He shook his head, too many curves in just the right places. It was a woman, a pint-sized one garbed in men's clothing, and she handled the sword that was almost her size with confidence. She pushed the point right between the folds of his thick neck.

"I'll not ask again," she warned.

Burke smirked when, with an effortless flick of the blade, she nicked his skin and a rivulet of blood cascaded down his chest to pool on his grimy shirt. The man eagerly fumbled keys over to her.

"Tanin," she said, tossing the ring to the tallest man.

The man reached out. The metal ring hooked on one of his long fingers, he then worked fast freeing everyone while two men trussed up the jailer like a fat pig for roasting.

"He'll need help." The woman nodded toward a man who was having trouble standing on his own. Then she searched the room with wide, stormy blue eyes. The color reminded Burke of a turbulent ocean just before a gale force hit. For a brief moment, he wondered if fiery red curls lay beneath her knit cap to match the squall surfacing in her eyes.

"I don't see him," she said, annoyed.

"This is where I was told he'd be." Tanin walked over to her, and together they searched the darkened corners of the cell.

It was obvious they were looking for someone in particular and Burke had the feeling he knew whom. The guards had brought the young man in only last night, but they acted as if they had captured a rare prize. They had strutted and pranced around him while gleefully detailing what they intended to do to him. His response hadn't been what they'd expected.

"They took a young man out of here a short time ago," Burke said now.

The woman approached him with confidence and not an ounce of fear. It did not intimidate her a bit to have to tilt her head back to gaze up at him, his height close to six feet.

"Do you know where he was taken, and is he all right?"

"He's a strong one for a skinny kid," Burke said. "Though I think it was spitting in the jailer's face that did him in."

The woman grinned. "That's Malcolm."

"I'm not sure where he is, but after he was dragged out by several guards, I heard a door slam not far off and the clink of a key in a lock."

"The cells at the end of the tunnel," Tanin said and handed her the keys.

The woman eyed the prisoners ready to leave. "There's no time to waste. Get them out of here."

Burke was shocked that the tall man turned and did as he was told. How the hell could he leave the small wisp of a woman on her own to free one of their comrades?

I'll help you," Burke offered.

"No. You'll go with them."

She gave him a shove that he didn't appreciate, and it only served to make him stand his ground.

"You'll need help," he insisted.

"Not likely," she said, sounding affronted. "It's none of your concern. Now go."

She dismissed him with the turn of her back and took off past the prisoners who were standing in a single file, eager to make their escape.

Tanin waved for him to take up the rear and he did, though reluctantly. He just couldn't believe all five men would allow a single, pea-sized woman to go off on her own to rescue a man. Where was their common sense?

Burke reminded himself that Scotland was far different from America. Sure there were strong women in America, especially in the Dakota Territory, where he came from, but a man protected a woman. He was stronger and more capable, and it was a man's duty to look after women. Hadn't his father taught him that? And wasn't his deceased father the reason he was here in this mess in the first place?

He shook his head as they quietly made their way down the passageway, a single torch guiding their way.

A clang of steel had them freezing in their tracks, and Tanin ordered everyone to hurry. Burke glanced back and spotted where the passageway veered off into a darkened tunnel.

He had only a moment to make his decision, but it was an easy one. There was no way he'd leave that woman on her own, whether she liked it or not.

Burke could barely make out where he was going. His broad shoulders bumped into the narrow tunnel walls now and again, and dust collected in his nostrils from the dry dirt his boots kicked up.

He wondered why he hadn't collided with the woman yet. She hadn't had that much of a head start on him. And with it being so dark, she couldn't possibly have traveled that fast.

The whining screech of rusty hinges stopped him dead. A clang of chains, muffled voices, and then suddenly hasty footfalls approached from the opposite direction.

Burke readied himself, intending to take the person down and find out his identity later. He waited in the dark, listening, judging the distance, and when the time was right . . .

His arm shot out and the man crumpled to the ground, probably not knowing what had hit him.

In an instant, the woman was in his face, her blue eyes the color of a gale storm that would put fear in the staunchest of sailors.

"I gave you orders," she snapped.

Burke was good at giving orders, not taking them, and certainly not from this wee wisp of a woman.

"I thought you might need my help—and I was right." He leaned down, grabbed the dirk in the guard's waistband, and held it in front of her face.

"You thought wrong. I would have handled him."

She shoved him aside. "We need to get out of here now."

The narrow passageway afforded little room, and in stepping over the unconscious man, she all but melded with Burke to brush past him. He felt her sleek frame coil, tense, and move off, all in a split second.

She once again issued orders.

"Malcolm, stay behind him. And you—" She jabbed at Burke's chest. "Do as I say."

Malcolm leaned into him. "Do what Storm says. Believe me, you don't want her mad at you."

Her name certainly fit her, but then he had weathered enough storms in his life. This little tempest wouldn't intimidate him.

"Make another mistake, stranger, and you're dead," she warned as if making a casual remark. "Let's go."

Malcolm nudged him this time. "Storm takes getting used to."

You could say that again, Burke thought. Sandwiched between the pair, he easily kept pace with them. He followed her sure-footed steps without complaint since he had no idea how to get out of there, and he didn't intend to be left behind.

They came upon a dimly lit passageway and made their way to a flight of steps, then up a circular stone staircase and out into the dusky night.

Pungent pine and crisp autumn air greeted him, and with a deep breath, he drank greedily of freedom. He caught that breath when stung by the warning in Storm's eyes for silence.

She signaled them to follow, reminding him once again to be silent before she crept cautiously against the stone wall of the prison.

Burke followed and as they came to the edge of the corner, he caught sight of the last of the prisoners disappearing into the woods a few feet away. Tanin gave a signal, then merged with the thick trees.

Storm stepped forward, just as a guard came into sight. While the young guard fumbled for his sword, Burke reacted instinctively, pouncing on him with a solid blow to his jaw that knocked him out cold. He turned to grab Storm's arm and head for the cover of the trees but she sidestepped him.

"Get him out of here, Malcolm, before I run my blade through him," Storm said, pointing her sword at Burke.

"Let's go," Malcolm said, grabbing his arm.

Burke yanked his arm free, and before he could say a word, he felt the point of a blade at his neck.

"I'll not warn you again about following my orders. Go with Malcolm or feel my sword. The choice is yours."

"You certainly don't respond well to a helping hand."

She pressed the sword to his neck, not enough to draw blood, but to warn that she meant business.

"Fine," Burke said through gritted teeth.

She withdrew the blade, and Burke, swearing beneath his breath, followed Malcolm.

Chapter 2

Storm couldn't wait to get rid of the American. He had done nothing but interfere with her carefully laid plans. She could tell that he wasn't used to following orders and that he could handle himself in a difficult situation. However, this was her command, her battle, her land.

Which was why, at the first possible chance, she would leave him somewhere safe enough, but she wanted to be rid of him. She couldn't take the chance of his messing things up any more than he already had.

She did wonder why he had been imprisoned, but then it didn't take much of an accusation to be incarcerated. He had probably been in the wrong place at the wrong time or he didn't have enough money to pay the bribe on trumped-up charges. Either way, it was not her concern.

He glanced back at her from where he walked a few feet ahead. He had done that from time to time, almost as if he watched out for her. She needed no one doing that. She was more than capable of looking after herself.

She did have to give him credit for keeping up the tough pace she had set for the group throughout the night. He looked sturdy enough, muscled arms and thighs attested to his strength. His dark trousers were torn at the knee and his white shirt ripped at the shoulder. Dark brown eyes were set in a rugged face marred by a few cuts and bruises and covered with dirt and sweat. His unkempt brown hair brushed his shoulders, and she had noticed that his hand had drifted often to his side—a common gesture for a man used to having a weapon strapped to his leg.

He looked back again and held her glance. There was determination and annoyance in his brown eyes, which suddenly widened as he rushed at her.

She mumbled an oath as her foot caught on an exposed tree root and she tumbled forward.

Storm felt his hands snag tightly around her slim waist and yank her up on her feet. She wobbled, and her hands shot out to grab hold of his forearms. There was a solid strength in them that could not be denied.

"I got you, don't worry."

She gave him a hefty shove and waved off Tanin, who approached. "Keep going. I'm fine. I need a few minutes with this man."

"No need to thank me for helping you, yet a third time," he said with a grin.

"I have no intention of thanking you and I don't need you rescuing me."

"That's debatable."

"No. It's not," she said firmly. "I do fine on my own. Now where is it you'd like to go? I'll see that you get there." She wanted rid of him as quickly as possible, or else she had the distinct feeling he'd forever get in her way.

"Dunwith."

"A day's journey. What takes you there?" she asked, curious.

"Personal business."

"Anything to do with what landed you in prison?"

"That was a complete misunderstanding," he said emphatically.

"It usually is, though the magistrate rarely sees it that way."

"A robbery, a fight, and a—"

"Setup," she finished. "They took all your money and you had nothing to pay the fine. Did you tell them you could get more money?"

"I'm not that stupid." He sounded insulted. "Besides, the money I had arranged to be brought here won't be available to me for two weeks."

"So you're presently penniless and homeless."

"Only for the moment, and, like you, I can take care of myself."

His brown eyes flared, giving his rugged features a devilish appeal that momentarily stunned her. "Good, then I'll see that one of my men makes sure you get to Dunwith."

"What of the others?" he asked.

"Those prisoners unable to walk much farther will be left with friends who will see them moved to a safe location. The others will be given a choice to go off on their own or to join with my group."

"What if I want to join with your group?"

She stopped short and glared at him. "Why would you want to do that?"

"Don't want my help?"

He was obviously amused by her remark, a half smile highlighting his sweat-dappled face. She wasn't at all amused. "No!"

"Why?"

"You don't take orders well."

"I don't take them at all."

"Obviously." She admired his abrupt honesty. "Why would you want to join us? I thought you said you had personal business in Dunwith."

"I do, but until my funds arrive, there isn't much I can do. Besides, I'm sure you could always use an extra pair of skilled hands."

She shook her head. "I don't think so. My men are well trained to obey me. Can you obey me?"

"I can follow orders."

"Can you obey me?" she repeated.

She could see the struggle in his eyes and in the pinch of his narrow lips. He was fighting with himself, though the answer was clear. He couldn't obey a woman.

"I've been taught to protect women."

"I don't need protection. I need obedience." She smiled when he cringed.

"I'll do my best."

"Not good enough. My men work together under my command. I never worry that they won't obey me and they never worry that I will fail them. That is why we've been so successful in our rescues. Go to Dunwith, Mr.—"

"Burke, Burke Longton," he said, holding out his hand.

Storm took it, his callused palm rubbing across hers and taking firm hold. The solid handshake told her he was a man who meant business, and that he didn't let go of her hand told her he was determined to have things his way.

"Once my funds arrive, I'll be on my way. Until then, let me help you."

Storm tugged her hand out of his, crossed her arms over her chest, and eyed him with a suspicious glance. "What is it you really want from me, Mr. Longton?"

"The name is Burke, Storm. And what I *need* from you is knowledge of this land and its people before I attend to my business. I had thought my task an easy one but I have realized it is going to be more difficult than I first thought."

"I have no time—"

"I will make it worth your time."

Storm hesitated. She needed funds, but was it worth it? This towering man could not follow the simplest of orders, and that could prove dangerous. Was she willing to put her men and people in jeopardy in exchange for a much needed filling of the coffers? And how could she be certain he spoke the truth that funds were on the way?

"I can be an asset," he continued.

"So far you have proved nothing but a liability."

"I beg to differ."

She ignored his remark. "How do I know these funds exist?"

"Good question," he said, running his fingers through his hair, "though not easy to answer. There really isn't any way I can prove that I have sufficient funds to offer you." He paused. "I can only give you my word."

Again, he was straightforward with his answer. However, was that enough to rule him an honest man? She thought herself a good judge of character—that was how she had been able to form her group of men. She had judged each one individually on his own unique merits, and all had proved worthy.

This man had a look of worthiness about him, and his concern for her safety attested to his honorable character. He would defend the defenseless, though his opinion on who needed defending was somewhat skewed.

Still, her main concern was his reluctance—actually his refusal—to follow her orders. The safety of her village depended on everyone obeying her rules. One person not following those rules placed the village in jeopardy. Burke's presence alone could do that.

"Have you given it enough thought?"

He sounded anxious.

"I have a duty to protect my people."

"I would bring no harm to your group."

"Not intentionally," she said.

"What of the money? Don't tell me you can't use it? Since my arrival in Scotland, I have seen with my own eyes the suffering of the less fortunate. Money would ease that suffering considerably."

He was right about that. Their food supply had dwindled to a dangerous low, and they would need to replenish it before winter.

"I can tell you are a sensible leader—"

"Yet you cannot obey me."

Burke shook his head. "Your head reaches my chest, and in those clothes you resemble a mere lad. You don't exactly look like a leader."

Her protest died at his outstretched hand.

"Let me finish. Your actions demonstrate your leadership abilities, and that your men obey you without question tells me they admire and respect you. Which means you will do what is necessary for your people."

He had that right. Her decisions were always based on the good of the whole, not merely the one. But his inability to obey orders could be a detriment to the group; his funds, however, would definitely prove beneficial.

"Let me think about this," she said.

"How long?"

"Until we reach our first destination, a couple of hours at least. Now let's get moving. We need to catch up with the others."

Storm waited for him to pass her, and for a

moment he looked as if he stubbornly refused to move. He stood stone still, his brown eyes fixed on her as if in a trance, and then suddenly he jolted forward and hurried past her.

The group's pace slowed at times in consideration for those few who found it difficult to keep up, and a persistent cloud followed them overhead. Otherwise, they met no obstacles.

Storm had no time to think further on her decision. She conferred with her men who scouted the area, adjusted her plan in case anyone had gotten wind of it, and determined which of the prisoners were in need of care.

She took a moment to stop for a breath and take in the beauty of the woods. Small pauses were necessary now and again, or else she would be forever lost in fighting to survive.

It hadn't always been like this. Life had been good once. She had loved each and every day, and then she'd lost the most precious thing in her life—her husband.

She chased the thought from her mind, or else it would consume her, beat her down, and devastate her all over again. She couldn't allow that to happen; she had people who counted on her. Which reminded her that she had a decision to make in regard to the American.

She had never turned away anyone in need of help. But why did he need to know about her homeland of Scotland? What had brought Mr. Longton to its shores? She had to be careful whom she trusted. There was a bounty on her head, but surely a man

15

from America would know nothing about that. Would he?

Shortly they would arrive at their first destination and she would need to make a choice. Let him join her group or cut him loose. She drifted back until she walked alongside him.

"Made your decision yet?" he asked.

"I've thought on it."

"Anything I can do to sway your choice?"

"Tell me what brought you to Scotland."

His brown eyes glared down at her. "I'm here to find my half brother and I don't intend to leave until I do."

Chapter 3

It's a long story and I don't want to bore you with it. Needless to say, it's imperative I find my half brother, and I've been told that I might find him in Dunwith," Burke said. He would feed Storm what was necessary for her to help him, for now, especially since he had discovered there might be a bounty on his brother's head.

"Does he know you search for him?" she asked.

"He doesn't know of my arrival." That his brother didn't even know of his existence wasn't something he was willing to share with her just yet. Her suspicion of his explanation was obvious in the tight set of her rosy lips and the squint of her turbulent blue eyes.

"What exactly do you want of me if I grant you permission to remain with us?"

He could tell that she was giving it thought, so he

was confident he could convince her to let him stay; besides, she intrigued him. She was a pint-sized bundle of courage and damned fair on the eyes. He couldn't help but wonder how she'd look without the stocking cap.

"I need to learn what I can of your land and its people."

"What in particular?"

"I'm not sure. I don't know exactly what will help me locate my brother. I think if I familiarize myself with Scotland and its people, it might help me to understand my brother and then eventually help me to find him. Otherwise I feel like I'm shooting at a target in the dark." That all wasn't exactly true, but it wasn't necessary for her to know that he had hired detectives to help locate his brother and they had given him a starting point.

She smiled, and he felt a catch in his heart. It was such a sincere smile and sparked a beauty in her face that he found hard to ignore.

"Targets can easily be hit in the dark, Burke."

Damned if he didn't like the way his name rolled off her tongue in her sweet Scottish burr.

He took a step closer to her. "You'll have to teach me the secret of hitting a target in the dark." Not that he didn't already know, but it would make for an interesting evening.

She shook her head, her smile never wavering. "I think you already have such skills."

Burke rubbed his hands together and grinned. "I think we'll get along well together."

"As long as you can obey me."

"Back to that again?"

"If you want to remain with my group, you will follow orders like everyone else," she said firmly.

"So if I agree to obey you, then you'll let me join the group?"

"Remain with the group," she corrected. "You won't be joining in any rescues."

"Somehow I doubt that."

She laughed. "We'll see about that, Burke."

Damn, he really liked hearing her say his name.

"So what do you say? Follow my orders and I'll help you find your brother for an agreed-upon fee."

He held out his hand. "I accept."

She hesitated. "I'd rather hear you say you will follow my orders."

She was going to be a challenge for sure, but, hell, he lived for challenges. Besides, she had amended "obey" to "follow," so he could live with that.

"I'll follow your orders."

She accepted his handshake. "Then we have a deal."

"As to the fee?"

"We'll talk on that later. I have things to see to."

"Anything I can help with?" he offered. He wasn't out to impress Storm, but he did want to show her that he would pull his weight.

"Something tells me you're a good hunter."

His grin turned to a low laugh. "Something tells me you're perceptive."

"Be wise and remember that."

"I've never been called a fool."

"There's always a first time." Storm smiled and

signaled Tanin, who hurried to her side. "Take Burke here with you to hunt for tonight's meal. He's going to be staying with the group for a while."

Storm walked off, stopped abruptly, and spun around. "Burke, Tanin's my right-hand man; obey him as you would me."

"Whatever you say, Storm," Burke said.

She laughed, shook her head, and walked off.

"We're limited in weapon choice," Tanin said.

Burke was forced to take his eyes off Storm's retreating back, actually her curvaceous hips. Her snug dark trousers let all eyes know that she was definitely female. And being male, he appreciated the beauty of her sensual sway.

"I'm versatile when it comes to weapons. What have you got?"

Storm watched the prisoners eat the roasted venison with gusto. They had made it across the river and into the thick of the woods hours ago. They would not be followed. The king's men feared her forest. They believed she had bewitched it to serve her purposes, and with good reason. Not one of the king's men who had entered had ever left or been found.

She smiled at the thought. A few of the soldiers had begged to join her group, while others took flight to freedom. And stupidity had claimed the lives of the rest.

Tanin approached with a piece of meat for her.

She took it with a warning. "Not another word of how proficient Burke is with a bow and arrow."

"I tell you, Storm, I have never seen anyone with such remarkable skill. He focused on his target, drew back on his bow, and—" He shook his head. "He fired on a fast-moving target and hit it dead on."

"So you have told me, what? Ten, twenty times now?"

"He will be an asset to the group."

"A temporary one," she informed him.

"Who looks forward to his time with all of you."

Storm would have toppled off the rock she was sitting on if Burke hadn't quickly wrapped his arm around her middle and held her firm.

"Easy now," he said, standing behind her.

"I didn't hear you approach," Tanin said with awe.

"A skill I learned from a tracker friend of mine."

Storm rested her back against his chest, his heat seeping into her, and for a moment, she felt relaxed and secure. The thought jolted her, and she quickly dislodged his arm and scooted across the large rock, turning to face him.

"I don't appreciate you spying on us," she said, annoyed.

"Not my intention," Burke assured her. "I simply took a brief walk, heard voices, and, recognizing them, decided to join you."

"Your friend can track in the dark?" Tanin asked, his awe still obvious.

"Don't you have duties to attend to?" Storm snapped at Tanin.

Tanin nodded, seeming unperturbed by Storm's annoyance. "I'd like to learn some of that skill."

"Any time," Burke agreed.

"More food?" Tanin asked.

Storm shook her head. "Thanks, I've had enough, but make sure you enjoy your share."

"Feel guilty you snapped at him?" Burke asked after Tanin walked away.

Storm almost snapped again but instead took a breath and measured her words. "Tanin is a good man. He knows my strengths and my weaknesses and exploits neither. That is why I trust him with my life."

"He speaks highly of you as well."

Storm chuckled. "Tanin would say little to you about me."

"That confident about him?"

"That confident," she assured him.

"You have beautiful blue eyes."

Surprise widened Storm's eyes. "How can you be so sure in the dark, Mr. Longton?"

Burke took gentle hold of her chin and lifted. "The moonlight makes the blue appear the color of the sea set to squall—beautiful, tempting, yet unforgiving. Are you unforgiving, Storm?"

"In some regards I am," she answered, her heart suddenly pounding in her chest, reminding her of the hurt and pain she had suffered and how unforgiving she had become.

"Suffering often brings strength."

She turned her head, her chin slipping from his fingers. "Easy words to utter when the suffering has finally passed, but suffering is suffering, Mr. Longton, no matter what way you look at it."

"Agreed, but strength is strength, Storm, and I

daresay your suffering must have been great to have given you the strength you now possess. Perhaps someday you will share your pain with me."

"You will not be here long enough for me to trust you with such a confidence. And besides, you have not fully trusted me."

"How so?" he asked.

"Your brother. There is more to your finding him, is there not?"

Burke leaned against the rock.

"If you withhold information about your brother, how will I ever be able to help you locate him?"

Burke crossed his arms over his chest and stared into the night.

Storm sensed he wrestled with the decision to trust her, but what choice did he truly have if he wished to find his brother?

He relented. "I've never met my half brother, Cullen, though my father had spoken of him to me since I was young. He told me how he left his year-old son with his deceased wife's sister while he journeyed to America to build a new life. He met and married my mother, and they staked a claim in the Dakota Territory together. My father returned to Scotland before I was born to get Cullen, but when he arrived, he discovered that his sister-in-law had died and no one knew where his son had gone.

"My father searched throughout the years, and on his deathbed two years ago made me swear to find my brother and bring him home, and to let him know he had never stopped searching for him. I gave my word I would. Besides—" Burke turned to look at Storm. "He's my brother, he's family, and he needs to finally come home."

"I understand," Storm said, "but he may not want to go to America. Scotland is his home, his heart is here."

"Perhaps he'll have no choice."

"Why is that?"

"I learned that there may be a bounty on his head," he acknowledged reluctantly.

"Why?"

"I don't know. It was secondhand information and I had no way of confirming it, but Dunwith was mentioned and I figured I'd see what I could find out there." That was all the information the detectives had to give him.

Storm slipped off the rock to stand beside him. "I'll have Malcolm take the group the remainder of the way. Tanin, you, and I will proceed to Dunwith tomorrow morning and see what we can find out."

Burke pushed off the rock. "Why?"

"Because it's a shorter journey from here than if we return to camp."

Burke shook his head. "No. I mean why are you coming along? Why not just send me with Tanin?"

"I have friends in Dunwith who may be of help."

"I appreciate your generosity."

"Your money is buying my help, Mr. Longton."

"Burke." He smiled. "After all, I am part of your group now."

"You are a visitor, not a permanent member," she

reminded. "Now I suggest we get a sound night's sleep. We'll leave with dawn's first light and should arrive at Dunwith by late morning."

"I appreciate your haste in helping me."

"I have good reason for it."

"To get me out of your hair faster?"

Storm laughed and patted her head. "My hair is well protected."

"Is it now?" he asked, and in a split second snatched the cap off her head.

Waves of silky black hair tumbled down around her face, over her shoulders, to finally rest at the middle of her back.

"I had thought fiery red," Burke said, swinging the stocking cap on his finger. "But the stark black color highlights your blue eyes. You are quite a beauty for a criminal."

Storm snatched her cap back. "Don't they teach manners in America?"

"We're not at a social function. We're in the middle of dense woods, two strangers who currently need each other. I wanted to know whom I dealt with."

"And you needed to remove my cap to discover that?"

"The Sioux Indian tribe, indigenous to the area I come from, believe that you must view the whole person with your eyes and heart if you are ever to know whom you truly deal with. Part of you hides beneath that cap."

"It disguises my gender, nothing more," she insisted.

"It disguises much more, and I intend to discover who you truly are, Storm."

She jabbed him in the chest. "Be careful, Burke. You may not like what you discover."

Chapter 4

Dunwith had once been a thriving village surrounded by tenant farms, all owned by the landlord whose manor house sat on a rise looking down over the land. Like many villages throughout Scotland, it had repeatedly suffered poor harvests. Poverty and famine were driving thousands to flee Scotland for the promise of rich land and bountiful harvests elsewhere.

Some Scots had left years earlier and had found that promise in America. Burke wondered if Storm had ever considered joining the throngs of disillusioned Scots.

"Stay here," Storm ordered, catching his attention. "I'll be right back."

Burke watched her disappear into the dense woods after she took the rolled bedding Tanin carried. He wondered what she was up to, but he didn't ask. Instead he had watched her actions and had begun to learn about her.

Storm knew the forest as if she were part of it, as if they beat to the same pulse. She never stopped to make certain her direction was accurate. She paced her steps and maneuvered around the trees and hills, never faltering in her footing.

"Storm handles herself well," Tanin said, drawing his attention.

"She's just a pint-sized thing. You would never expect—"

"She counts on people thinking her fragile."

"I have to ask you," Burke said. "Didn't she ever think of looking for a better life elsewhere?"

"You mean emigrate like so many have been forced to do?"

Burke nodded. "Exactly. What does she have here?"

"Her dignity and her home," Tanin answered with pride. "Storm couldn't watch helpless as her people suffered. She took action and was immediately forced into the thick of things."

"And into the thick of danger," Burke reminded him with concern.

"It was her choice."

"Was it?"

The crunch of leaves alerted them to Storm's approach. He turned to greet her and was struck speechless. She was dressed in a brown skirt, long-sleeved tan blouse, and brown wool vest. A deep green shawl hung loosely over her shoulders and around her arms, and her black hair bounced in waves around her lovely face with each step she took.

That she was a beautiful woman was undeniable.

"Ready," she said, handing Tanin the rolled bedding to carry at his side.

"So this is the real Storm," Burke said with a smile.

"Don't be so sure." Storm grinned and bent down to dust her hands with dirt. She applied some to her face here and there, though to Burke it did nothing to mar her beauty.

"Disguise?" Burke asked.

"We're weary, hungry travelers in search of food. We need to look the part if we want to be trusted and so my friends are not made suspicious when we speak with them."

Burke nodded at her sensible reasoning, though he didn't need to copy her actions. His face was already grime-ridden. He couldn't wait to wash the dirt off him.

"We stay no more than thirty minutes," Storm said.

"Is that enough time to find out about my brother?"

"If we haven't found out anything by then, we won't, and I won't place us in jeopardy."

Burke didn't respond, though he would have liked to tell her that he intended to stay longer if it meant it would help him find his brother. But that was his impatience gnawing at him. Storm was right, and he'd defer to her orders—this time.

The people cast suspicious glances at them when

they entered the village. Some even stood guard over what little crop was left to harvest in their gardens. Lack of food was obvious in their gaunt faces, and hopelessness weighed heavy on slumped shoulders.

Burke was reminded of a similar scene, when one especially hard winter had hit the Dakota Territory and crops were slow in harvesting if they harvested at all. He had ridden with his tracker friend who had been raised in the white world but whose mother had been full-blooded Sioux to see how the village had fared.

It hadn't, and much work was needed to help the people recover, and to make certain they didn't suffer again.

"You need food?" a stout woman asked, walking over to Storm.

"We would be grateful for any you could spare," Storm said softly, her head bowed.

"I have bread and mead to share," the woman offered. "Follow me."

"Accept the mead, not the bread, " Storm murmured to Burke before entering the small cottage the woman took them to.

Tears pooled in the woman's green eyes. "You are safe, Storm, thank God. We had heard you had been captured."

Storm laughed and gave her a hug. "Please, Hannah, you insult me."

Hannah giggled. "I told John you would never be caught. The heavens protect you."

"Where is that husband of yours?" Storm asked,

casting a quick glance around the single, sparse room.

Hannah brushed at her falling tears. "Taking his life in his hands so that we do not starve." She shook her head. "The fool is hunting on the earl's property."

"Tanin," Storm said, though the tall man was already at the door.

"What direction did he go in?"

Hannah blessed Tanin after telling him where to find her husband, and Storm told him to meet her in the woods when he finished.

Burke waited silently. Storm obviously knew what she was doing and it would not do him any good to interfere. Besides, he marveled at her compassion and understanding.

He had been furious the day he rode into the Sioux camp and found people starving, no food to be found. The little food he had brought with him had still been offered to him first, for it would have been rude for them not to share what little they had, just as Hannah did now.

He wished he had money with him so that he could give her enough to flee this wasteful life and start new in America, on his ranch if necessary.

"I need your help," Storm said, taking Hannah's hand and sitting at the table with her.

"Whatever I can do for you," Hannah obliged, and filled two tankards with mead from the pitcher on the table.

"I search for a man," Storm said, handing a tankard to Burke. "His name is Cullen Longton."

31

Burke stood beside Storm, since there were only two chairs.

"I was told he may have passed through here, and there may be a bounty on him."

Hannah's eyes widened. "There was a man accused of poaching on Dunwith land, but he was taken to Glencurry."

"Why?" Storm asked.

Burke didn't like the tone of her "why." Something was wrong.

Hannah shook her head. "None understood why. If he poached on Dunwith land, then here is where he should be tried and convicted, but he was whisked away."

Burke took a step forward, but Storm's hand shot out and jabbed at his thigh. He heeded her warning and stood still, fighting the urge to question the woman.

"More mead?" Hannah asked Burke.

He nodded and held out his tankard.

"When did this occur?" Storm asked.

"Three, maybe four weeks ago."

"Do you know for certain if his name was Cullen?" Storm asked.

"I cannot say for certain, but the name does sound familiar."

Storm stood. "We must go." She took Hannah's hand and dropped several coins in it.

"I cannot," Hannah protested. "There are those needier than me."

"And this man beside me has agreed to help them, leaving you free to accept this gift."

Burke finally spoke. "Storm is right."

Hannah wept, hugging the coins to her chest. "You are a godsend, Storm."

"Some claim I'm the devil." She laughed.

"No, an angel. This will feed my family and others. God bless."

After quick hugs and more tears, Storm and Burke took their leave and made their way to the woods unnoticed.

"We wait for Tanin," Storm said, pacing the forest floor, the crunch of leaves distinct beneath her booted feet.

"You're upset. Why?"

Storm stopped pacing. "It makes no sense that this man was taken to Glencurry. His crime was here in Dunwith."

Burke reached out and took hold of her arms. "What's wrong with that?"

Her hesitation upset Burke even more, but the rustle of branches had them both taking cover. Burke wrapped his arm around her slim waist and dragged her behind a thick bush. Her waist was tiny. He could practically wrap his arm clear around it. How she swung a sword, he'd never know. There was strength in her small frame and feminine curves that reminded him that she was a woman, a woman who felt good in his arms.

He wanted to hold on to her, offering security, safety, sanctuary.

She, however, broke free once she saw that it was Tanin.

"Food is stored for them where none will find it

and there is enough to feed more families," Tanin said, holding the rolled bedding out to her.

Storm nodded and took the bedding, disappearing into the woods.

"You found what you needed?" Tanin asked.

"We found that we may have to go to Glencurry," Burke said.

Tanin's head jerked, his eyes turned wide.

"Glencurry seems to cause an adverse reaction in people. Why?" Burke asked.

"Earl of Balford at Glencurry is not a man you want to deal with," Tanin advised.

"Why?"

"He cares little for human suffering."

"Then my brother could suffer at his hands?"

"More than he can humanly endure."

Burke grew alarmed. There was no way in hell he'd let an earl or a duke or whatever some such nonsense-titled man harm his brother.

"How far is Glencurry from here?"

"Two, two and half days."

"Then we leave right away," Burke said.

"No, we return to camp," Storm said, tossing the rolled bedding to Tanin and once again clothed as a young lad, stocking cap and all.

Burke approached her. "I need to get to my brother."

"We need to make certain your brother is at Glencurry," Storm argued. "It will do us little good to go there uncertain and without a plan. When we go, we go to free him."

Burke wanted to argue but there was nothing to

argue. She was right. If he charged in there like a fool, he could wind up imprisoned as well. What good would that do?

"I will send men to find out all they can. Then we will decide what is to be done," Storm said and turned. "Come. We need to get back to camp. There is work to be done."

Burke didn't want to follow. He wanted to head in the opposite direction and demand to see his brother, if it was indeed his brother, and then he would demand his brother be freed or he'd buy his way out of prison. One way or another, he intended to free Cullen, his brother, and take him home to America. He had promised his father, and he intended to keep his promise. Besides, he wanted to get to know his brother; he was all the family Burke had left.

Nightfall found them camped behind a large boulder, a single fish serving as their meal. Storm ate little, though Burke insisted she eat more. She insisted she wasn't hungry, and he wondered if that was her standard response when little food was available.

Tanin was quick to seek his bed. Burke realized he was a man of few words but of great courage and compassion and a man who thought highly of Storm. He wondered what had brought the pair together and what bond kept them together.

Burke approached Storm where she sat perched on the edge of a boulder, staring into the night.

"Tell me of the Earl of Balford."

Storm didn't even turn and acknowledge him.

"He is not a man of his word."

"You've dealt with him before?"

"Yes, to my regret," she said.

Sorrow clearly filled her voice and Burke ventured to guess, "You lost a man to him?"

"Yes," she admitted reluctantly and looked about to say more, but remained silent.

Burke waited, giving her time, realizing the memory hadn't been a pleasant one and that perhaps she didn't wish to recall any more of it.

She took a breath and continued. "He has a small dungeon beneath his manor house. He imprisons tenants on whatever charges he creates—"

She paused, and Burke wondered how many such painful memories she must have endured while helping people.

She sighed and went on. "He then charges the families for the food and the cell."

"What if the family has no money?"

"The prisoner starves to death and then the family is charged to remove his body or it's tossed in the woods for the animals to feed on."

While the information disgusted Burke, it also gave him a shred of hope. "Then there's a good chance I can buy my brother's freedom."

"I'm not sure about that."

"Why?"

"That someone who poached on Dunwith land was taken to Glencurry for imprisonment doesn't make sense."

"What do you think is going on?"

"That's what we need to find out, but first we have to determine if it's your brother being held at Glencurry."

"Tanin and I can go and find out," Burke suggested, anxious that his brother might need his help this very minute and he was wasting precious time.

"No. I will send what men I choose."

"I will not see my brother suffer," Burke said firmly. "If I go and discover it is Cullen, I can make immediate arrangements to have him freed."

"How? You have no money."

That stopped Burke, but only for a moment. "I'll make certain the earl understands that he'll receive plenty of money in two weeks."

"In which time your brother will more than likely starve if he hasn't already."

Burke raked his hair with his fingers in frustration. "I can't stand by and do nothing."

"You're not," Storm assured him. "If my men ascertain it is your brother and they believe they can easily free him, then they will do so and return to camp with him."

"I want to be part of the rescue," Burke insisted.

"You would only be a hindrance. You are not familiar with Glencurry land or the manor itself. I will send men who know it well. The best thing you can do for your brother is to wait here."

"You ask a lot."

"I give a lot—your brother's freedom."

Burke reluctantly admitted to himself that she made sense but it didn't ease his annoyance. He made one more attempt. "I could wait along the trail."

"You can wait at camp, and that settles it."

Burke held his tongue, realizing she tested him.

Would he follow her orders or not? If he didn't, would she refuse to help him any further? He wouldn't take a chance with his brother's life. He would do as she instructed though it rankled him.

"We'll do it your way."

"We will always do it my way, Burke." She smiled.

He grabbed her chin and gave her a quick kiss on the lips. "Don't count on that."

Chapter 5

Storm was relieved that they would reach camp shortly. She had kept her distance from Burke since last night. She was still stunned that he had kissed her—not that it was a passionate kiss. It was over as fast as it started. It was the idea that he had the audacity to even do it.

And what had she done?

She had stood there speechless and watched him walk away and bed down for the night. She had not even reprimanded him or warned him never to do it again.

Why? Why hadn't she reacted?

The last time she had been kissed was by her husband, Daniel. It was a quick kiss good-bye. It was also their last kiss. No man had touched her lips since then, not until last night when Burke had kissed her.

It had stunned her and made her consider Burke as a man and not just an annoyance. He wasn't anything like her Daniel. Her husband had possessed a quiet strength and had often teased her about her demanding nature. He'd say it was her young age, she being barely twenty then.

She was, however, now twenty-and-five years, no longer a young lass in more ways than just age. She wondered over Burke's age. He seemed older to her, perhaps thirty or more, or perhaps life had made him appear older.

Burke was the complete opposite of Daniel. The American was brash and vocal about his opinions and wants, where Daniel had been gentle in tone and demands—not that he didn't get his way; he just did it with a gentle love.

She couldn't see Burke being gentle. He exuded an arrogant confidence that demanded things be his way. Yet he had deferred to her, with reluctance, but again in the end it was for him to get what he wanted—his brother's freedom.

She couldn't blame him. She had fought so very hard for her husband's freedom, but to no avail. She had lost him, and it had been her fault.

"How far are we from camp?"

She jumped and nearly tripped if it hadn't been for Burke's quick reaction. He slipped his arm around her waist and plopped her back on her feet to continue walking.

"You really need a keeper, and, lucky you, I'm available."

Storm couldn't help but smile at his grin. He wasn't

handsome, as her Daniel had been. His features were more rugged, each line and groove a distinct map that proved he was a man who had traveled life's trails with strength and had emerged victorious. He was a man you knew would be there for you in the thick of things and would never leave your side.

Her heart fluttered at the thought of such strength and honor.

"So, am I your keeper?"

Storm shook her head. "More like my jester."

He laughed. "I like your sense of humor."

"You are the only person who believes I possess one."

"I can attest to it since I have seen it firsthand," he said with a thump to his chest.

A strong chest, she thought. His shirt had spread wide, revealing thick muscles, and his shoulders were broad and in a way defiant, as if he challenged any who approached him.

"So I claim myself your official keeper," he said emphatically.

"I don't need a keeper."

"This is, what? The fourth time I've saved you?" he reminded.

"You only think you've saved me. I can assure you that I can save myself."

"When you can prove that to me, then you'll no longer need me as your keeper."

"I need to prove nothing to you," Storm insisted.

"Afraid you do." He was even more insistent. "You see, my father raised me to protect women. Not that I haven't met women who can protect themselves, but there comes a point when a man is needed."

Storm laughed. "No, there comes a time when a man *thinks* he's needed."

"I disagree," Burke said with a shake of his head. "You mark my words, there'll come a time you'll need me."

"I don't believe so, but I will keep your prediction in mind."

"Good, then when the time comes you won't deny my help."

"I would never be foolish enough to deny *necessary* help."

"Then you'll be sure to accept it," he said much too confidently.

"We're home," Tanin said, rushing past them.

Burke looked around.

"Don't let your eyes mislead you," Storm advised and took his hand. "Stoop," she instructed, and together they ducked beneath a thorn-covered arched bush, then squeezed through a row of dense trees to emerge into a clearing.

"I'll be damned," Burke said.

"Be careful of your words, Mr. Longton," Storm warned with a smile. "Some claim this is the devil's lair."

Storm was proud of the home she and her group had carved out of the forest. Homes were fashioned in the trees, pulleys were constructed to provide water and necessities, weapons were stored in the hollow of hundred-year-old trees. Life was lived here with purpose and joy.

"This is amazing," Burke said, his neck arched back as he examined the housing in the trees. "It must have taken much work."

"It was a labor of love by many," Storm assured him.

"It would certainly appear that way."

People called out hearty welcomes to Storm and she responded in kind. She watched as Tanin greeted his wife, Ellie, a tall, slender, red-haired beauty whom Tanin had loved since they were young. It always relieved her when she saw the two reunite in a hug. They were so very much in love, and Storm didn't intend Ellie to suffer her fate of losing a husband.

"I know you will always return him to me safe," Ellie called out with a wave.

"Count on it," Storm said.

"That's a strong promise," Burke said.

"And one I intend to keep. Now let's see where we're going to put you."

"Right beside you," he demanded.

Storm raised her brow.

"I am your keeper."

She poked his chest. "Not likely."

He grabbed her finger. "I'm about to invest a large sum of money in you, which gives me the right to remain close by your side. Keeper or not, I intend to be your shadow while I'm here."

"You are persistent."

"Some call it demanding."

"I'm the demanding one here," Storm said.

"I thought you were commanding."

"Finally you have it right."

"Good, so where's your place in the trees?"

Storm walked off with a shake of her head, leaving him to follow. He was right on her heels.

"Grab hold of me," she said after wrapping her arm around a thick rope.

"Now there's an order I can follow," Burke said, slipping his arm around her waist and grabbing hold of the rope with her.

With a kick of her foot to the counterweight at the base of the tree they took flight, gliding up until they came to rest on a platform built between two thick branches.

Storm secured the rope to a broken branch and joined Burke at the wooden railing, his awe obvious in his wide brown eyes.

"It's breathtaking," he said.

"It's safe," Storm corrected. They could see the forest for miles in all directions. In addition, she had sentries posted at various positions throughout the forest. No one could approach the hideout without their knowledge. Their home was impenetrable.

Storm walked past Burke to enter her home tucked in the confines of the sprawling branches of the generous spruce.

It was one room, large enough to hold a narrow bed and a small table. A chest sat at the end of the bed, and pegs in the wall held a cloak and a nightdress.

"This doesn't look big enough for both of us," Burke remarked upon entering.

"It's not," Storm advised.

"I'm not leaving your side and don't—"

"Follow me," she instructed and walked out of the room around the walkway that circled the thick tree trunk to enter another room similar to hers, though it contained only a single bed and small bench with a candle on it.

Burke tried out the bed and shook his head. "This bedding needs stuffing."

"That's something that will keep you busy."

"There's that sense of humor of yours again," he chided with a smile.

"We all pull our weight here," Storm said seriously.

"You won't find me slacking. I'll do what's necessary, though a good commander uses the talents of his troop and doesn't waste them on petty things."

"Which is why you'll be joining Malcolm to hunt for food today."

Burke nodded. "Now you're using my talents wisely. What about my brother? Shouldn't we see to sending the men right away?"

"I'll see to it."

"I want to be there when you talk with the men you send."

"It's not necessary," Storm said and turned to leave.

He grabbed her arm and swung her around.

"It's necessary to me. I want to know whom you send. I want to hear their plans and offer advice if called for."

"We've been through this. Leave me to my talents

as I leave you to yours." She reached out, placing her hand over his. "If it is your brother, my men will bring him back."

Burke relented. "I should find Malcolm and go hunting."

"A wise choice. Have him also take you to Janelle. She will supply you with clothing while she repairs your garments."

"You have a seamstress?" Burke asked with a laugh.

"She is Tanin's mother and a healer and excellent with a needle."

"You have no talents with a needle?"

Storm had once enjoyed stitching garments for her husband and herself and was quite skillful with a needle. Daniel had remarked that she should start stitching baby garments, for it wouldn't be long before a wee one was on the way.

She had started a wee garment, in hope that it would soon be needed, just the day before her life had plunged into darkness.

"Storm?"

She shook the painful memories from her head. "I have no time to stitch."

He pulled her slowly toward him. "You should rest."

"No time." His brown eyes reminded her of the rich earth. She had loved to dig in the soil with her hands when planting her garden. It was almost as if she could feel its potent fertility.

That's how it felt looking into his brown eyes— potent and fertile.

She yanked her arm free and stepped away. "Burke, about that kiss."

"What kiss?" he asked, shaking his head. "If you thought that was a kiss, then you haven't known a man. That was just a friendly peck."

"No friendly pecks then," she ordered, feeling her neck grow hot and knowing in a second her cheeks would glow bright red.

"Fine with me," he said, walking past her to the door.

She took a deep breath, attempting to stem the tide of heat rushing to her face before she turned to catch up with him. She gave it a second or two and swerved around.

Burke stood in the open doorway, his hands clasped overhead to the frame and a wicked smile on his face.

"Can't let you go without tasting a real kiss."

She had no time to protest. He scooped her up into his strong arms and planted his lips against hers, soft, smooth, hard, rough; the mixture titillated and passion tingled her body down to her toes. When he finished, he set her on her feet, making sure she was steady before he released her and walked to the door.

"Now *that's* a kiss," he said without looking back.

Chapter 6

Burke rode down the rope with a fire in his loins. He had wanted to make certain Storm tasted a real kiss but he never intended to get such pleasure from it. She was a mere wisp of a woman, a beauty for sure, but not his type. He liked women large and sturdy with good hips that could bear him children without his worrying he'd lose his wife in childbirth.

No, Storm wasn't his type. He'd forever worry about her. Lord, a good gusty wind would blow her away, not to mention what a harsh Dakota winter would do to her.

He shook his head. Why the hell was he thinking of her in Dakota Territory? He wasn't here to find a wife. There were plenty of women back home interested in filling that position. He was here to find his brother, and he'd do well to keep his mind on that.

She lived in the trees.

Damned if he didn't admire the home she had carved out of the forest for her group. Only a woman with extraordinary strength and courage could manage to create and sustain a home in the wilderness. She really wasn't that different from the women who braved the American frontier.

But she was so tiny. Where did she find the strength?

"Heard you are hunting with me today," Malcolm said, coming up to him.

How did he know that? Storm had just informed Burke of it.

Malcolm slapped him on the back. "Storm gave orders to Tanin to relay to me and others before entering camp."

"She certainly stays on top of things."

"She devises plans before we even finish discussing the issue." Malcolm shook his head. "She's amazing."

It was obvious the good-looking youth admired her. Burke also wondered if he had feelings for his leader, but then it wasn't his business.

"Did other men receive orders as well?" Burke asked.

Malcolm nodded. "They already left camp."

Burke almost swore aloud. Damned if she hadn't played him for a fool, making him think she had yet to talk to the men she would send to rescue his brother when all along her decision had been made and the men sent on their way.

"Ready to hunt?"

He sure was. He was ready to hunt Storm down and give her a piece of his mind.

"I'd rather have gone with William and Philip than hunting," Malcolm continued. "They've had the most success in rescues. Storm always sends them on the difficult missions. They're the most skilled."

Burke immediately regretted his anger. Storm hadn't wasted a minute in seeing to his brother. She had sent her best men, and for that he was grateful. He would make sure to tell her.

"Come on," Burke said. "I'm going to teach you a thing or two about hunting."

Malcolm proved a skilled hunter, and with a few tips from Burke and an hour of practice, he was fast becoming an expert. In no time they easily snagged several hares.

"Is it true that everyone is rich in America?" Malcolm asked on their way back to camp.

"It depends on how you define rich," Burke said, seeing in Malcolm what he had seen in so many young foreigners who arrived on the shores of America—the promise of hope.

"Money, land, food aplenty for family and friends," Malcolm said.

"With hard work and some sacrifice, it's possible," Burke assured him.

"I heard those same words told to friends who left Scotland to seek a better life in Canada, only to discover more hardships."

"Forging a life out of the wilderness takes courage, sustaining it takes hard work."

"Especially if you're an outlaw." Malcolm laughed.

"How did all of you come to be together?"

"Storm has rules we all agreed to follow. One of them is never to discuss the group with strangers. You, Burke, are a stranger."

He was candid and emphatic and Burke respected both.

"Storm's quite a woman," Burke said, attempting another approach.

"Can't discuss her either. You need to direct all inquiries to Storm. She's the only one with the authority to give you answers. She's probably by the creek over there." He pointed to a barely visible path to the right. "She usually washes up at the creek after returning from a mission. I'll see that the women get the game for tonight's meal."

Burke nodded and followed the path, if it could be called that, the forest having reclaimed most of it. It did, however, lead him to the creek and Storm. She sat on the ground a few feet from the creek in clean trousers and a tan shirt, combing her wet hair with her fingers.

"How did the hunting go, Burke?"

He approached her with a laugh. "How did you know it was me and not Malcolm?"

"A couple of weeks in prison leaves a man with a distinct odor." She held up a bundle of clothes. "I stopped to see if you spoke with Janelle. When I found out you didn't I took the liberty of picking up some clothes for you."

Burke took them from her. "Intended to find me, did you?"

"No. I knew once you discovered I had already sent men after your brother, you'd find me."

Burke dropped the clothes beside her and stripped off his shirt. "I wanted to thank you for handling the matter so quickly and efficiently."

He held on to his shirt and noticed that she kept her eyes focused on his face. He had never considered himself a handsome man; years spent out in the rough winters had toughened his skin and added a flurry of lines around his eyes. He probably looked well past his twenty-nine years.

"Feel free to strip and wash up, Mr. Longton," she said to his surprise. "I don't wilt at the sight of a naked man."

"Seen naked men before, have you?" He had to ask.

"Yes," she answered with a smile and shook her head, to fluff her drying hair with her fingers.

The silky black strands fell together like a fine piece of wool cloth woven to perfection. Her skin was the color of rich cream, and he wondered if the taste was as potent.

He turned abruptly and walked to the creek. He needed to cool off. He bent down and stuck his head in the refreshing cool water, and as he came up, he wiped his face and neck clean with his hands. He then rinsed off his arms and chest, not caring that the water ran down to soak his trousers.

He wanted to make certain he freed himself of the heat that had set his blood on fire and had him ready to crawl out of his skin. And all because of a woman who obviously was familiar with naked men.

He dried himself off and marched back over to her. "How many men?"

"Excuse me?"

"How many men have you seen naked?"

"I don't see what business that is of yours," she said calmly.

"I don't either but I'm curious," he admitted.

"Your honesty at times amazes me."

"My father taught me to be an honorable and honest man."

"Do you wonder if your brother is like you?"

Burke tossed his wet shirt aside and sat down beside Storm. "I have wondered since first learning about him when I was young. Had anyone helped him? Was he still alive? Had he had a harsh life? My father searched tirelessly for him and blamed himself for what had happened."

"He couldn't have taken a babe to America with him. He did the right thing. It wasn't his fault his sister-in-law died."

"Tell that to a grief-stricken father who beyond death continues to search for his son, through his other son. I don't intend to fail my father. I will find Cullen and bring him home."

"What if he doesn't want to go?" she asked.

"When he discovers the wealth that awaits him, he'll go."

"Tell me of this wealth," Storm said, reaching for the clean shirt and handing it to Burke.

A cool autumn wind had suddenly interrupted

an otherwise warm day, and she offered him protection against it, handing him the clean shirt.

He accepted, slipping it over his head. "The Dakota Territory can be unforgiving and generous at the same time. My father claimed over three hundred acres. Longton Ranch raises the best cattle in the territory, not to mention the horses we train and sell. The town of Longton prospers also, thanks to my father's generosity. He built the town, started the first bank, brought a doctor there, built a church and a school, all while remaining friends with his Sioux neighbors."

"That must have been a feat."

"If you knew my father you would know it was his nature to treat everyone fairly and honestly. He believed that a man was nothing without integrity. He lived it every day of his life. That was the attribute my mother so loved and admired in him, and, as she had often told me, made her feel so very safe with my father."

"How lovely that she should trust him so unconditionally."

"She told me he had earned it. He was a good man, a good husband, and a good father. She couldn't have asked for more."

"Your mother has also passed?"

"She died one week after my father. I expected it. They were too much in love to live without each other."

"How sad for you."

Burke shook his head. "No. I'm happy that they're together. And once I find my brother, I know they both will be at peace. My mother had looked forward to raising Cullen as her own and was just as disappointed as my father when he was not found." He turned to her. "What of your parents?"

"Not worth talking about."

"That bad?"

Storm shrugged. "I barely remember my father. He left when I was young. My mother thought I ate too much and was too much of a burden. She gave me away to a family, but after a couple of months they gave me to another family, who treated me decently enough."

"That's horrible," Burke said, appalled at Storm's loveless childhood. Was that why she rescued people? Had she felt so abandoned that she reached out to others suffering the same fate?

"It is the way of things here. You survive or you surrender. I prefer to survive."

"I can see where you got your courage."

She smiled. "Life gave it to me many times over."

"What of the future?" he asked. "You can't remain an outlaw all your life."

"I don't think of the future." She turned to stare at the creek.

What she really meant was that she believed she had no future. She was an outlaw and would forever be hunted and perhaps one day caught. The thought chilled his bones. He could not fathom the idea of Storm rotting in a jail cell or, God forbid, being tortured endlessly, death her only chance to escape.

"You should think of the future," he insisted.

"What will you do when your outlaw days come to an end?"

"I doubt they ever will."

He didn't like the hopelessness he heard in her voice. "You don't know that for sure. Anything can happen."

"It would take a miracle. This is my life and I accept it."

"Why? You fight for others. Why not fight for your own future?"

"I do not live beyond this day, for I do not know if I will see tomorrow. I will do what I must and leave the rest to fate."

"Not good enough," he said adamantly. "Fate is what you make it. You said you'd rather survive than surrender. Leaving your life to fate is surrendering."

A soft smile lit her face and sent a jolt to his heart. He convinced himself it was out of concern he felt for her. She was a young, beautiful woman who had the right to a good life. She needed a good man who would love her, protect her, and provide for her.

"Fate cannot be swayed, Burke. It is there whether we like it or not. But enough talk of fate. Let me tell you of the Scottish people. Hopefully it will help you better understand your brother."

"If you're an example of the Scottish people, then I already know something of them. They're stubborn fighters who refuse to surrender even if it's for their own good."

"That we are," Storm agreed, "but we don't

56

surrender for we are bound to this land through generations who have spilled their blood for it, and its people will fight to their last breath to keep us free."

How could he argue with her? He fought for his land and the freedom it brought him. He would die defending his land if necessary.

"So what you tell me is that my brother Cullen will not leave this land."

"Would you leave yours?"

Burke shook his head. "No. It is my home. But many are leaving Scotland. There is a chance he may want to emigrate."

"Many have no choice."

"Perhaps Cullen won't have a choice."

"The wealth you say is his will grant him a choice," Storm said.

He'd never thought of that. He'd just assumed Cullen would want to return to America with him and claim his share of the inheritance, though his return wasn't necessary. The money was his whether he lived in Scotland or in America.

Burke rubbed his chin. "You have given me much to think about."

"It is good to be prepared for all possibilities."

"Even miracles?" he teased.

She laughed. "Are you promising me a miracle, Mr. Longton?"

"If it were in my power I'd make certain you get one."

"You are a strange man."

"Good strange?" he asked with a cautious laugh.

"I believe so. You demand and yet you have a tender heart."

"Shhh," he warned, pressing a finger to her lips. "That's a secret that cannot get out."

She nodded, assuring her silence.

He stared at her a moment, caught by the beauty in her blue eyes. The color had settled to the bold blue of a sky after an angry storm. He slowly slipped his finger away from her mouth, running it down her petite chin to stroke the gentle flesh beneath.

"You are beautiful."

Her eyes remained fixed on his as if caught up in their depths, and then suddenly she turned her head away, his finger drifting off. She stood and walked away from him.

He watched her go even though he wanted to run after her and keep her beside him, just a bit longer.

"One," she called out.

Burke stood but remained where he was. "One what?"

"One man," she said, continuing to walk. "I've seen only one man naked, and he was my husband."

Chapter 7

Storm woke before dawn's first light. This was the time she felt most alone. This was the time she missed her husband the most. She pushed the painful memories away. It did no good to dwell on them. He was dead, and nothing would bring him back. No amount of tears would ease her pain, though she had shed them endlessly.

Nothing but time would relieve her suffering. It had been three years since his death, and still at times the hurt felt raw, as if it had been yesterday that she had felt his arms around her, his lips kissing her.

She ran her fingers over her lips, recalling Burke's kiss. Dare she admit that it actually felt good?

She attempted to dismiss the thought as she quickly jumped out of bed and dressed with equal haste. Unfortunately, the disturbing thought refused to be ignored and lingered in her mind.

She was being ridiculous. So what if she enjoyed Burke's kiss? What difference did it make? It meant nothing, and there would not be another kiss. It wasn't worth wasting her thoughts on.

Storm slipped on a brown wool vest over her long-sleeved tan shirt, the morning chill reminding her that autumn had finally arrived. She descended the rope ready and eager for breakfast.

Activity around the campfire alerted her to a possible problem. The mornings were always quiet around the camp. She and Janelle would share the morning meal, Malcolm sometimes joined them, but Tanin was never seen until after sunrise.

He was there now, however, along with Malcolm and Angus, which meant something had happened.

Storm approached them and they all turned quiet. "What's wrong?"

Tanin answered. "We received word that William and Philip were captured before they could reach Glencurry."

"Where were they taken?"

"They're on their way to Mullvane, where I was held," Malcolm said.

"Probably caught by the soldiers sent to find the escaped prisoners."

Everyone around the campfire jumped at the sound of Burke's voice as he stepped out of the darkness.

"I thought you were still sleeping," Storm said.

"You'll find I'm an early riser." Burke tossed a slim stick into the fire. "So what do we do about freeing William and Philip?"

"*We* see to that," Storm said. "You remain here."

"I feel responsible for them."

"*I* gave them the order, not you."

"Still, they went to rescue my brother. I can't sit by and do nothing," Burke said emphatically.

"If I order—"

"*If* you order, which I ask you not to do," Burke requested firmly. "You are short two men to help with the rescue. You know I'm skilled—"

"And I know that you don't—"

"I'll follow orders. I give you my word on it," Burke promised.

He was right about her needing the help, and though her men remained silent, she knew they thought the same. She had always considered their suggestions when an escape was planned and she had no doubt they agreed with Burke.

"You promise you will obey my every command—" She held her hand up to prevent his quick response. "My *every* command, even if it means you leave me behind."

The shock on his face answered for him, but she had to admit he was quick to rein it in.

"I'm not saying it would be an easy thing for me to do. My first response would be to protect you and get you the hell out of there under any circumstances. But I respect your command and will respect your orders. I can't promise, however, that I won't object now and again."

"But you will follow my orders," she confirmed.

"I give you my word."

"Then we appreciate your help in rescuing William

and Philip." Storm moved aside, making room for Burke to join them at the campfire. "We need to find them before they reach the prison."

"I thought the same," Tanin agreed. "We should leave immediately."

"We'll need to be careful of any soldiers that may have been left behind in hopes of finding the rest of us," Burke offered.

"True, and we'll need to split into two groups and cover the two possible paths they could have taken," Storm explained. "We'll reunite where the two paths converge. And if anyone should be captured, it will be up to the other group to free everyone."

"Hear that, Malcolm?" Tanin teased. "Don't make us free your sorry ass again."

"Watch it, Tanin, or I might be tempted not to rescue you when you get caught."

Angus gave a hardy laugh, his wide girth rolling with the timbre. "Tanin has never been captured."

"There's always a first time." Malcolm grinned.

Storm let the men have their fun. It was their way before a rescue, teasing one another, yet knowing each one of them would do whatever was necessary to help the others. Her small group had formed a bond that had strengthened with time and would no doubt grow even stronger.

Her instincts had been right about each man she had chosen. Their personalities had varied, but they possessed equal strength and determination and were willing to work for a common cause—the betterment and equality of the Scottish people.

"Ready yourselves," Storm informed them. "We leave in ten minutes." She turned to Burke. "Go with Malcolm. He will show you what weapons are available for your use."

"Do you trust him?" Tanin asked when Burke was out of sight.

"I see no reason not to, though sometimes it is what we don't see that can harm us."

"It's odd, don't you think, that William and Philip should be captured while on a mission concerning him?"

The thought had crossed her mind briefly, but she had dismissed it. Should she have? Should she be more vigilant about Mr. Longton? Or had her character judgment been correct? Was he truly an honest man?

"It may be a coincidence, and I got the impression that you favor Burke Longton," Storm said.

"He is a skilled man, but he's not a Scotsman."

She smiled. "So are you saying he can't be trusted?"

"I'm saying that he has skills that can help us, but we should still be cautious until we can determine for a fact that he can be trusted."

"I would not place the group in jeopardy."

"I know that, and I know if it proves necessary you will rid the group of Mr. Longton," Tanin said. "Now it's time for me to get ready. I will take Burke in my group."

"No," Storm said. "You and Angus will take the

creek path. Malcolm and Burke will travel the north-east path with me."

"As you say," Tanin said with a nod.

It was easy for her to tell when Tanin disagreed with her decisions. His manner became rigid, his responses curt. "You don't agree. Speak your mind, Tanin, I expect it of you."

He didn't waste a minute. "Malcolm has yet to rein in his overzealous enthusiasm when on a mission and Burke is still a stranger to us. Leaving you to—"

"Teach Malcolm the finer skills of fighting and learn more about Burke. Trust me."

"I always have or I wouldn't follow you. But know this—if either one gets you in trouble, they'll be answering to me."

Storm smiled. "I'd have it no other way."

Hours after they left the camp, Storm signaled for Burke and Malcolm to stop. This was the point where she expected the soldiers to be waiting. The three crouched down and Storm used a stick to scratch a diagram in the earth of where she felt the soldiers lay in wait.

Burke offered a plan of action and Storm agreed. It took only minutes to capture the three soldiers, two of whom had been sleeping.

Hands tied, mouths gagged, the soldiers were led along the path with them. It was another hour before they heard the clang of swords and surmised that Tanin and Angus were in the thick of battle.

Storm ordered Malcolm to tie the prisoners to a

tree before she and Burke took off and leaped in to join the melee.

They were outnumbered for sure, but not out-skilled. Storm attempted to make her way to free William and Philip of their restraints. It proved difficult until Burke caught on to her actions and jumped in front of her, fighting off the enemy with a sword. A weapon he had claimed he had no skill with, though it looked otherwise.

She had Philip nearly freed from the thick ropes that bound his wrists, when he shouted a warning to watch out. She gave the rope one last slice and swung around to face her attacker, but not fast enough. His blade sliced her shoulder, though she had moved quickly enough to avert serious damage.

Philip grabbed her sword and ended the man's life in one swift thrust, then quickly freed William, who picked up the dead man's sword and joined in. Philip threw Storm her sword and grabbed another off a dead solider.

Storm ignored her wounded shoulder, and in no time, the soldiers were conquered. A few ran off in the end, dragging a couple of wounded with them.

"Gather what weapons and items we need off the dead and be ready to leave," Storm instructed. "There could be more soldiers close by."

"We didn't see any when we came along the creek," Tanin informed her.

"We caught three from where we approached," Malcolm said.

"Then this could be the lot of them," Philip said.

"I don't want to take any chances. Hurry," Storm ordered.

"You're hurt," Burke said loudly and shot the men heated glares. "Can't you see that she's bleeding?"

"Looks like a flesh wound. Time for that later," Tanin said without concern and walked off, as did the other men, to follow Storm's instructions.

"Let me see that," Burke demanded and reached out.

Storm stepped out of his reach. "I gave you orders."

"The others can see to it. Your shoulder needs tending."

"Tanin was right. It can wait."

Burke shook his head. "I don't think so. That wound needs cleansing and dressing."

"And we need to be out of here in two minutes. So either help the men or I will." She plopped down on the rock, the throb in her shoulder causing her stomach to roll.

"Tanin," Burke called out, and in a second the tall man was at his side. "This is more than a flesh wound."

"I gave orders—"

"Be quiet," Burke ordered. "Your injury needs tending now."

"He's right, Storm," Tanin said after examining the wound. "It's deeper than it looked at first glance."

"Then bandage it, and Janelle can see to it when we reach camp."

Burke pushed Tanin out of the way. "I'll take care of it. Finish helping the men so we can get out of here."

Much to Storm's surprise, Tanin took off.

"I didn't know you were in charge," she snapped.

"I issued the same orders you would have and Tanin knows it," Burke said and shook his head. "I'm not trying to usurp your command, and if you weren't so stubborn you'd admit that this wound does need immediate attention. So let's get it wrapped and you back to camp as quickly as possible."

Storm marveled at how fast Burke worked. He tore her ripped sleeve off her shirt and used it as a bandage. She winced from the pain and he apologized for hurting her.

The man did have a tender heart and nice eyes. Storm really liked his eyes. They were deep brown and filled with confidence. He was a man who knew what he wanted and went after it.

"She's lost some blood," Storm heard Burke say.

She suddenly felt light-headed, weak almost, as if she were about to faint. The thought shocked her. She couldn't faint. She reached out, grabbing the arm in front of her.

"Tanin!"

"It's all right, Storm, I've got you."

That wasn't Tanin. It was Burke.

"You need to sit," Burke said firmly.

She leaned on his arm and attempted to push to her feet.

"Stay put," Burke ordered.

"I need to stand," she said adamantly.

"Not when you're about to faint," Burke said.

She turned to Tanin, trying to shove Burke aside. "You know what to do."

Tanin responded with a strong slap to her face.

Chapter 8

Burke lunged at Tanin with a roar and would have beaten him senseless if Malcolm and Angus hadn't grabbed him and held him back.

"What the hell is the matter with you?" Burke yelled, his face red with anger.

"Mind your business," Angus said harshly.

"She's hurt and needs—"

"To stay on her feet and stay strong," Angus finished.

"She's a woman—"

"She's our leader first," Angus corrected.

"Let me go," Burke all but snarled.

"Let him go," Storm ordered sharply after shaking her head clear, and the men obeyed.

Burke walked over to her and got more annoyed when he spotted her red cheek. "That wasn't necessary. I would have helped you."

"By letting me faint and delaying us from leaving?" She shook her head. "That isn't helping me. We're leaving now," she called out.

"You're in no shape to walk," Burke argued, though he doubted it would make a difference. Storm was a stubborn one, and as Angus had pointed out, she was their leader.

"I have no choice," she insisted. "We must get back home before nightfall or we risk being caught. Now if you don't want to be left behind, Mr. Longton, I suggest you keep up with us."

She turned and set a quick pace, her men following suit.

Burke mumbled several oaths, scooped up his bow and arrows, and took off after them. He was still reeling from the vision of Tanin slapping Storm across the face. Her head had jerked to the side and she would have stumbled if Tanin hadn't grabbed her arm.

That Tanin's action had prevented her from fainting didn't matter to him, she had suffered an injury and needed tending, not abuse.

"Couldn't have done it, could you?" Malcolm asked, having slowed to walk beside Burke.

"If you mean slugged her, no, I couldn't have."

"Then you would have failed her. Would you have preferred that?"

Burke didn't answer, and not another word was spoken until they reached camp hours later.

"Tanin, see to things," Storm ordered. "I'm going to see Janelle." She walked off, her strides slow.

Burke looked at Tanin.

"Go. If she does not find my mother in the shelter on the ground, she will need help getting up the tree," Tanin said.

Burke took off and would have whether Tanin approved of it or not. He had worried about Storm on the whole journey home. She had kept a quick pace, which couldn't have helped the pain in her shoulder. Yet she had not complained once. He wasn't certain if she had been courageous or stupid. What did it matter now, as long as she was all right.

He found her with her hands held firm to the thick rope. Her head rested against it as if uncertain she had the strength to keep hold.

He didn't bother to ask her if she needed help. He walked over, slipped his arm snugly around her waist, tucked her against his body, and ordered, "Put your arm around my neck and hold on."

She looked up at him, her blue eyes filled with pain.

He almost spewed a plethora of oaths but instead ignored his anger and addressed her pain.

"Hold on to me. I won't let you go. I won't let anything happen to you," he whispered his promise in her ear.

Her eyes drifted shut and her head descended slowly to rest on his shoulder.

"I'm here, Storm, I'll take care of you." His words alarmed even him, but then he felt compelled to look after the pint-sized, stubborn woman. No one else did, at least not the way he would—leader or not.

He continued to hold on to her as he walked her through the open door of the tree house.

A tall woman with long white hair that lay in a single braid over her shoulder turned at their entrance. She had remarkably beautiful skin with few wrinkles, though one sensed her advanced years.

"Her shoulder took a deep slice," Burke explained, reluctant to release Storm.

Janelle hurried to his side. "Help her to the chair."

Burke did as directed, anxious for Storm to receive adequate care. He feared her wound could prove deadly. He had seen much lesser wounds prove someone's demise.

"I wrapped it as best as possible," Burke offered, stepping aside but not too far. He felt the need to remain close to her side. Storm might need him, if only to hold on to a friendly hand against the pain.

"This requires stitches if it is to heal properly," Janelle said when she finally uncovered the wound.

"Do what you must and get it over," Storm encouraged.

"I'll help," Burke offered.

"There is nothing for you to do, begone," Storm ordered.

Burke laughed. "I don't think so. I'm staying right here."

"And if I don't want you here?"

"It doesn't matter," he said, squatting down on his haunches beside her. "I'm staying by your side."

Storm reached out hesitantly, finally pressing her hand to his cheek. "You are a stubborn one."

"Dependable, Storm," he corrected. "I'll be there for you when necessary."

Her smile was sad and touched his heart. He didn't

know what it was about this woman that made him feel so protective of her. It made no sense, and yet he didn't fight the notion. He simply did what he felt was right, and it felt right to see to her safety.

"This will be painful," Janelle said.

Burke winced while Storm simply nodded.

"What can I do?" he asked, anxious to help in any way he could, though more anxious to ease her pain if possible.

"Hold her," Janelle said. "It will be easier for me and less painful for her if she remains still."

Burke grinned, pressing his nose to Storm's. "How lucky am I? I have an excuse to hold you."

He almost regretted his words after they left his mouth, especially when he witnessed the confused look on Storm's face. She didn't seem to know what to make of his remark, though it was obvious. He enjoyed holding her.

"Have you ever felt the sting of stitches?" Storm asked, resting her head on his.

He wrapped his arm around her waist and moved in close beside her, leaving her injured side free. "Sting, you say?" He guffawed. "I'd say more like a needle pulling your flesh together."

"Thank you for so vividly reminding me."

Burke was quick to amend his response and take her mind off her pending pain. "I'm a coward at heart."

"I don't believe that for a moment."

Burke was impressed by the seriousness of her tone. "Why not?"

"You have proven yourself a courageous warrior

in the short time I have known you. I doubt the sting of stitches would upset you."

Janelle cleansed the wound, then signaled him that she was near ready to begin, and Burke hoped to distract her as much as possible.

"Twenty-five stitches is what did the trick," he said, keeping his head rested against hers.

"Tell me," Storm said, her hand reaching out to grab hold of his. "Was it a blade, an arrow, a fierce fight that won you the honor of a scar?"

"It was . . ." He paused, meeting her eyes so close that he could tell that one eye was slightly bluer than the other. "A pitchfork."

"A pitchfork?" Storm asked with a gasp as the needle pierced her skin for the first stitch.

"A mighty weapon, I might add," he said dramatically. "I was but a lad of ten years and challenged by friends to take a dive into the haystack."

Burke hurried to continue when Storm squeezed his hand as Janelle made the next stitch. "It was a dare I could not refuse."

"Your honor was at stake," Storm agreed.

"You understand," he whispered, and his lips drifted to her ear as her hand squeezed his harder.

"Honor must be defended," Storm said with difficulty as Janelle made a third stitch.

"And I did a superb job," Burke bragged, and was relieved to hear Storm chuckle and rest her head to his shoulder. "I positioned myself just right for the dive."

Storm glanced up at him, and he was caught in the depths of her blue eyes. Her pain was obvious but so was her strength. They battled for dominance, and he had no doubt which would be the victor.

"Without making certain of what awaited you?"

"I was ten," he offered as an excuse.

"And about to learn a hard lesson," she said with a cringe.

He pressed his cheek to hers and whispered in her ear. "I now look before I leap."

Storm laughed as Janelle finished the last stitch. Burke stepped away so that Janelle could bandage her shoulder.

"What happened after your plunge into the pitchfork?" Storm asked with a teasing smile.

Burke stuck out his chest. "I screamed through every stitch and was comforted by my mother for three days straight."

Storm's smile faded. "I have no time for rest or comfort."

She walked out and Burke followed. He silently admonished himself for his remark. He should have remembered that Storm had never had the comfort of a loving mother. Her childhood had been harsh and lonely. Even now, he knew she had to feel alone. She was a leader, and her men and people came first.

Of course, there had been her husband, but he had yet to find out about him. He knew her men would offer no information, and though he was curious, he thought it inappropriate to ask her directly about him. He had a feeling that her penchant for rescuing the helpless might have something to do with her husband and the reason she was now an outlaw. In time, he would discover the truth.

He caught up with her as she was about to grab the rope to descend to the ground.

"I'll get you down." His hand caught the rope at the same time hers did.

She hesitated, but he could see that her common sense took over and she nodded her approval.

They descended much differently than they had ascended. She no longer leaned on him. Her strength had returned, and she placed a distance between them even though he held her close. It was as if she had erected a shield to protect herself against being protected.

How he would penetrate that shield, he wasn't certain. That he would penetrate it, he was certain.

"There is nothing so urgent that you cannot rest," he said when they reached the bottom.

She pushed away from him with a wince.

He reached out, and she stepped out of his grasp.

"There is your brother to see to."

"The men need rest," Burke said. "It will have to wait."

"There may not be time," Storm insisted. "If it is your brother Cullen being held, then he has been there over a month. He could be close to death by now."

She walked away, and Burke once again followed, annoyed at being reminded of his brother's precarious position. He needed no such reminding. He worried that he would be too late to rescue Cullen and not only that he would fail to fulfill his father's dying wish, but that he would never get to know his only sibling.

"Glencurry must still be dealt with," Burke heard her say as she approached the campfire where her men sat.

"We have been considering the matter," William said, his meaty hand reaching out to assist her to take a seat next to him.

Burke joined them, squeezing in between the lean Philip and Malcolm. That they even considered the failed rescue so soon after returning from a mission amazed him. He thought Storm would order the men to rest, and here she ordered that another mission be discussed, and the men did so willingly.

He remained silent, watching the motley crew work. They argued, agreed, and argued some more, and Storm never stopped any one of them from voicing his opinions. She showed them all respect, as they did her.

"What say you?" William asked, turning to Storm.

"We all agree on one thing—that Cullen, if it is him, cannot survive much longer. The rescue attempt must be immediate if he is to be found alive."

The men nodded their agreement.

"Which means we cannot waste another minute," Philip said and stood. William rose with him.

"You need to rest first," Burke said.

"The few hours they rest could mean your brother's life," Storm said. "Are you willing to risk that?"

"It's as much a risk sending them on little rest. A couple of hours' sleep should help revive them and then they can be off."

"It also could be enough time for the soldiers to

regroup and return," Storm suggested. "So which then is the better choice?"

"Are you leaving the decision to me?" Burke asked, surprised.

"He's your brother."

She hadn't considered that when she made the decision to send the men in the first place. She hadn't even consulted him, so why did she do so now?

"Let the men rest," he said.

Storm nodded and looked to William and Philip. "You leave shortly; get ready."

Burke jumped to his feet, the two men hurried off, and the other men drifted away from the campfire.

"Why give me a choice when you had no intention of honoring it?" That he was annoyed resonated in his gruff tone and his stoic stance.

"I wanted to see what you would do."

She sounded as if she judged him, and his annoyance grew. "And you don't like what I did?"

"You thought of the men, not the prisoner."

"I thought of both."

"There is only one who can be considered," she said sharply. "His life depends on it."

"If the men are too tired—"

"They'll get over it and do what they must."

"Like Tanin?" Burke challenged.

To his surprise, she smiled.

"Are you angry because Tanin did what was necessary and you could not?"

That fired his defenses. "I would not have slapped you. I would have handled it differently."

"And gotten the same immediate results?" She

didn't wait for an answer. "I need my men to follow my orders without hesitation. It could mean the safety or loss of a life or lives. Each one of them understands this and does what he is told. You, Mr. Longton, find it impossible to do."

"There is a simple answer for that, Storm."

"And what is that?"

"I don't follow; I lead."

Chapter 9

Storm marched right up to him. "There's room for only one leader in my group, Mr. Longton. If you cannot accept that, then you can leave." She turned and hurried her pace since she felt an overwhelming need to punch the arrogant American.

One minute he was tender and caring and the next minute he was claiming himself a leader. Well, not here was he, nor would he be. She had warned him, and she had the feeling she would continue to warn him about following orders. It was already tiresome, but the money—

She halted so quickly that she kicked up a cloud of dirt around her.

She hadn't had time to discuss an exact fee with him, and she suddenly wondered if it was worth keeping the American around.

Storm turned, intending to do just that, and almost collided with Burke.

"Were you following me?" she accused.

"We weren't finished," he said

"There is no room for discussion. You either—"

He cut her off. "I didn't say I wouldn't follow your orders. I also didn't say I wouldn't object now and again. From what I've seen in the short time I've been here, it's obvious that you not only allow your men to voice their opinions but you also consider them. I'm expressing my opinions, maybe a little more forcefully, but it's only natural since I'm accustomed to leading."

"Since you are a leader, you know only one person can lead."

"Believe me," he said with a shake of his head. "I'm trying to remember that."

"I'll keep reminding you," Storm said with a chuckle.

"I have no doubt of that, but be aware you may tire of reminding me," he cautioned, his smile spreading slowly.

"A leader must chastise when necessary." Her smile grew as his faded. She knew her words stung his pride, but then they meant to remind.

"Were you returning to speak with me?" he asked.

She was relieved he'd changed the subject. There had been enough debate. Any further discussion would not change the outcome.

"We never discussed a fee."

"I thought the same myself," he said.

They entered into a brief discussion since the sum Burke offered was more than generous for what he asked of her in return. The money would sustain them for a year or more if they were careful.

He baffled her, this American who had entered her life so chaotically and continued to cause anarchy. Yet she could not help but respect him and admire his courage.

She watched him walk off to wait for her beneath the tree. After she told him she would speak with William and Philip privately before they left, he insisted he'd wait to help her get to her quarters.

She hadn't argued with him, perhaps because she felt it more sensible not to irritate her injured arm, or had she liked the comfort of his arms?

Storm was shocked by her own thoughts and shook the nonsense from her head. Wherever had that idea come from? She had known the man barely two days and he had annoyed her more than not.

It had to have been the kiss, she reasoned, returning to the campfire. It reminded her of bittersweet memories, memories she thought she kept tucked away. It had been three long years since her husband had last kissed her, held her, made love to her.

She shivered and hugged herself tightly. She missed the warmth of Daniel's arms, his body next to hers at night. They would cuddle in each other's arms and fall asleep content. She hadn't been able to sleep for weeks after his death. She had felt a constant chill without him beside her.

It had taken time to cope with his death, to make sense of it, accept it.

She shook her head. She really had done neither. His death made no sense and she had never truly accepted his demise, she had simply learned how to live with his absence.

Now this brash American appeared and stirred long-buried emotions that she preferred remain buried. She didn't want to be reminded and feel the dreadful pain of losing Daniel yet again.

"You're cold."

Storm jumped and glared at Burke as he dropped to his knee and added more wood to the dwindling fire.

"You must stop sneaking up on people," she admonished, holding her hands out to the rekindled flames to warm her hands.

"I wasn't sneaking, and besides, you looked deep in thought and I didn't wish to disturb you." He sat on the log beside her. "Is something troubling you?"

You.

She shook her head. She had no time to let nonsense interfere with her mission. No time for a man and no desire to love again. She had sworn over her husband's body never to let another suffer so senselessly, and she would spend the rest of her life fulfilling that oath.

"Are you sure?"

She appeased him with an answer. "I have much on my mind and it sometimes overwhelms."

"The way of a leader. That is why a leader should have a diversion now and again."

"And what do you do for a diversion?" she asked, curious.

"I ride across my ranch, sometimes for two or three days. Its vast, raw beauty puts everything into a clearer prospective. What once overwhelmed then seems inconsequential, and I return a much more satisfied man."

"That sounds appealing. Unfortunately, I don't have the luxury of time. A moment by the creek, a brief glance from the tree house, or catching the flight of a soaring hawk are my diversions on occasion. Minute ones, though I do cherish them."

"Do you ever rest?"

"You sound as if you accuse me of a crime," she said and was suddenly caught in the depths of his rich brown eyes. They explored her face with an intensity that made her wonder what he searched for. That he had many questions was obvious. That he asked few disturbed her. He was patient in his exploration, which meant he was determined.

"A good leader knows rest is essential to performance and accuracy."

"A good leader knows she will be called on to perform and make decisions, whether rested or not," she recounted. "Why do you try so hard to get me into bed, Mr. Longton?"

A wicked grin spread across his face, and she laughed at her ill-chosen words.

He leaned in closer to her. "Given the opportunity, I don't think it would be hard for us to fall into bed together."

"Confident in your prowess, are you?"

"Astute when it comes to attraction."

Storm didn't have a chance to respond, for William

and Philip approached and Burke took his leave.

She saw the two men off once the plans were finalized. It was agreed that if they had not returned in a week's time, Tanin and Angus would come after them. She said a silent prayer for their safe journey and returned to sit for a moment alone at the campfire.

What had Burke meant by "astute when it comes to attraction"? Was he attracted to her? Did he think she was attracted to him? They barely knew each other. How could he surmise anything?

It hadn't taken Daniel a long time to make his attraction known to her. He had stopped one day at the farm where she lived, and she had given him and his horse water. He returned every day after that until finally, a month later, he proclaimed his love for her and asked her to marry him. He told her he was a tenant farmer two villages away, and while his plot of land was small, it could sustain them both.

She left with him, but her dream of finally finding someone who would love her and never leave her ended when Daniel died only two years after they wed, leaving her alone yet again.

The crunch of leaves alerted Storm to someone's approach.

"Deep in thought again?"

"Taking a moment for myself," she said as Burke stepped out of the dark. "Thank you for letting me know of your approach."

"Didn't want to startle you again and I don't want to intrude on your privacy." He turned to walk away.

"You're not intruding. I had my moment."

He turned around and sat beside her. "It was awfully brief."

"I would ask how you knew that, but no doubt you have been watching me."

"Keeping a safe eye on you. You were injured only a few hours ago," he reminded with a glance to her shoulder.

"I appreciate your concern, but I really am fine and I can really look after myself."

"You've proven that, but I"—he tapped his chest—"feel better keeping an eye on you. You never know. You may faint again."

"And you'll be there to give me a good solid slap."

Burke laughed and shook his head. "Not likely. You'd be in my arms before you could hit the ground. Then I'd carry you to bed, where you should be now resting, and would see that you stayed there until properly healed."

Storm cut loose with a hearty laugh, and when she was done and holding her side from the laughter, she said, "That will never happen, Mr. Longton."

"You're sure of that?"

"I'm sure," she said with the last snicker of laughter escaping. "I've never fainted, and I seek my bed when I'm ready and rest when I want to. So what you suggest could happen is simply impossible."

"Never faint?"

She shook her head. "Not once, and as you've seen today, I prevented it. And as far as carried to bed?" She stuck her booted feet out and wiggled them. "I have two good solid feet to get myself to bed."

Burke stuck out his arms. "And I have two good solid arms to carry you."

Before Storm could scoot out of his reach, he had her up in his arms and was walking off with her.

"Put me down," she ordered calmly though firmly.

"I will," he agreed.

"Now."

"No."

"I order you—"

"To put you down and I will," he said.

"Now," she reiterated.

He dropped her to her feet, grabbed her around the waist, and coiled the rope around his arm to have them springing up the tree.

Before she could voice her objection, he once again had her up in his arms and carried her into her quarters to plop her down on the narrow bed.

"Is this supposed to prove me wrong and you right?" she accused, hurrying off the bed, only to be stopped short by a searing pain to her shoulder. She stumbled and would have toppled over if Burke hadn't grabbed hold and eased her down on the bed.

"You are stubborn," he said, keeping hold of her.

"I'm vigilant," she corrected and took a deep breath against the throbbing pain that remained. "I must be, and dare I say, you're just as obstinate?"

"You can, but that doesn't mean I agree."

"You are forthright."

"And that you can always count on," he said and released her to stand. "You and I clash for a reason."

"And what is that?"

87

"We are alike." He walked to the door and turned. "Which means we understand each other more than we realize. Sleep well."

He disappeared out the door, and Storm sat there staring after him.

Chapter 10

Burke searched the gray sky. Heavy rain clouds drifted in from the distance, promising a downpour. He checked the perimeter of the camp once again and saw nothing. He took his frustration out on a rock, kicking it with his boot and sending it tumbling.

It had been six days since Storm and Tanin had left. He hadn't been informed of their absence. It was the day after he had dumped Storm on her bed. He had intended on rising early to see that she took it easy for the day, giving her shoulder time to heal.

She wasn't in her quarters and no one would tell him a thing until Malcolm finally returned to camp and told him she'd be away a few days. He would say no more, and Burke had no choice but to accept the snippet of information.

He had advised Malcolm that he could have helped. Malcolm had told him not this time, which made him worry even more.

He hoped it didn't have anything to do with Cullen. It would annoy him if Storm had gone off on a matter concerning his brother without him, but then they had never agreed that he would be privy to all information regarding his brother, only that she would help locate him.

Being it was the sixth day, he was growing concerned, though no one else seemed to. Activity went on as usual, and he had become familiar with the camp in Storm's absence.

It ran smoothly, with everyone tending to specific chores and none complaining or shirking their duties. They were a fine group working together to survive. That his money was needed was evident in the tattered and patched clothes, the sparse food, and the lack of adequate weapons.

Laughter, however, was prevalent, as were smiles and camaraderie. They were a contented lot for outlaws.

Burke kept busy hunting with Malcolm, making repairs to weapons, and getting to know those in the camp. But there wasn't a day that he didn't think of Storm and worry over her.

What was so urgent that it took her away when she needed to recover from her wound? Why didn't she send someone else or ask for his help? Why was he so annoyed that she left without him?

He finally joined Malcolm and Angus to feast on the rabbit cooking on a spit over the campfire.

"Eat. Rain comes soon," Angus said, already biting into a fat piece of meat.

Conversation was sparse and the rabbit near cleaned to the bone when the first drop of rain hit. It sent everyone scurrying for shelter.

Burke scanned the edge of the woods. Disappointed that nothing came into sight, he hurried to his quarters in the trees. He stripped off his damp shirt and threw it over the chest to dry, then stretched out on the bed, cushioned his arms beneath his head, and listened to the rain.

He wondered if Storm had safe, dry shelter, or if she huddled cold and wet somewhere. Knowing her, she'd survive either way.

She intrigued him. She had since they first met, dressed as a man, though more resembling a lad. Her face betrayed her gender. She was much too beautiful to be anything but a woman. Add stubborn to that and it rounded out her gender, but then obstinate women were a challenge, and what man could turn down a challenge?

He grinned as night crawled into the room and laid claim to it, except for the small glow of the hearth fire. It amazed him the way a hearth was constructed in the tree houses. It was small but functional, and Burke wondered about the designer's identity.

Storm had seen to making this a safe haven for them all, but nothing lasted forever. What would happen when a rescue failed, men were lost, and funds ran out?

The future didn't look bright for the outlaws, but then did a fugitive really have a future?

He recalled Storm when she dressed as a woman and how lovely she looked. He could only imagine how her beauty would shine if she was dressed in new garments. But what good would new garments do her here in the forest, fighting the soldiers?

She could return to America with him.

The unexpected thought rattled him. This was her home, her land, and her people. She was born and raised here and had even warned him that Cullen might very well refuse to leave. He imagined she would as well.

He could do only so much for her, and the thought saddened him.

His eyes drifted shut as he thought how much she might like the Dakota Territory and what a shame that she'd never get a chance to see it.

A crack of thunder woke him with a start and he jolted up in bed. He could hear the rain still, and something else. He swung his legs off the bed, and cocked his head at the sound, his ears trying to determine its origin.

Footsteps. Had Storm returned?

He hurried out of his room, forgetting his shirt. Her door stood ajar, and he thought he heard voices, so he entered without knocking.

She stood naked before the burning hearth, her back to him and her slim body glistening from the rain that dotted her pale skin. She was exquisite; a narrow waist that curved to round hips and taut buttocks, and skin that appeared as soft as a fresh rose petal.

She shivered, her skin running wild with goose-flesh, and he quickly grabbed the blanket from the bed and wrapped it around her, drawing her back into his arms to rest against his chest.

She didn't object, didn't push him away or insist that she needed no help. She simply lingered in the silence of his protective embrace.

He hugged her tightly, wanting to keep her warm and wanting to chase away whatever worries haunted her.

After several silent minutes he whispered, "Are you all right?"

She didn't answer immediately and he simply waited.

"I wasn't in time."

The despair in her voice jabbed at his heart. "You can't save everyone."

She turned around in his arms. "I would have gone immediately if I had known. I didn't know."

"You can't blame yourself."

A single tear rolled down her cheek. "He was my brother."

Burke almost reeled from her remark, and he had the good sense to walk both of them to the bed to sit.

A tap at the door preceded Janelle's entrance, and she smiled when she saw him there beside Storm.

"I brought a hot brew to warm her and cloths to change her wet bandage." Janelle placed the items on the table. "Could you see to it for me, Burke? I have more pressing matters."

Burke nodded. "I'll take care of her."

Janelle closed the door quietly behind her.

He left her side to get the hot brew, placing the cup in her hands, and ordered her to drink.

She took a sip.

"I didn't know you had a brother," he said.

"He wasn't my blood brother, but we spent a good portion of our lives together working for the same family."

Burke understood the camaraderie of such a relationship. Sometimes it could be stronger than blood relations.

"How did you learn of his plight?"

Storm hugged the warm cup. "I received a message in the middle of the night."

"Why didn't you wake me? I would have gone with you."

"Tanin was the logical choice and he was familiar with the area. You would have only slowed me down and time was of the essence, though time had run out."

Burke listened while he redressed her wound.

"He was imprisoned for stealing food and then left to starve. It makes no sense."

"Life never does," he said, relieved to feel that her chilled skin had warmed considerably. He'd like to think his arms had warmed her, but probably the hot brew had chased the chill from her bones.

"I want it to," she said adamantly. "I want something to make sense. Tell me something that makes sense."

"Love?" Burke questioned his own suggestion.

"You don't sound as if you believe that yourself."

"It was my first thought so I went with it." He finished tying off the dry bandage. "When you think about it, though, love might just make the most sense. It's what brought me here and what makes you rescue the helpless. It's a driving force that has people accomplishing extraordinary things. And once love takes hold there's no stopping it."

Storm looked as if she contemplated that as she sipped her brew, then she asked, "Have you ever loved?"

"There's many people I've loved, but if you ask if there's a special woman, then the answer is no."

"You've never been married?"

"Not even close," he confirmed with a laugh.

"You don't wish to wed?"

"I will only wed when I fall in love, completely, foolishly, deeply, and without doubt. I intend to share the pitfalls and the joys of life with her until our dying day."

"What a lovely thought. I wish you success in your quest to find such a love, but then you're stubborn enough to be successful."

"A trait we have in common," he reminded, and thought to ask about her husband, but realized it wasn't a good time. She had suffered enough with losing a brother. She didn't need memories of her husband adding to her pain.

"Leaders are never stubborn, Mr. Longton." She smiled. "We are wise."

He smiled along with her, pleased that she had acknowledged him as a leader sharing the same quality.

"Thank you," she said softly.

"For what?"

She tucked the blanket around her. "For covering me up and warming me."

"I never meant to intrude on your privacy," he explained. "The door was ajar and I hoped you had returned safely from your journey."

"Weary, but safe," she confirmed.

He wanted to reach out, wrap her in his arms, and take her to bed—to sleep. She needed rest, and he'd make sure she got it. He wouldn't let her out of his arms until she slept a good many hours.

"Now if you will excuse me, sleep will be a welcome reprieve for me."

"I couldn't agree more," he said, relieved she'd finally get the rest she needed, and walked to the door. He turned, holding the door ajar. "You won't be going off somewhere in the middle of the night, will you?"

"To tell the truth, once I fall asleep I don't think anyone will be able to wake me."

He grinned. "Sounds good to me." He stopped again before going out the door. "But if by chance another emergency arises, please wake me. I'd be only too glad to help out."

"I'll keep that in mind."

He wanted to insist, but thought better of it. Storm would do what she wanted regardless, so he'd have to sleep lightly and keep aware of sounds and make certain she didn't slip past him once again.

The rain continued for a few hours throughout the night, then stopped. Burke slept on and off, his sleep disturbed by dreams and sounds. Finally, as the first hint of dawn rose on the horizon, he tossed the covers aside and got dressed in his trousers, shirt, and the brown leather vest Angus had given him.

He hadn't heard a sound from Storm's room all night. He assumed she slept soundly but he wanted to make sure for his own peace of mind. He kept his footsteps light and with a gentle push of her door, he peeked inside.

Several oaths spilled from his lips.

Storm wasn't there.

He descended the rope in an instant and made his way through the camp searching for her. She had an uncanny way of disappearing. It seemed that no one had seen her. He knew better. No one would tell him where she went. He wasn't really one of them, and therefore he wasn't fully trusted.

Why hadn't he heard her leave? His sleep had been restless enough and he'd been alert.

Janelle bid him good morning but knew nothing of Storm's whereabouts or those of her son, Tanin. Malcolm had also disappeared, as had Angus.

Had they all left on another mission?

Damn, he hated being left out.

He was going to have to make it very clear to Storm that he wanted to be advised of her whereabouts at all times.

He laughed, as he knew she would. What right did he have to demand anything from her? He was a stranger and therefore a safety risk. Why should she tell him anything? She really had been generous so far with him. She had searched for his brother immediately and provided a safe haven for him while he awaited his funds. He had no right demanding anything.

Angus stepped out of the woods, a big man, the size and width of a bear, though gentler. He carried fresh fish on a pole and smiled as he approached.

"Where is everyone?" Burke asked anxiously.

"A good morning to you," Angus said, walking past him to the campfire and kneeling to prepare the fish.

Burke followed him. "Tanin, Malcolm, and Storm are gone—"

"Sit," Angus instructed with a nod. "They'll be here shortly."

"You know where they went?"

"Aye."

Burke wanted to rip the answer from the man. He was tired of his questions being evaded, tired of secrets, tired of being treated like the enemy.

"Tell me," he demanded.

Angus glanced up at him. "All you had to do was ask."

"I'm asking."

"We got word hours ago that William and Philip were near and needed assistance. They have your brother with them. He's injured."

Chapter 11

Storm entered camp just ahead of her men. She wanted to speak with Burke privately but he rushed at her, not giving her a chance.

"Are you all right?" he asked anxiously.

Stunned that his concern for her preempted his concern for his brother, Storm merely nodded her head.

"Make certain you have Janelle take a look at your shoulder."

Again not a mention of his brother, his concern focused on her, and it reminded her of how Daniel used to worry over her. It was heartfelt, and the endearing thought near pierced the protective armor she kept wrapped around her.

Burke Longton was simply a considerate man, no more.

William and Malcolm entered the village supporting a man barely able to walk. Tanin followed, and they rushed to Janelle's hut at the base of a tree where she tended the ailing and injured during the day.

Burke rushed alongside them and Storm followed, anxious to speak with him.

The man was placed gently on a makeshift bed of thatch. He had been beaten so badly that his face was indistinguishable. The rest of his body looked to have suffered the same fate, and from his woeful moans, his pain was obvious.

Storm stopped Burke from going to the man's side with a hand to his arm. "Let Janelle see to him. We need to talk."

He hesitated.

"It's important," she insisted and tugged at his arm.

"Have you eaten?" Burke asked, leaving the hut.

She shook her head, amazed that his concern for her seemed neverending.

"There's fish at the campfire."

He took her arm as if he thought her weary and needing help, and walked with her to the campfire, where the smell of cooked fish filled her with joy, her stomach agreeing with a rumble.

She was surprised that he hadn't immediately demanded to know why she had taken him away from his brother.

"Your stomach sounds anxious," Burke said.

Storm sat on the log. "It's been almost a day since I ate."

Burke picked the fish clean of meat and gave her a handful. She accepted it gratefully.

"Eat some," he urged, "before you deliver the news about my brother."

She took a small bite, but not wanting to delay the inevitable, she said, "The man we freed isn't your brother."

"How do you know this?"

That he hoped she was wrong was evident. "Once he knew we neared camp he admitted his name was Peter, not Cullen."

Burke nodded knowingly. "Cullen had a chance for freedom, he feared Peter would not."

"Exactly," Storm said. "Peter admitted that a man had just been removed from there, though he did not know if his name was Cullen."

"It is the only lead we have; we must follow it. Where was he taken?"

"He doesn't know."

Burke paced the opposite side of the campfire, then stopped abruptly. "Philip did not return with you. You left him behind to see what he could learn, didn't you?"

Storm nodded, swallowing a piece of the delicious fish. "If the man had just been removed, his trail would be fresh. We could not lose the opportunity to follow if possible."

"I am lucky to have found you."

He never ceased to startle her with his generous and honest remarks.

"If not for you, I wouldn't have made it to Dunwith, and even if I had, I doubt anyone there would have spoken to me. I am grateful for your help."

"You are paying me a sizable fee," she reminded him, feeling uncomfortable with his praise and turning her attention to picking the last of the meat off her fingers.

Burke suddenly plopped down on his haunches in front of her and proceeded to help her, popping the pieces he picked into her mouth. "You have been a great help, and I want you to know it."

His actions startled her but she managed not to show her unease, though it was difficult. The tips of his fingers brushed her lips and dusted her chin of crumbs. An innocent enough gesture, and yet it produced a shivering effect she thought had died with her husband.

No one had touched her intimately since Daniel.

Storm gently pushed his hands aside. "Your generous fee requires my immediate attention."

"My fee?" he asked, placing a hand to his heart as if wounded. "You mean you care nothing for me?"

Storm smiled, though she wondered how serious was his jest.

"I care for the plight of the defenseless. I will not abandon you or your brother in your time of need."

"Why do you fight so relentlessly for the helpless?" he asked, sitting beside her.

"Who else fights for them?"

Burke shook his head. "Something had to have

happened to make you such a staunch defender of those in need."

"My land, my people, that's cause enough to fight against injustice. You can't tell me you haven't done it yourself."

"True enough."

"I imagine you've even stepped outside the law on occasion."

"A necessary evil," he admitted, "as now."

"You do realize you take your life in your hands by residing among outlaws."

Burke shrugged. "I am not known here in your country and I do not plan on remaining here. I hope to convince Cullen to return with me."

"No desire to remain in Scotland?" she asked, wondering why she would even think he would give credence to such a thought.

"My home is the Dakota Territory. I miss it even now."

"I feel the same," she admitted. "There's no way I'd leave Scotland."

They sat silent for a moment, both digesting their declarations and both wondering why they felt disturbed by the news.

Burke broke the silence. "When Janelle says he's able, I'd like to speak with Peter."

"A good idea," Storm agreed, anxious to move away from the fact that while they were much alike, she and Burke were also worlds apart. "You may be able to learn something that might determine if the man removed from prison was your brother."

"I thought the same myself, though I know so little of my brother," Burke said with sorrow.

"He could resemble your father. Do you?"

Burke grinned. "My father often commented that I was spared his features and lucky to have my mother's good looks."

"So you have no idea what your brother looks like?"

"Not a hint, which is what makes this search all the more difficult," he admitted.

"Difficult, but not impossible," Storm encouraged.

"You really do enthrall me."

"You, Mr. Longton, continually stun me."

"My honesty can do that at times, but then at least you know who you deal with, and damn if I don't love the way my name rolls off your tongue in that thick Scottish burr of yours."

"Pardon if I don't find my name sounding as titillating on your tongue. Your American accent is a bit harsh on the ears."

He laughed and attempted to pronounce her name with a Scottish burr. It wasn't long before they both were laughing.

"I prefer your American accent. It does less damage to my name," Storm said after calming her laughter.

"It was worth a try," he said and reached out his fingers to her chin.

She pulled away, uncertain of his intentions.

"No, no," he urged, holding his hand steady. "You have a piece of fish—"

She let him dust the piece from the corner of her mouth, a light dusting as if he barely touched her, and yet he left his mark. He stirred her senses and sent a shiver through her though she concealed her reaction, remaining perfectly still.

"You haven't known a man's touch in some time, have you?" he asked, his hand drifting off her.

"Storm!"

She turned to see Tanin signaling her from Janelle's hut.

"Peter must be conscious enough to speak coherently," Storm said and stood.

"I'll have an answer from you sooner or later," Burke said as he walked off ahead of her.

A chill ran through her, seeping into her bones and causing her to shiver. Was she imagining things, or did Mr. Longton seem interested in her? She shook her head. She felt foolish for even giving the idea credence. He was nothing more than a brash American who spoke out of turn every chance he got.

She was a woman who missed her husband and the intimacy she had shared with him. There wasn't a night she hadn't ached for Daniel's touch, for his hard, warm body next to hers, for the way he held her close when they slept or the way he teased her body alive with his fingers and his lips.

Somehow, Burke had managed to spark those memories and ignite them. However, it would do her little good to feed the flame. Mr. Longton would eventually return to America. She would never see him again.

But then her life was far from conducive to finding love. Perhaps she should allow herself to enjoy a brief interlude with Burke and fill the emptiness inside her, if only temporarily.

She could make no commitment to a man or promise a future with children. More than likely she would eventually be caught, imprisoned, and perhaps put to death, or she would live out her days in the woods as an outlaw.

She had no future, a fact she accepted, so therefore she had to live life for the moment, and Burke was here for the moment.

"Storm!" Tanin called out again.

She hurried off, trying not to think about Burke.

"I did not see the man," Storm heard Peter say upon entering the hut.

"Is there anything you can tell me about him?" Burke asked.

Storm noticed that Peter breathed slowly as if it hurt him to take the slightest breath. "Take your time," she said, kneeling beside him.

The injured man attempted to smile and winced. "I do know he was given extra attention."

"Treated special?" Burke asked.

"If treated worse is special," Peter answered sadly. "His size probably helped him. He was a big man, wide with muscle and tall. He had to bend his head to enter the torture room."

"What color was his hair?" Burke asked.

"Like yours," Peter said with a nod to Burke.

Storm watched Burke tense.

"He was a brave one, or perhaps foolish," Peter

said. "He refused to speak, answer any questions, deny any accusations."

"What did they accuse him of?" Storm asked.

"Stealing from the Earl of Balford. A horrendous fate awaited him is what they promised when they finally dragged him away."

"What did he steal?' Burke asked.

"I don't know," Peter said.

"You never heard him called by name?" Burke asked anxiously.

"If I did, I don't remember. I wish I could be of more help." A tear spilled from the corner of his swollen eye. "I am forever grateful for the rescue and am sorry to have misled you."

"Don't worry," Storm said, patting his arm gently. "We would have rescued you whether you were the man we were after or not."

The man reached out a feeble hand to Storm. "You're the woman whispered about in the prisons. The one everyone prays will free them."

"I do what I can for those in need."

"You must be careful," Peter urged. "I heard them talking about plans to capture you and make you pay for your crimes."

"Do not worry about me."

"No. No," Peter protested anxiously. "You must take care. You must not meet such a horrible fate."

Janelle stepped in, chasing everyone out, insisting that Peter had to rest and shoving clean bandages into Burke's hands. "See to Storm."

Storm took the bandages from Burke. "I can see to my own wound."

Burke snatched the bandages back. "Janelle ordered me to see to it and so I shall."

Storm grinned. "Since when do you obey a woman?"

"Since the order is no chore at all."

They were standing beneath her tree house and in an instant, Burke had her around the waist, the rope around his arm, and they were gliding up to the treetops.

She liked the feel of his embrace. He cuddled her against him, holding her firm as if he never intended to let her go. She let her defenses down for a moment to rest her face on his chest and breathe in the scent of him, loving the pungent mix of earth and pine.

His warmth and his strength both penetrated her to the bone and filled her with a sense of peace. She hadn't felt such peace since Daniel had last held her.

Her head snapped up along with her guard, and when they entered her quarters she said, "I can tend to my wound."

"Better that I do it," Burke insisted, turning the chair around for her to sit after placing the bandages on the table.

She didn't move. "The wound is healing fine."

"Show me," he said, gesturing her to sit.

When she hesitated he asked, "What are you afraid of, Storm?"

"Not you, Mr. Longton," she said, stepping almost nose to nose with him.

"Then prove it. Let me help you."

She could not take a challenge lightly or allow this man to think she was afraid of him.

"All right, Burke, tend my wound," she said and slipped her shirt over her head to stand bare-chested in front of him.

Chapter 12

"**S**it," Burke ordered with a tap to the wooden chair. It was apparent Storm had tried to shock him. He hoped his reaction wasn't as apparent, though it sure had surprised him how quickly he had sprung to life. The quicker he could get his eyes off her breasts the better. They were round and full and her nipples a dark, rosy color and hard, possibly as hard as he was right now.

Relief flooded him when she sat, and though her breasts were partially out of sight, they weren't out of mind. He worked quickly at changing her bandage and was pleased to see that her wound was healing nicely.

"The stitches should come out soon, don't you think?" she asked looking up at him.

He was forced to meet her eyes and catch a glance of her naked breasts. Damn if he didn't ache to touch them, so round and perfect and the hard nipples so deliciously inviting. He could almost feel his tongue exploring them, his teeth nipping at them, and his mouth—

He nodded. "I'd say tomorrow or the day after." He turned away from her. "All finished." He wanted her to put her shirt back on. Actually, he needed her to cover up. Her breasts were just too damned tempting. All of her was just too damned tempting.

"Thank you," she said.

He turned just as her shirt slipped over her breasts, and relief mixed with regret.

"You're welcome. So what now?"

"What do you suggest?" she asked, tucking her shirt around her trim waist and into her trousers.

It was an innocent enough question, but with where his mind had wandered, it was now a dangerous one. He found Storm attractive, which was surprising. He had reminded himself time and time again that she wasn't at all his type.

She was too petite, and yet here he found himself responding to her like a young buck in heat. He had always maintained control when it came to passion. There had never been a woman who got him hot and bothered with just one glance. Until Storm.

"No suggestions?" she asked again.

He had suggestions but he was sure she wouldn't approve.

"We continue to question Peter when he feels up to it. If we continue to probe, he may remember something."

"I thought the same myself," she agreed and walked to the door.

"Aren't you going to rest?" he asked, wondering if Storm required any sleep at all. She didn't look tired. She actually looked refreshed, and he wondered how she maintained her chaotic pace.

"No time," she said, stopping at the open door. "On the way back we were alerted to a lad barely ten who was recently imprisoned for hunting on the manor lord's private grounds. He is being held in the village of Mewers. His family has no funds to get him released."

"So you will."

"Wouldn't you?"

Burke walked over to her. "I'm right beside you on this one."

Once again, the group gathered around the campfire to discuss another rescue mission, and they also hoped to obtain some supplies that were desperately needed.

"Mewers's prisoners are sequestered in a building behind the manor house," Tanin informed the group.

"An easy rescue?" Burke asked, not feeling as much of an outsider, thanks to the last few days spent with the people in the camp. He had become more aware of their plight and their pride and could empathize with them.

"Unfortunately not," Storm said. "Mewers is the one village that has a thriving market which attracts many people as well as thieves, the hungry, and the needy. The manor lord maintains a large troop of soldiers to see that his prisoners remain imprisoned and that his market is safe from those who don't have the coin to spend."

"A stronghold of sorts," Burke said.

"That it is," Tanin agreed.

"The manor lord there, the Earl of Henwood has close ties with the Earl of Balford. Their properties adjoin and Henwood has been known to hold prisoners for Balford," Storm explained.

"My brother could be there," Burke said.

Storm nodded. "There is that possibility, which is why Philip has been sent ahead to gather information."

"This could prove a difficult rescue mission," Angus said.

"Not if we plan for it," Storm said. "Philip will provide us with the information we need concerning the guards' routine. That leaves the market." She turned to Malcolm. "You've been there, haven't you?"

"I've managed to steal an item or two without being caught," he boasted.

"Then you and Burke will see to canvassing the market—"

Burke interrupted her. "I'd prefer to be part of the prison rescue."

"And you may be, but for now, you will learn what you can about the market so that our thievery goes on undetected."

Burke had learned there was a method to her decisions that usually proved accurate and successful, so he would bow to her expertise and follow her lead. For now.

"When do we leave?" Burke asked.

"Early morning," Storm instructed and then proceeded to give detailed instructions as to the mission itself.

When the plans were finalized, Burke informed Storm that he intended to speak with Peter again. He was surprised or perhaps disappointed that she didn't ask to join him. She simply acknowledged his intentions with a nod and turned to speak with Tanin.

He found out soon enough that Peter was in no condition to talk and took his leave, intending to look over the weapons that might prove useful on this mission.

He caught sight of Storm entering the woods alone. While everyone there was accustomed to her independent nature, he still had trouble with it. So he followed her.

She appeared set on a destination, remaining focused on the trail she traveled. Burke didn't find it difficult keeping pace with her though he was amazed at her stamina. She had barely returned from a six-day journey, and here she was walking the woods yet again.

The forest grew thick with trees and brush, making tracking her a bit more difficult but not impossible. Then suddenly the density gave way to a clearing and the ruins of an old structure.

He remained concealed by the brush and watched Storm approach the crumbled edifice. She took a seat on what had once been a stone wall that now looked like nothing more than a few stones haphazardly piled together.

She tilted her head back to the bright sun, and he was captivated by the graceful beauty of her pose. The sun's rays kissed her slim neck, giving it a translucent sheen and inviting soft, subtle nibbles.

Damn, he couldn't stop thinking about kissing her. He was going to have to satisfy his temptation sooner or later or he'd drive himself crazy. The one kiss they had shared had lingered much too long in his memory and probably was the cause for his wanting to taste her again.

One more kiss. One more kiss would do it and he'd be satisfied.

"Why don't you join me, Burke?"

He eagerly stepped out of his hiding place. "When did you realize I was following you?"

"When my sentry signaled me that I had someone on my tail."

He shook his head. "I forgot about the sentries you have posted."

"In all honesty I would have never known you were following me," she admitted. "Who taught you to track like that?"

"Johnnie, a half-breed friend of mine. We grew up together. Johnnie's father worked for mine and resided on the ranch. We were inseparable. Maybe one day you'll get to meet him."

"Not likely, since I have no plans to leave Scotland, and I doubt your friend plans on traveling here."

"You never know," Burke said. "Who would have ever thought I'd be sitting on the rubble of a stone wall with a female outlaw in the woods of Scotland?"

Storm laughed softly, and the light tinkle sent a ripple resonating throughout his body until it accumulated in a rush of gooseflesh down his back.

"Actually, you're sitting on the remains of one of the oldest churches in Scotland." Storm laughed again. "You look surprised, Burke."

He grinned at the injustice of it all. He couldn't kiss her in the middle of the ruins of a church. It just wasn't right.

"I would have never thought this a church." What he truly meant was that he would prefer that it wasn't a church.

Storm glanced over the decayed structure. "It was small, barely fitting ten people. I was married here."

"Here?" he asked, looking around. "How long ago were you married?'

"Five years."

"But this structure—"

"Had long been decayed before then," she finished. "But many couples believe that if they wed among the ruins they will have a strong, long-lasting marriage." Her eyes saddened as she whispered, "A myth."

She had opened the subject of her husband so he felt comfortable to probe. "How long were you married?"

"Two years."

"That's barely time to get to know each other."

Storm smiled. "It was as if Daniel and I knew each other our entire lives from the very start. We loved the same things, never grew bored of being with each other, and laughed often. He told me that

116

the heavens had designed us specifically for each other and we would never match with another. I agreed."

"So you think you will never love again?"

"I *know* I will never love again."

"That doesn't seem fair to you or your husband," Burke said.

"Why do you say that?"

"You are young and have your whole life before you. It would not be fair to you never to know love again. And as for your husband, if he truly loved you as you claim, then he would not want to see you alone. He would want you to love again."

"I could never love someone the way I loved Daniel."

"Of course it would be different. Daniel was your first love. There is nothing like a first love, but don't deny yourself the chance to taste love again. It may be a bittersweet taste at first but you never know. You may develop a liking for the flavor. All I'm saying is at least take a taste."

Storm stared at him for a moment, and he thought that she would argue the point.

Instead, she said softly, "I'll keep that in mind. And you, Burke? You mentioned once that you have yet to find love."

"It hasn't struck me yet."

"Is that what you expect it to do, strike you?"

"Dead in the heart," he said, slapping his hand over his heart.

Storm laughed. "It could sneak up on you and gradually claim your heart."

"I think I'd see it coming," he said confidently.

"I don't know. Love can be sneaky," she warned.

He shook his head. "It's going to hit me fast and hard and suddenly I'll be in love."

"You know, Mr. Longton, love is the one leader no one can usurp."

He stood and held his hand out to her. "I'll keep that in mind, but you might be wise to do the same."

Chapter 13

It took three days to reach Mewers and they camped in the dense woods that skirted the village. Storm and Philip had arranged a time and location to meet, and after instructing the men and posting guards, she and Tanin were about to leave for the appointed meeting.

"I want to go," Burke said, approaching Storm as she tucked her dirk into its sheath at her waist.

"It's not necessary."

"Not to you, but to me it is, and besides, you've ordered us to stay put until you speak with Philip. What else is there for me to do?"

She reiterated her order. "Stay put."

"No."

His stance was as adamant as his declaration. His legs were spread, his boots dug in, and his hands rested firmly on his hips. He did not intend to be denied his request, and Storm couldn't blame him. If it had been her brother, she'd make certain to be along every step of the way.

"I'll follow whatever orders you give." He winced. "Let me rescind that. I'll follow any orders that don't involve causing you pain."

"At least you're honest."

"And always will be," he confirmed with a sharp nod.

Storm gave it a moment of thought and decided there was no reason for him not to join them. "You can come with us but—" She walked up to him and poked him in the chest as she spoke. "You will in no way interfere if orders are given that should cause me pain."

Burke looked ready to protest when she poked him again.

"Think twice, Mr. Longton, before you agree."

Burke let out an agitated sigh. "I won't interfere."

"Your word on it."

Another agitated sigh. "I give you my word, though reluctantly."

Burke had proven himself an honorable man, and Storm knew he would keep his word once given whether he agreed with the circumstances or not. It seemed when it came to her, he was overly concerned, but then to him men were meant to protect women. He was doing what he had been raised to do.

"You'll follow between Tanin and me. I don't want you getting lost." She smiled and shook her head. "But then you wouldn't get lost; you're too good of a tracker."

"True enough, but there's no time to waste so it's best I do as you say."

Storm stumbled in jest, her hand to her chest. "Did I just hear you agree with me?"

He cracked a smile. "It's easy to agree with you when you make sense."

"I make sense all the time."

"Women rarely make sense," Burke said on a laugh.

"Amen to that," Angus said, passing by.

Storm grinned and sauntered off. "Have your fun, but do remember that it's a woman who leads you."

They didn't have to wait long for Philip to join them at the designated meeting place. He arrived shortly after them, and they huddled beneath a large spruce to hear what he had learned.

"They took a prisoner out of here just before my arrival," Philip informed them. "It is whispered about in the village as if it is a secret that cannot be divulged."

"Was a name mentioned?" Burke asked anxiously.

Philip shook his head. "No, though mention was made of the size of the man, and from what Peter told us, the description fits."

"Then it could be Cullen," Burke said.

"Don't get your hopes up," Tanin advised. "We have yet to learn of a name. We could be chasing after the wrong man."

"Which is why we must free the young lad," Philip informed them.

"He knows something?" Burke asked.

Philip nodded. "The lad spent a good two days with the man in the same cell."

"He would know his name," Burke said, excited.

"He would know something," Storm said.

Burke agreed. "Enough for us to learn if it is my brother we chase after."

"A good chance of it," Philip said. "And with the prized prisoner gone and only the lad remaining, there is a bare minimum of guards around the prison."

"Any idea where he may have been taken?" Burke asked.

Philip shrugged. "I can't even make sense of why this man has been moved around as much as he has been. Usually a prisoner is kept in one location or perhaps moved once, but this many times?" He shook his head. "It makes no sense."

"He's right," Storm agreed. "I've never known a prisoner to be moved as much as this man. Something isn't right. Perhaps the lad will enlighten us."

"The village has many items we can use," Philip advised.

"Malcolm, Angus, and Burke will canvass the village tomorrow."

They returned to camp in silence. With no campfire set, the group munched on the bread and cheese they had brought with them and retired early.

"A moment of your time?" Burke asked after the others had bedded down.

Storm nodded and they walked over to a large rock and sat with their backs against it.

"You seemed worried earlier about the prisoner being moved so often. Why?"

The half moon cast enough of a glow for Storm to see the concern in Burke's dark eyes, and while she wished to ease his worry, she knew he'd prefer the truth.

"It's as if someone wishes to hide this prisoner."

"Why would that be?"

"I'm not sure," she said, shaking her head. "But we aren't dealing with a simple crime, which means it isn't likely that you will be able to buy your brother's freedom, if this man is truly your brother."

"You can't be sure of that."

She shrugged. "As you've often said to me, you never know, though the evidence does prove otherwise."

"I can't have come this far to lose my brother this way," Burke said adamantly. "Money speaks loudly and often erases crimes. It will aid in my attempt to free Cullen."

"I agree that money can buy almost anything, but be aware there is that small segment money can't buy."

"I've yet to find something money can't buy, Storm. It bought you."

Her eyes narrowed and she sat up straight. "I was never for sale, Mr. Longton."

"I apologize," Burke said quickly. "I phrased that inappropriately. I admire your courage and conviction and meant no disrespect."

"Then why say it?" she snapped.

"Frustration, foolishness, exhaustion? Have I found one that suits you?"

She laughed softly and relaxed once again against the rock.

"This is difficult for me, though I don't like to admit it."

"I understand. You don't wish to fail your father. You gave your word, and your word is your honor."

He looked at her, startled that she understood. "My father died with a smile when I gave him my word that I would find Cullen. He knew I would not fail him."

"Yet this land and its people are foreign to you and you must depend on the assistance of a stranger to help you keep your promise. Which means you have no control over the situation, and that alarms you."

"You are damned perceptive and damned beautiful."

"It surprises you that the two mix so well together?"

"You are quick-witted," Burke said with a smile.

"Part and parcel of being perceptive."

"Your husband must have found you a handful."

Storm smiled with joy. "Daniel claimed he wouldn't have it any other way."

"Neither would I."

Storm felt her heart catch and she quickly stood. "It's best we turn in."

"If you say so," Burke said and stood.

"Good night," Storm said and turned to leave.

Burke took hold of her arm and pulled her to him. "Not so fast, pretty lady."

He leaned down and claimed her lips in a gentle kiss.

His tenderness did her in, or perhaps tenderness was what forced her response. Whatever it was, she soon found herself lost in a kiss that stirred her long-dormant passion. It had been so long since he had kissed her, and she allowed herself the pleasure of enjoying the taste of him.

He knew how to kiss, how to titillate with his lips and his tongue.

She pulled away suddenly and ran off without a word, her husband's face vivid in her mind and her heart in pain at betraying his memory.

Morning found Storm busy with Tanin and purposely ignoring Burke. She didn't wish to address her sudden departure last night, and least of all did she want to discuss their kiss. It had been a mistake and one she would not make again.

She finished with Tanin and intended to make herself scarce until Burke and Malcolm left, but then she turned to find Burke standing in front of her.

"Was my kiss that bad or that good?" he asked.

"Neither. It was a mistake." She tried to push past him.

He held her in place. "I don't think so."

"It doesn't matter what you think. Now let go of me," she ordered him quietly and calmly, not wanting to attract attention.

"Not until I have an answer."

"I gave you one."

"Not good enough," he insisted.

"You need to be going. Malcolm is waiting." She gave a nod to where the young man stood near the edge of the woods.

"He can wait. I told him I needed to speak with you first."

"This mission is too important to be held up by a kiss," she scolded.

"My sentiments exactly, so give me an answer and be done with it."

"I can order—"

His eyes narrowed. "An answer, Storm, here and now."

She knew he'd go nowhere until she responded and she thought to lie to him, but she had a feeling he'd see through it.

"Like or don't like," he reminded. "It's that simple."

He was right. It was that simple, and she was being foolish. It would be her choice whether he kissed her again. Her answer would make no difference.

"Like," she said, getting it over with quickly.

Burke grinned. "I liked it too."

Her cheeks burned red as he walked away, and she turned so that no one would see her blush. She did not have a problem baring her naked breasts to this man, and yet knowing that he liked the kiss made her blush like a young lass enamored of a lad.

But then removing her shirt had been her choice and had also been meant to put him in his place. The kiss was entirely different.

I liked it too.

She hadn't considered how he had felt about their encounter, and learning that he had enjoyed it only made her more uneasy. And more apt to think that he would attempt to kiss her again. She would have to speak to him about this and make it clear that he should never kiss her again.

Why not?

The question nudged at her mind. She did not intend to fall in love again and Mr. Longton would return to America when this was over. So what harm would there be in enjoying a few kisses with him now and then? It would be nice to have a man's arms around her once again, share a kiss, a gentle touch.

Storm walked over to lean against the rock she had sat by last night with Burke.

Would it be so wrong for her to think of herself? Hadn't she thought of others for most of her life? She hadn't considered the consequences of her actions when she attempted her first rescue. It was simply necessary, and when it was done she had been marked an outlaw. With little choice left to her and a burning need to fight injustice, she set out to free the helpless with no regard for her own life and no thought of her future.

It didn't matter anymore. Her reputation had grown, and as Peter had warned her, there were plans for her capture. She always thought it would happen someday and she'd be sent to Weighton to await her death.

Weighton housed the most wanted criminals, those whose acts branded them traitors to Scotland. She didn't think of herself as a traitor, and many believed her a savior to the common Scot. However, the ruling class thought otherwise and they were the law.

So what was left to her but to enjoy what she could of the life she had left? Perhaps a kiss or two from Burke would brighten her day and lighten her heart, if only for a short time.

She glanced at Tanin, who was speaking with Angus and William. She had advised him long ago that when the day came that she was caught and sent to Weighton, he was to disperse the group and direct the members to make their way out of Scotland. He was not to help her, for they both knew he would die trying. Tanin had objected, but she insisted that she wouldn't see Ellie suffer the pain of being a widow. He had finally agreed and given her his word.

Burke would never have agreed.

She smiled and whispered. "He would foolishly attempt to rescue me."

Her smile faded and she recalled her husband's words.

There isn't anything I wouldn't do to save you, I love you that much.

She had felt the same, but unfortunately, she had been too late.

Chapter 14

It didn't take long to determine that the market would pose no problem for them. The amount of activity kept everyone busy, with children laughing and running around the tables. A sleight of hand could easily go on unnoticed, and in no time the group would have the few items they needed.

Burke made his way through the market stalls, taking note of areas that were more private and therefore more conducive to a successful theft. He wandered along slowly, taking in everything he could, when out of the corner of his eye he caught a woman staring at him. She quickly turned away when he looked in her direction.

She certainly was no peasant, dressed as she was in silks and brocade and accompanied by a slew of servants. She was stunning, her auburn hair in a pile of ringlets atop her head with a string of pearls weaving through the mass of curls.

Though her features were sharp, she was a beauty, with milky white, flawless skin, and she stood a good seven inches over five feet. The servants followed her like an army of guards protecting her from anyone who came too close.

"Lady Alaina, I have a lovely silk for—" one of the merchants said drawing her attention.

Burke watched as she examined the rich purple material. She looked to be studying it, when actually she glanced out of the corner of her eye at Burke.

"Lady Alaina likes what she sees," Malcolm teased quietly behind Burke.

"It's my good looks. The women can't resist me," Burke shot back.

Malcolm laughed and slapped him on the back. "You wish."

"Why else would she stare at me?" Burke asked with a smug grin.

"Maybe she thinks she knows you," Angus offered, joining them.

Burke glanced again at the woman.

She was now staring after him and suddenly started to wave. A servant followed her line of interest, changing direction once she began waving.

"Let's go. Storm's waiting," Malcolm said, picking up the pace.

Burke reluctantly turned away and followed the men into the woods. They reached the campsite, the others already there and waiting for them so that plans could be formulated for a combined rescue and theft.

It was determined fast enough that the mission didn't seem difficult and that if all went as planned, they could be on their way home by noon tomorrow.

"We'll just have to keep Burke away from the market," Malcolm said with a laugh.

"Why is that?" Storm asked with curious concern.

Malcolm continued his teasing. "Lady Alaina found him appealing."

Angus disagreed. "No, she stared at him as if she thought she recognized him, but wasn't certain."

"Your opinion, Burke?" Storm asked.

"That Lady Alaina isn't as beautiful as you."

The men snickered and laughed and made fun of the bold American.

"Tell me why you think Lady Alaina found you interesting," Storm asked, ignoring her men.

"Who is Lady Alaina?" Burke asked, needing to settle that bit of information before he pursued a thought that had been simmering.

"The Earl of Balford's daughter," Angus answered.

"The man possibly responsible for my brother's capture."

"I get it," Malcolm said, excited. "If you and your brother resemble each other, then it's possible that Lady Alaina had seen your brother Cullen and then was surprised when she caught sight of you."

Burke nodded. "She may have information that could prove helpful."

"You'll stay away from her," Storm ordered so sharply that all the men turned wide eyes on her.

"She could be of help," Burke suggested.

Storm maintained her authority. "I can't have you jeopardizing the lad's rescue."

"I won't—"

"That's right, you won't," Storm said. "You won't go near Lady Alaina, for the lad's safety and your own."

He could tell she was angry; her blue eyes blazed like a storming sea. God, he loved seeing the color of her eyes rage like a tempest; the startling blue always set his blood to boiling and his heart to pumping.

Storm continued, "If the Earl of Balford is responsible for your brother's capture, then he's also responsible for moving him from prison to prison, which means he has an intense dislike for Cullen. If Cullen's brother should suddenly appear, do you really think that the earl will welcome him with open arms?"

Damn if he didn't find her intelligence just as attractive as her gorgeous eyes.

She did not give him a chance to respond. "You'd put not only yourself in danger but my men as well."

"Your men?"

"That's right, my men." Storm stood with a shout. "They would be the ones who would risk their lives to rescue you." She pointed a finger in his face. "You, Mr. Longton, will do nothing without my permission."

Burke stood, grabbing hold of her finger. "You think so?"

She yanked her finger free. "It's an order; you have no choice." She marched off.

The men coughed from the cloud of dirt she'd kicked up as she stomped away.

Burke started to go after her, but Tanin grabbed his arm. "I'd give her a minute or two."

"Hour or two is more like it," Angus said.

"Neither will really make a difference," Burke said and went after her. Her anger disturbed him. She might resort to sudden anger when on a mission, but he had never seen her grow so militant when planning or discussing a mission. Something else had to have disturbed her.

"Wait," he called out to her since it didn't look as if she planned on slowing down or stopping any time soon.

Storm spun around. "Stop following me. I prefer to be alone right now."

He caught up with her. "Too bad, I'm coming with you."

"You are a persistent annoyance."

"And you are angry. Why?"

She looked ready to lash out at him when suddenly she shook her head, turned, and walked over to a large spruce, its branches mushrooming out and creating a haven beneath, which she sneaked under to sit.

Burke joined her, noticing she had drawn her legs up near to her chin and wrapped her arms around them as if huddled in protection. He wanted to reach out and pry her arms loose and tell her not to be afraid, that he wouldn't hurt her. He wouldn't let anyone hurt her.

"Talk to me, Storm. I'm a good listener."

She rested her head on her raised knees, her glance directed at him. "I didn't mean to get angry."

"I know. You weigh your decisions carefully, even decisions made with no time to spare. You still give thought to each and every one of them, no matter how brief, though never unwisely."

"You make me sound like a sage."

"I believe at times you are," he said. "It's the mark of a good leader."

Her head came up. "You're right. A good leader must always see to the safety of her men, even the foolish ones."

Burke nodded and grinned. "You're referring to me."

"I don't wish to see you added to the list of those needing rescue."

"Don't worry, you won't have to rescue me," he said with confidence.

"Funny," she said with a tap to her chin. "I recall rescuing you once already."

He slapped his hand to his chest. "Must you wound my manly pride and remind me of that?"

Storm scoffed. "Somehow I don't think your manly pride wounds that easily."

This time he thumped his chest. "That's because I'm a confident man."

"Arrogant too."

"That does help," he admitted without remorse.

"Are all Americans like you?"

He smiled. "Only the lucky ones."

Storm laughed, stretching her legs out and relaxing back against the thick tree trunk.

Relieved that he had eased her tension, he joined her relaxing against the tree. He had questions concerning the lad they were to rescue and the Lady Alaina, but they would have to wait. She looked so lovely sitting there, even dressed in lad's garments. There was softness to her every curve and a defined beauty to her features. It could steal the breath if one gazed too long, or rob the senses, or make a man think on things that women deemed wicked.

Damn if he didn't want to be wicked with Storm.

He wondered if perhaps she felt the same.

Hadn't there been a spark between them on first meeting? Had he imagined it, or was it a clash between their need to take command? How would that work when making love? Who would take the lead?

The thought excited him and made him anxious to discover the answer.

"Nothing to say, Burke?"

He had plenty to say but time was needed to court the lovely lass and see if she was as willing as he was eager.

"I didn't want to disturb your peace."

"Peace is relative, Burke," she said. "I have found it in the strangest of places."

"We share a common interest, for I have done the same myself and know the serenity such places can bring."

Her gaze locked with his. He loved her eyes, could get lost in them, could swirl in their stormy blue depths and never care if he were rescued. He had to clear his mind of her or the next thing he knew he'd be kissing her, and now was not the time or place.

"I've been thinking of the lad we will rescue," he said to distract himself.

"I expected you to speak of him to me," she said, her posture turning rigid.

He regretted disturbing her peace, but then it was necessary in more ways than one. "You claim to know my mind?"

"No, but I know what I would think if it were my brother we searched for."

"And that would be?"

"I would think that if the lad could not provide me with sufficient information concerning my brother, then perhaps Lady Alaina could. I would want to know all I could about her and possibly find a way of talking with her, though not personally. I wouldn't want to take the chance that my resemblance could in any way harm my brother."

"Good, you agree with me," he said, pleased.

"Yes, but that doesn't mean we will be contacting Lady Alaina."

"Why not?" he asked, attempting to keep the irritation out of his tone.

"Our first concern is finding out if this man we've followed from prison to prison is your brother. If he is, then we must find out why he is being moved so frequently and where he goes next. Once these questions are answered I have a feeling we'll learn what part Lady Alaina plays in it all, and then we can decide if talking with her is necessary."

"That will take time."

"Much will depend on what information we learn from the lad tomorrow."

He let out a frustrated breath. "I'm impatient."

"Which is why it is better that I am in command."

Burke smiled. "You really like reminding me of that."

Her smile matched his. "A little reminding is good now and again."

"You know, you're right."

He grabbed hold of her chin and planted a kiss on her lips that just about curled both their toes. His tongue went deep, his taste hungry and his passion strong.

He yanked himself away, his body responding much too strongly.

"Just a reminder," he said on labored breath and jumped to his feet and walked away.

Chapter 15

Storm's blue eyes blazed when she entered the small cell and caught sight of the lad. He lay on his side curled in a ball, his arms tight to his chest, his knees meeting his elbows. Bits of straw strewn on the floor provided bedding. It stuck to his worn, soiled clothes and to his brown hair.

The stench of neglect permeated the thick air, and Storm raised her sleeve to her nostrils. She hurried to the lad's side, and he cringed and tried to move away.

"I'm here to free you," she whispered and laid a gentle hand on his shoulder.

He peeked from beneath his folded arms, then raised his face. "I prayed you'd come for me. Every night I prayed."

Storm's heart ached. She had heard those words time and again from prisoners she had freed, and all she could think about was the prisoners who had prayed and whom she had failed to rescue.

"I need you to do as I say."

"I will, whatever it is I will do it." He uncurled himself, groaning with every move.

"Wait," Storm urged. "Do nothing yet."

He nodded and stilled, relief in his tear-filled eyes.

"What is your name?" she asked, taking his hand and gently stretching out his thin arm.

"Henry Doddle," he said and reached his other hand out to her.

Storm tenderly rubbed the lad's stiff and injured limbs before she asked him to stand. She took stock of his bruises and determined that while he had been beaten badly, he suffered no broken bones.

"We'll be setting a fast pace, Henry—"

"I'll keep up," he said adamantly.

Storm patted his shoulder. "You are a brave lad."

Burke suddenly appeared at her side. "Does he require help?"

"I can walk on my own," Henry insisted.

"Good," Burke said. "Then let's get going."

Storm went with the lad, leaving Burke to carry out the remainder of their plan. He was to devise a dummy of sorts to serve as a decoy. Philip had determined that the soldiers barely paid heed to the lad. If they thought him asleep, it would provide more time for their escape. They could place a good distance between them and Mewers before the lad's absence was realized.

Storm wanted out of the area as fast as possible,

knowing that the Earl of Henwood would be furious when he discovered a prisoner had escaped. It would mean his reputation, since he boasted loudly about his impregnable prison cells. He would surely have his soldiers out hunting down the culprits.

"We don't rest," she ordered as they set a fast pace for home.

"The lad doesn't look fit enough to make it," Burke said from behind her.

"The men will carry him if necessary," Storm said, "Now be silent and keep up."

It was a relief when night finally came, for it was only then they stopped. No fire was allowed though the night air held a good chill. Storm saw to it that Henry was fed and a blanket wrapped snugly around him. The poor lad was asleep in no time.

Storm assigned the men to guard the perimeter. Tanin disappeared into the woods, his post being the most important. After all had been arranged, she settled down to take the first watch.

"Sleep, I'll take guard," Burke offered, leaning against the large boulder she perched on.

"The first watch is always mine."

"Don't trust anyone?" he teased.

She didn't find him funny. "A good leader knows when her men need rest."

"And a good leader knows when to rest herself."

"True enough," she agreed, "but I'm not tired."

Burke braced his hands on the boulder and hefted himself up to sit next to her. "I don't understand how you can exist on such little rest."

Storm shrugged and attempted to ignore her

sudden need to cuddle next to him. She blamed her impulsive desire on the chilly night, convincing herself that she sought his closeness to warm her, chase away her chill and nothing more.

"It's been my life. Little rest, much work."

"No time for fun or laughter?" Burke asked.

"Afraid not. My day begins before sunup and lasts long past sunset."

"Even when you were married?"

"Daniel and I had our moments. Even though our farm was small, there was still much work to be done. The landlord fees were high and climbed each year. We barely had food one winter, but we survived." She was silent for a moment, and then whispered. "We were always there for each other— always."

"You need a day of fun," Burke said firmly.

"That sounds like an order," Storm said, glad to have her thoughts diverted. Her heart forever ached when she thought of her husband.

"Does it have to be?"

No, it didn't really need to be. It would be lovely to spend a fun day with the brash American. She could forget all her cares and pretend, if only for a few hours, that life was normal and she was happy.

She shook her head. It was a foolish thought. She had no time for fun.

"You shook your head, therefore I'm going to have to make it an order."

"An order?" She laughed.

He shook a finger at her. "I'm warning you. You had better take me seriously, or one day soon, I'm going to capture you—no, I'm going to rescue you for a fun day."

The idea appealed to her, spending a day without worry, without plans, without having to lead and make decisions.

"You can try," she challenged, and secretly wished that he might just do as he warned.

"I won't just try," he assured her. "I will be successful in my rescue and you will have a fun day, even if you attempt not to."

"You will force fun on me."

He leaned into her. "I will torture you with it."

She doubted he would need to torture. She enjoyed his company and would find spending time with him pleasing, perhaps much too pleasing. Since for the moment she thoroughly favored the warmth of his body seeping into hers.

"You'd have to capture me, and being the king's men are unable to do that, it's doubtful you could." She hoped he didn't hear the regret in her voice.

He laughed and leaned his face next to hers. "You failed to realize one thing."

"What's that?"

"I'm an arrogant American who believes he can accomplish anything, therefore, I can do what the king's men can't."

"You truly believe you can capture me?" she asked with a grin.

"Rescue," he corrected. "I'd always rescue you. No matter where you are. I promise you that."

His tenacious pledge caused a chill to race through her.

"You cannot promise me that," she insisted, moving away from him to the edge of the boulder.

He followed. "I most certainly can."

"You must not. I need your word on it."

"I will do no such thing," he snapped.

She had given these same such orders to each person in her group and it had never disturbed her as it did now. She felt an ache within her that she didn't understand as she relayed her orders to him.

"It is understood that if I am captured, the group will not attempt to rescue me."

"That's ridiculous," Burke said empathically.

"You don't understand."

"Enlighten me."

She sighed to release her own frustration. Why did it disturb her so to say to him what she had said countless times before?

"If caught, I would be taken to Weighton, an impregnable prison. Anyone attempting to rescue me would surely be caught and killed. I will not have that on my account. There will be no rescue."

"Your men agreed to this?"

He sounded annoyed and she attempted to explain, "You must understand—"

"Never would I understand your men leaving you to rot or be tortured in a prison, impregnable or not. I would give my life trying to save you."

Storm jumped off the boulder and turned to face him, her hands firmly planted on her slim waist. "You will do no such thing."

Burke joined her on the ground, standing near

nose to nose. "You'd be in prison, you'd have no say in the matter."

"Which is why I have given orders now, so my men would know exactly what to do."

"Abandon you."

"No. They would save their own lives."

"You never leave a comrade behind, not when you have fought side by side with each other. It just isn't done," Burke insisted.

"It is if your leader orders it so," she claimed.

He put his nose to hers. "Your men can do as they wish, but if you're caught while I'm here with the group, then I will rescue you. Count on it."

She stepped away from him and groaned. "You are the most frustrating man."

Burke walked over to her. "And you're not the most frustrating woman?"

Storm was about to argue when she suddenly changed her mind, walked over to him, stood on her toes, threw her arms around his neck, and planted a kiss on his lips that shocked both of them.

She leaned against him, needing to feel his strength, needing his warmth, needing his close-ness. He wrapped his arms around her waist and obliged her desire, yanking her up against him.

She pressed her chest hard against his while she commanded the kiss, drinking as deeply as she could of him. She couldn't get enough of him, and even when she surfaced to take a breath, she nibbled at his lips before delving in for more. She relished the play of their tongues, teasing, sparring and tasting. It was a kiss of hunger long denied, and she felt as if she would never get her fill.

A rustle of branches tore them apart and had both reaching for the weapons strapped to their sides. It took a moment to realize that no one was about, the sound probably caused by a nocturnal animal making its way through the woods.

"I've neglected my watch," Storm said and scrambled on top of the boulder in an effort to put a distance between them, or else she feared she would kiss him again.

"I'll join you," he said, ready to hoist himself up.

"No," she said curtly.

He remained where he was staring up at her. "Why?"

She thought to lie, but what good would it do? "I cannot have you near me right now."

"Why?" he asked again.

"You distract me."

"As you do me," he said.

She smiled softly. "Then it is better I sit here alone."

He looked ready to object, then shook his head. "I suppose you are right."

"For once we agree," she said, laughing softly.

"I leave reluctantly," he said, turning away.

"I let you go reluctantly," she said to her surprise.

He turned around. "Be warned, I will have a day of fun—and more—with you."

Chapter 16

Once home Henry was made comfortable after Janelle pronounced rest and nourishment would heal his bruised and battered body. He had suffered no broken bones. It was as if his captors had enjoyed toying with him, like children tormenting a small, helpless animal.

Burke waited impatiently outside Angus's hut. Being there was room for only one person in Janelle's hut, and Peter's injures required more attention, Henry was placed with Angus. Storm had ordered that no one speak with him without her being present. So here Burke stood waiting for her, anxious to speak with the lad, but respecting her edict.

He watched as she approached, Tanin walking beside her. It amazed him how refreshed she appeared after days of endless walking. Her step was spry, her movements not at all labored, and her lovely face glowed. She seemed invigorated and yet she had gotten only a few hours' sleep over the last six days.

Tanin parted company with her when he reached his tree house, his wife standing at the base waiting for him.

Storm continued toward Burke with a smile.

Damn if it didn't go beyond attraction. She had haunted his mind constantly since the night she had initiated a kiss, not that she hadn't tormented his thoughts before that, but now she was forever planted in his mind.

He wanted to spend time with her, just the two of them. He wanted to get to know Storm the woman, not Storm the outlaw. He knew what he proposed could prove dangerous. She would not leave Scotland and he would not leave his home. How then could there be a future for them? And why did he even consider a future with her?

His thoughts and emotions were playing havoc with him, and damned if he knew what to do about it. What had his father warned him of love? That nothing would make sense. Nothing had made sense since he'd met Storm. Did that tell him something?

He shook the nonsensical thoughts from his head. Storm seemed a willing partner when it came to passion. Why not enjoy her while he could and leave it at that?

Maybe because she haunted the hell out of him day and night and he worried about her safety all the time. Did he really think that would change once she was out of sight?

"Something troubles you?" Storm asked once she was beside him.

"Trying to clear my head."

"By shaking it?" She grinned and took hold of his arm.

He felt as if he'd been struck by lightning by her simple touch, so strong was the passion that assaulted him. What was it about this woman that made him respond so carelessly, so eagerly, so wantonly?

"I've tried that myself. It doesn't work," she assured him.

"It's worth a try," he admitted, glad she kept her arm hooked with his. "Anything is better than endless chaos in your head."

"Haven't you heard?' she said with a tease. "There is wisdom in madness."

"Only a madman would claim that."

Storm laughed, though it quieted fast enough. "Sometimes I wonder if madness isn't a reprieve from sanity."

"A double-edged sword that cuts the same."

Storm sighed. "Exactly. What difference does either make in the end?"

They turned silent, each one lost in thought, Burke's thoughts once again centered on Storm and her dangerous life. How did one stop being an outlaw? In the Dakota Territory, outlaws were outlaws. They were hunted until captured, and few if any escaped the law.

It was in essence a chosen life with a predictable ending.

Burke didn't care for the thought and wondered how, in the time that remained to him here in Scotland, he could change the ending for Storm.

"Feel up to talking with us?" Storm asked Henry upon entering the hut.

"Of course," Henry obliged, pulling himself up in bed with a groan or two.

Burke watched as Storm assisted the boy, helping him to sit up and arranging a pillow behind his back for comfort before sitting on the bed beside him. That she was an angel to these freed captives was obvious. They gazed on her with eyes of gratitude. He doubted there was anything they wouldn't do for her if asked.

He dragged the only chair in the room over to the side of the bed where Storm perched and joined them.

"We heard that another prisoner shared the cell with you," Storm said.

Henry nodded. "A big man."

"Tall, wide?" Storm asked.

"Both," Henry said, sounding impressed. "I had thought for certain he would break the chains they kept on his wrists and ankles, so large and thick were his arms."

"Do you know his name?" Burke asked, hopeful.

Henry thought a moment and then shook his head slowly. "He never shared his name with me."

"Do you know of his crime?" Storm asked.

"I heard the guards mention a theft and I asked the man one night what he had stolen. He told me something of great value that could never be replaced and that he would do it again if given the chance."

"What else did you speak of?" Storm inquired.

Henry once again pondered the question. "We talked of family and discovered we both lacked one, his mother dying when he was young as did mine."

Burke felt as if one of the pieces of the puzzle had just fallen into place.

"He didn't know his father, nor did I. We both drifted among helpful strangers."

"Can you think of anything else this man might have said?" Storm asked.

Henry once again gave the question thought and looked about to shake his head when suddenly he blurted out, "Love. He told me to find love, that it makes all the difference in the world."

"Can you describe him to us?' Storm asked.

Henry nodded staring at Burke. "He resembles him, same hair color, though longer, eyes, mouth the same, though bigger in size, a broader chest and shoulders and taller by a good four to five inches."

"Good, that helps us," Storm said. "If you should remember anything else about him, please tell me or Burke."

Burke held his hand out to the lad. "Glad to meet you, Henry, and thanks for the help."

Henry shook his hand. "Pleased I could help and I'm grateful for the rescue."

Storm and Burke left the hut and wandered over

to the campfire. They sat side by side on the decaying tree trunk.

Burke stared at the flames, his thoughts on his brother and all the years spent alone while he grew up with a loving family. It didn't seem fair, but life wasn't fair. If it was, his father would have found Cullen as a child and they would have been raised as brothers. They were nothing but strangers right now, and Burke wanted desperately to change that.

He felt Storm's hand slip over his and lock fingers. He grabbed on to her offer of comfort, not letting go.

"I can only imagine how difficult this must be for you."

"He wandered all those years thinking no one loved him, no one cared, while my father frantically searched for him." He shook his head. "I am here only a short time and I find his trail. Why? Why couldn't my father have found him?"

"I think it is easier to trace a man than it is to find a child. There are so many homeless children that it would be near impossible to find the one you search for. Would your father have recognized him if he had found him? He had left when his son was a mere babe and returned when he could walk. It was a difficult mission in more ways than one."

"He blamed himself his entire life for leaving his family behind."

"Your father attempted to find a better life for his son, and that he searched for him proved how much he loved him."

"I won't leave Scotland until I find Cullen," Burke said stubbornly.

"Are you threatening me?" Storm teased. "Must I find your brother just to be rid of you?"

He raised their joined hands. "We're stuck with each other until then." He paused, staring at her. "Is that so bad?"

His query flustered her and she fumbled for an answer.

She finally calmed. "No, it is not so bad."

He squeezed her hand. "Thank you for helping me. I would never have gotten this far without your help."

"You are paying for that help," she reminded.

"Somehow I think you would have helped me whether I paid or not. You just wouldn't leave a man imprisoned if you could help it, though logically you can't free them all."

"I can try," she said with a smile and a tilt of her head.

"A heroic gesture, but foolish."

To his surprise, she didn't disagree.

"So I've been reminded time and time again."

"Then why do it?"

He noticed she glanced down at their joined hands, and for a moment, he thought he saw tears glistening in her eyes, but then she raised her head proudly.

"Someone has to help the helpless."

"Are you pushing for sainthood?" He sounded petulant, but couldn't help it. He worried about her safety, and yet each day she willingly placed her life in jeopardy. It irritated the hell out of him, though he did admire her courage.

She shrugged, her thin shoulders falling slowly down as if a heavy weight descended on her. "Don't ask me to explain. It's something I must do."

"So you woke up one morning and decided to be an outlaw," Burke said, needing her penchant for her work to make sense, needing to understand her more.

He realized he struck a nerve when she wiggled her fingers free of his, and her silence warned him that she was not about to share the truth.

Finally she stood. "I have things to see to." And walked away.

He let her go. There was no point in stopping her. Obviously, she didn't wish to discuss the topic, which made Burke all the more curious to find out about it. In time, though, he would.

He stretched his legs out in front of him and rolled his shoulders, easing the ache in his back. He had walked his fair share back home, but never the distance he had covered while here in Scotland. He much preferred a horse to his legs, but the terrain surrounding the camp wasn't conducive to riding horses.

He wondered if Cullen was a horseman, or had he only his legs to depend on?

He was anxious to find his brother and get to know him. He hoped Cullen would agree to return to America with him if just for a while. Burke thought if he could get him there, Cullen just might like it and decide to stay.

Actually, with Cullen being a wanted man, there was no way he'd be able to remain in Scotland. He would always be hunted unless, of course, he could buy his way out of his crime, and he would certainly have the money to do that.

Their father had been brilliant when it came to investing, and money really was not a problem for either of them. They could live an entire life and not spend the wealth their father had accumulated, which continued to grow each day.

He wanted to make certain Cullen shared in that wealth, and he hoped to find in Cullen the brother he had missed while growing up.

But what of his brother? Was he a thief or falsely accused? Was he a good man or a troubled man? Would he welcome a brother into his life or take his share of the wealth and want nothing to do with Burke?

There was so much to learn and Burke was eager. But once Cullen was found it would mean that Burke would need Storm no more. They would part ways, never to see each other again.

The thought disturbed him, and try as he might not to think about it, she refused to leave his head. She had remained stubbornly fixed in his thoughts, and like a fool he had nourished those thoughts and allowed them to flourish. Now she was there to stay until he faced the fact that he desired the pea-sized outlaw and ached for intimacy with her.

"Damn," he muttered.

"Talking to yourself?"

Burke jumped up at the unexpected sound of Storm's voice.

"It's one person who never disagrees with me."

"I don't know," she said with a smile. "You sounded agitated."

"Were you looking for me?" he asked, feeling as agitated as she had suggested.

"Peter remembers something and I thought you'd want to hear what he has to say."

"Let's go," Burke said, walking past her, though she was at his side in a flash.

They entered Janelle's hut to find Peter sitting up in bed and looking somewhat better than he had. The swelling had gone down but the bruising hadn't noticeably faded.

Burke and Storm squatted down on opposite sides of Peter.

"I don't know if this is important," Peter began.

"Anything you can tell us might prove helpful," Storm encouraged.

Peter nodded eagerly. "I remember how the man grew angry when he learned they were removing him from Glencurry."

"He wanted to stay there?" Burke asked.

"He claimed he belonged there," Peter confirmed.

"How so?" Storm queried.

"I don't know," Peter said. "But whatever it was, he wanted to remain at Glencurry. Even with the torture they inflicted upon him he—"

Burke didn't allow Peter to finish. "How badly was he tortured?"

"Not as badly as me, which I found strange since he seemed such a prize to them, but then maybe the jailers were instructed not to harm him."

"Who would give such orders?" Burke asked.

"The Earl of Balford decrees the punishment for each crime," Peter advised.

"You've done well, Peter," Storm said. "We appreciate your help."

"Anything. Anything I can do," he insisted.

Storm smiled. "Rest and get well."

Burke hurried out of the hut, and when they were a few feet away, he turned to Storm. "I think I should go speak with this Earl of Balford."

"That would be a foolish thing to do."

"Why?" he demanded. "Perhaps I could buy my brother's freedom."

"There is always that possibility."

"See, you agree," he said anxiously.

"But not now," Storm insisted. "Not before we know for certain if this man is your brother—"

"All things point to it."

"But we are not certain. Until we know without a doubt, you will sit tight and wait."

"If I don't want to?" he challenged.

"Then you will jeopardize not only your life, but your brother's as well."

"I hate it when you make sense," he said, knowing she was right, though it didn't help his concern for his brother.

She placed her hand on his arm. "I know how anxious you are, but if we move too fast we could do more harm than good. We will find your brother, but you must be patient."

He agreed with a nod, and tucked the idea of contacting the Earl of Balford in the back of his mind in case it should prove necessary.

Chapter 17

❝I don't understand it," Storm said, walking alongside Tanin through the camp. "It's been a week or more and we haven't gotten any closer to finding out where the prisoner was sent after leaving Mewers."

"It is strange," Tanin agreed. "First he's moved around and then he can't be found. You know what that can mean when a prisoner simply vanishes."

Storm hadn't wanted to voice her concerns, but with no news of the prisoner's whereabouts, it was growing more likely that he had been disposed of, his body never to be found.

"We should have heard something by now," Tanin said. "Philip and William have talked with people who have consistently provided us with accurate information and yet none of them know anything."

"Either that or they're not talking."

"What are you thinking?" Tanin asked.

"That people might be afraid to speak of the matter. But why would the imprisonment of a man accused of theft cause such fear? I believe there's more to this than we know."

"What do we do?" Tanin asked. "The American grows more impatient by the day. He looks about ready to take matters into his own hands."

"Which will not help us or him in the least."

"We also need to consider who will take Burke to St. Andrew Harbor where he claims his ship with the money should have arrived by now," Tannin said. "He insists that you go with him. I don't think he realizes just how infamous an outlaw you are and how dangerous such an excursion can be for you."

"The trip at least would distract him from the matter of his brother and provide us more time to hunt down his whereabouts."

Tanin scrunched his brow. "You're not thinking of going with Burke, are you?"

"Going where with me and why not?" Burke asked, stepping from behind a tree Tanin and Storm passed by.

Storm halted and shook her head. "You must stop lurking."

"I'm not lurking. Now what about going where with me?" Burke asked.

Tanin answered him. "To the harbor to get your money."

Burke smiled. "Yes, you must come with me. I'll

have it no other way. You deserve time away from here and a day of fun."

Storm had often thought about the day of fun he promised. It was a foolish idea, and besides, if she tasted such a pleasant day, wouldn't she want more of it?

"She can't do that," Tanin insisted firmly.

"Why not?" Burke challenged just as firmly. "She deserves a break from this place."

Tanin was blunt. "She's a wanted outlaw with a high price on her head. She's sure to be caught and imprisoned."

"Tanin is right," Storm agreed, though she hated admitting it. It would have been nice to spend a day as an ordinary person, doing ordinary things. "I'd risk not only my life but the safety and well-being of this camp. I cannot do that."

"There must be a way," Burke demanded.

"There isn't," Storm confirmed. "One of the men will go with you."

"What if I devise a way for you to go without the chance of being caught?"

"That's not possible," Tanin said.

"But if I do," Burke said, his eyes fixed on Storm. "Will you go with me?"

"Why not?" she said, confident he wouldn't be able to guarantee her safety.

"You heard her, Tanin. She's agreed to go with me."

"If there's no chance of her being caught," Tanin added. "Which there isn't, so it doesn't look like she'll be going with you."

161

"But she did agree and you heard her," Burke said. "Now about my brother."

A gust of wind swirled the dirt and leaves around their feet and fat raindrops followed.

"My quarters," Storm said to Burke and told Tanin she'd speak with him later.

In minutes they were safely tucked away in Storm's room while the rain beat down on the pine thatched roof.

Storm removed her worn brown jacket, slipped her stocking cap off her head, and shook her dark hair free. She settled both items on the bed then joined Burke at the small table. He had removed his gray wool jacket, and his white shirt was rolled up at the sleeves, which seemed to be a habit of his. She rarely saw him with his sleeves down.

"Haven't found out anything new, have you?" he claimed more than asked.

"Unfortunately, no," she admitted reluctantly.

"Why do you think that is?"

Storm folded her arms on the table. "You aren't a fool, Mr. Longton. I imagine you have assumed the same as I have."

"That my brother could very well be dead?"

"Precisely, though for some reason I think someone wants more than death for him."

"And what would that be?" he asked.

"Possibly revenge. Remember Henry told us that the man had claimed to have stolen something of great value that could never be replaced. That certainly would be a motive for revenge."

"What could be irreplaceable?"

"That's what we need to find out," Storm said. "And if it is true, then no amount of money offered would save your brother's life."

"How do we find out what was stolen?"

He paid no regard to her warning, though she knew well enough he understood the severity of such actions. He wasn't a foolish man, but then wise men could be pushed to foolishness when feeling helpless. And right now, she knew Burke felt helpless to assist his brother. She felt his pain and empathized, for she had been there once herself.

"I'm not sure," she said, feeling helpless herself with the situation. "Nothing new has been found and we seem to have hit a dead end."

"One thing I discovered that is the same in all cultures is that people love to gossip. It seems in this case no one dares open his or her mouth. Which means they fear to, so it would lead me to believe that the person who holds my brother prisoner has the power to make people fear him. Who would be the logical candidate for that?"

Storm admired his intelligence. He was much like her in thinking things through and reaching a conclusion that made sense, though he wasn't as patient as she was.

"Logic would follow that it would be the Earl of Balford. His connection to the king is known. He asks and gets what he wants," Storm informed him.

"Then we can go with the idea that Cullen stole something irreplaceable from the earl and he now seeks revenge."

"It would be reasonable to surmise and a new starting point for us."

Burke rubbed his chin. "Everything has a price, even a priceless object. Perhaps Cullen tried to sell the object, in which case, where would he go to do that?"

"It depends on the object," Storm said, a crack of thunder making her jump.

"Afraid of storms, Storm?" Burke smiled. "Is that your true name or do you hide your real identity?"

"It is who I am now," she said, not wanting to recall her birth name, not wanting memories to haunt her. Stormy nights had always proved disastrous for her.

Burke leaned his arms on the table. "Tell me how Storm was born."

She would tell him, but only so much. "She was born out of necessity. I was unable to tend the farm myself and so I lost it and found myself homeless."

"There was no one who would help you?" he asked.

That he sounded offended reminded her he was a caring man. She enjoyed gazing on his handsome, rugged features. There was strength in his square jaw and chiseled cheekbones, and though his lips were narrow, they were potent. His kisses attested to that.

She nodded. "Of course, but the price was too steep."

"Damn," he said, and pounded the table with his fist. "Men took advantage of you in your time of mourning?"

"What better time to do it? I had nothing. They offered food, a roof over my head."

"Yet you refused."

"There were times I thought myself a fool for my decision," she admitted on a soft laugh. "But I knew it was the only decision I could have made. Besides, I began meeting other people in the same predicament and we joined forces. We began to forage on the landlords' precious estates and steal from wealthy travelers along the roads. One rescue led to another, then another. That started my career as an outlaw."

"And that's when Storm was born."

"Exactly. I arrived on a stormy night, an avenging angel to free the innocent, and I will probably leave this world on a stormy night defending the innocent."

He reached out and grabbed hold of her hand. "You will not."

"It isn't your decision."

"You will not sacrifice yourself senselessly."

She yanked her hand away and stood, nearly tumbling the chair over. "Perhaps you should tell that to Henry or Peter, that what I did for them was senseless."

Burke stood slowly. "I did not mean—"

"What you said? It was clear to me." She folded her arms firmly across her chest, waiting for him to explain, though why she would even give him a chance to redeem himself was beyond her.

He approached her with cautious steps. "There will always be the less fortunate, those who need defending. Every society has them."

"And there will always be those who choose to defend them."

"You didn't choose," he reminded. "It was forced on you out of necessity."

"I accepted my role freely."

"It doesn't mean you have to continue it for the rest of your life."

He stood directly in front of her, and she thought for a moment, a sheer moment, she heard the beating of his heart, solid, strong, and steadfast.

"I have no choice," she said softly and with regret.

He reached out and gently unfolded her arms. "There's always a choice, Storm." He drew her to him. "Like now. You have a choice to walk away, or a choice to let me hold you. It's up to you."

Her breath caught as he stilled all movement and waited for her decision.

It wasn't a difficult one to make. She stepped into his arms without hesitation.

Storm sighed and rested her head on his solid chest and this time heard the strong beat of his heart. She sighed again when he wrapped his arms around her and cuddled her close to him. He then rested his chin on the top of her head.

She relished the feel of his arms snugly around her, the heat of his warm body seeping into hers, the safety of his embrace. She felt content.

"Life changes, Storm," he advised gently.

"Not for me," she said regretfully.

"For everyone," he insisted. "It never remains the same, and for that we should all be grateful."

She sighed. "For me life will only get worse."

"You have a choice, Storm in which way your life will change."

"I wish I could believe that, but I think fate waits for me and there is no way I can avoid her."

"Perhaps fate sent me here to intervene," he said.

"You certainly have done that." She chuckled.

He lifted her chin and stroked her bottom lip, sending tingles racing through her entire body.

"You are a good person, you do good work, but sacrificing yourself serves no purpose. Living is what makes the difference."

She thought at first to argue, but her tingling body advised otherwise and she whispered, "Kiss me."

"With pleasure," Burke said and claimed her lips.

Her arms swept up around his neck and she pressed her body firmly against his while his lips worked their magic. She was soon lost in a haze of passion that escalated as the kiss deepened.

She didn't protest when he lifted her off the ground and lowered them to the bed together. They remained locked in each other's arms and locked in a kiss. Storm didn't want it to end.

His hand stroked her back and slipped down over her backside, which he gently squeezed and moved her up more firmly against him.

She felt all of him and she relished the thought of his strength penetrating her, filling her, bringing her pleasure.

She moved against him in a provocative invitation.

His lips drifted to her ear in kisses along her cheek. "This is your choice?"

"It is," she said.

"You are sure?"

"I have not a doubt."

His hand moved to her waist, working to free her shirt, while his lips returned to hers. This time Storm was the impatient one and her hand joined his pulling her shirt out of her trousers.

"Storm!"

The shout broke them apart and had them jumping off the bed. Storm shoved her shirt back in her trousers as she ran out of the room. She looked down from the walkway high in the trees.

Tanin looked up at her. "Philip has returned with information concerning the prisoner."

Chapter 18

Burke, Storm, and Tanin joined Philip at the campfire. He sat stuffing his mouth with roasted venison and looked exhausted.

Burke would have given the man time to digest his food, but not Storm. She plopped down across from him and wanted to know what he had learned.

Her lovely face was flushed with the heat of passion, her lips rosy and plump from their endless kisses, and Burke wondered if the men noticed. He sat beside her wishing that the news could have waited for a few moments more. But moments wouldn't have been sufficient time to make love to Storm. He would have preferred hours.

Philip shook his head. "You're not going to like the information, though I can't confirm it as truth or gossip," Philip told them.

"Either way we need to hear it, so tell us," Storm said.

"Someone heard that the prisoner was moved to Weighton."

Burke felt the stunned silence descend around him like a heavy burden that would be hard to lift, and he grew anxious.

"Why does this disturb all of you?" he asked.

Storm responded bluntly. "There is only one way out of Weighton—death."

Burke felt as if he'd been punched in the gut and the blow silenced him.

"It makes no sense," Tanin said. "Only those accused of crimes against the king and country go to Weighton. Why would this man be sent there for being a thief?"

"It would depend on what he stole," Storm said.

"It could involve treason," Philip offered.

"You weren't able to learn any more?" Storm asked.

Philip shook his head. "I heard even that tidbit secondhand."

"Then we can't be certain it's true," Burke said, hoping the information would prove wrong. "Where is Weighton?"

"Not far from St. Andrew Harbor where your ship is docked," Tanin informed him. "But make no mistake, it's the most highly guarded prison in all of Scotland. No one has ever escaped its confines."

"We still need to determine if the man we chase after is Burke's brother, Cullen," Storm reminded. "Philip, did anyone know the prisoner's name?"

"No, I could find no one with that information."

"It's as if his identity is purposely being guarded," Tanin said.

"Of course. Then he can't be tracked and found," Storm concluded.

"Would he have reached Weighton by now, or is there a chance we could intercept?" Burke asked.

Philip shook his head. "Too late for that; he'd have reached the prison by now."

Burke didn't like feeling helpless, and he felt that way too often of late. He had followed Storm's orders since arriving, but things weren't going as he had hoped. He needed to move things along, and sitting here without funds wasn't doing that.

Burke stood. "I'd like to get to the harbor as soon as possible."

"Money isn't going to solve this problem," Storm said firmly.

"Presently, nothing is solving this problem," Burke snapped.

"We need to confirm the identity of the prisoner before we do anything," Storm reminded.

"We haven't been very successful at that, have we?" Burke asked as if he was waiting to hear a different response.

Philip cleared his throat, and everyone looked at him. "Actually money may be the very thing that can help us."

Burke sat down again. "Tell me."

"The man I learned the information from second-hand advised me that I could probably learn more for a steep price, since he felt that the fellow was taking his life into his hands by divulging more."

"What if it's a ruse?" Tanin asked.

"Scam or not, it's the only lead we have," Burke said. "I'm willing to take the chance."

Tanin and Philip looked to Storm.

"It makes sense," Burke said, turning to her. "We have no other lead or prospect of a lead. I'm willing to pay the price and see what we learn."

Storm shook her head slowly. "It doesn't sound right to me. It could be more than a scam. It could be a setup, the law looking for anyone connected to this man. Anyone who might make a fuss over his disappearance."

"But his identity isn't even known," Burke argued.

"Yet we look for him," Storm said.

Burke was adamant. "I say we take the chance."

"Since it's our only lead, I must agree," Storm said, "though reluctantly."

"Noted. You and I leave for the harbor tomorrow," Burke said to Storm.

"No!" shouted Tanin and Philip in unison.

"She'll be safe with me, I promise," Burke said. "I have a plan."

"We hear the plan and then see if we agree," Tanin informed him curtly.

Burke stretched his shoulders back and his chin went up. "I intend to make it known that Storm is my wife and that we arrived together on my ship on business."

"What of her Scottish burr?" Tanin asked.

"I will explain that she suffered an ailment on the journey and has temporarily lost her voice. Believe me, she'll be dressed in such finery that no one will question me. They will be more interested in what money I have to spend."

Philip nodded. "That could work."

Tanin chuckled. "If Storm could remain silent."

Philip laughed. "Tanin's got a point. She's used to having her say."

The two men quieted as soon as they glanced at their leader. She wasn't smiling.

Storm dismissed both of them, then turned to Burke. "Why is it necessary for me to go with you?"

"I promised you a rescue and this is it. Don't deny yourself a short reprieve," he urged, when she looked ready to protest. "Besides, who knows what we can find out while at the harbor? Gossip always flies freely around a port."

He leaned his face next to hers. "And we'd have a night on my ship together, in my cabin, in a very comfortable bed."

Her expression softened to a teasing smile. "I'm not sure which offer is more promising."

"Then you have no choice but to find out."

"Ah, but didn't you tell me I have a choice?"

Burke brushed his lips over hers ever so lightly. "What do you choose?"

She sighed. "To be rescued."

"You won't regret it," he murmured. "I promise."

"I know I won't."

He wondered if she did so to ease her own doubts

rather than to appease him. "We leave tomorrow."

She agreed. "The sooner the better. If this prisoner isn't your brother, we'd have wasted all this time."

"I don't know," Burke said with a shake of his head. "Peter thought the man resembled me, only larger. I'm almost sure it's Cullen, and the longer I hesitate, the worst his situation grows."

"Again I agree, but tell me," she asked with a scrunch of her eyes. "What is your ship doing in St. Andrew Harbor?"

"My father started many lucrative businesses, an import business being one of them, and Longton ships dock at St. Andrew. I made certain that the ship was stocked with specific cargo for my use."

"Ladies' dresses?" she queried with a crooked grin.

For a moment she resembled a young, carefree lass ready to be adventurous, and he wanted to give her that—give her joy, good memories, and love, if only for a day or two.

"My warehouses are stocked with a wealth of items for export, ladies' items included. I'm sure we can find you something suitable to wear." He intended to make certain of it. She would have a day of fun she would never forget and a night of memories that would linger long after he was gone.

"A fine skirt and blouse will do," Storm said.

Burke near laughed; instead he kept it to a generous smile. "My wife would wear finer garments than a mere skirt and blouse while visiting a foreign port. You'll be wearing silks, linens, and fine wool."

"But only the manor ladies wear such finery."

Burke stretched out his arms. "I am a wealthy American and my wife will dress accordingly. No one will even consider you the infamous outlaw Storm, and since I can't call you that, what would my wife's name be?"

"Let's keep it simple," Storm said. "Call me Mary."

"Is that your given name?" he asked, curious.

"My true name was buried along with my husband and there it shall remain." She stood. "I must talk with Tanin and Philip. I want Philip to arrange a meeting with that man who, for a handsome fee, will provide us with further information. This way we can meet them on our way home."

"Will it take us long to reach the harbor?"

"We'll walk to Barkell, about three villages from the harbor. There we'll meet with friends to get horses and ride the remainder of the way, saving us time. Then we'll need to sneak aboard your ship—"

"Where we'll depart the ship as Mr. Longton and his wife, Mary."

Burke stood and Storm walked over to him. "While your wife, I will remain silent for the sake of our mission, but be aware that if necessary I will speak up."

"At the *appropriate* time," he teased.

"Do you prefer a wife who is seen and not heard, Mr. Longton?"

"My wife will have her own mind and speak it. I want no delicate flower that wilts on the vine. She will need strength to survive the wilderness and respect its beauty."

"Your homeland sounds similar to Scotland. I can understand why you wish to return to it."

"I could live no other place," he admitted.

"I feel the same."

He thought how unfortunate that was for both of them. There could be nothing between them but a brief interlude, and for some reason the idea terribly disturbed him.

They parted, and Burke returned to sit by the fire. A strong breeze swept through the camp, chilling the late afternoon air even more. The fire kept him warm enough, and besides, he had too much on his mind to even consider the dip in temperature.

He'd need to see to the ship's business while there, and though the ship was due to leave port shortly, he had a feeling it would be better to delay its departure. He might have to make a hasty exit from Scotland once he found Cullen, and his ship would give him that ability.

He didn't know how Cullen would feel about leaving, but given the circumstances, he might not have a choice.

Choice.

He had told Storm she had a choice and she did. She would choose to remain in her homeland and fight her crusade no matter how difficult her life. She stubbornly refused to see that she fought an endless battle that would never know victory.

He wished he could get her to understand the uselessness of her cause. That what she did would change nothing and affect only a few lives, and in the end, was it really worth the sacrifice?

To those she had saved it most certainly had been, but on a larger scale, what did she really accomplish? And none of this should make a difference to him, so why did it?

He shook his head and held his hands out to the fire, rubbing them together to warm them.

Storm was much too beautiful and much too intelligent to be wasting her life away in the woods, a wanted outlaw. She should have a home and children and a husband to look after her and protect her.

If she were his wife, he'd protect her with his life and provide generously for her and their children.

He smiled at the thought of a dark-haired little girl as obstinate as her mother running into his arms to be scooped up and hugged.

He gave his head a good shake this time. Was he crazy for thinking of having children with Storm? They came from different worlds. Worlds separated by a vast ocean and love of homeland. He couldn't afford to fall in love with her.

It would cost him dearly to love her and then be forced to leave her here in Scotland. He wouldn't be able to do it. And he didn't see Storm leaving her beloved home.

Another shake of his head warned that his musings were just that, thoughts that meant nothing and would amount to nothing. He and Storm understood each other. They each had an agenda to keep and the stubbornness to stick to it.

He would love Storm for the time he was here but he would not *fall in love* with her. He couldn't, for love was a commitment he took seriously. When he loved, it would be forever, and that would mean that he couldn't leave Storm behind in Scotland. She would have to return to America with him whether she liked it or not.

In that, she would have no choice.

Chapter 19

Their journey went smoothly, and Storm and Burke arrived at St. Andrew Harbor early in the morning. Not a good time to sneak aboard a ship, but there was no time to waste. Philip and William had left camp the same time, and had probably already contacted the mysterious man who possessed the information they required. If all went well they would meet in four days to exchange money for information.

Therefore, they had to get to the ship as soon as possible, see to their business, and leave within two days' time.

"We can't be seen together," Storm said, concealed by a stack of crates at the end of the harbor. Burke could tell she was impressed by the massive ship, the gangplank bustling with men unloading crate after crate.

"Agreed," he said with a nod. "I need to get on board, give orders to my crew, and change clothes so that it looks as if I've arrived with the ship. Then we need to get you on board as well."

"We may have to wait until evening when there is less activity and the cover of darkness."

"Not an option," Burke said. "I won't have you here alone along the harbor. You resemble a lad, and with three ships anchored in the harbor, I guarantee in no time you'd be a crew member ready to set sail on one of them."

Storm resented the idea that he felt her incapable of looking after herself, when by now he knew otherwise.

"You forget who I am," she reminded.

Burke was quick to disagree. "It is exactly who you are that makes me worry over your safety. I gave my word you'd be safe and I intend to keep it. Besides, today is to be a day of fun for you."

"Then what do you propose?" she asked, the day of fun beckoning her to play.

"You remain hidden until I return for you. Then we'll make it appear as if I've taken you on as a cabin boy, and make sure to keep your face smudged. We don't want anyone discovering what a lovely face you have, at least not until you're my wife."

Wife.

While it was nothing more than a charade they played, the title still startled her. It had been three years since her husband had called her wife, and Daniel had an endearingly proud way of using the title on occasion. It had filled her heart with joy. Not so this time.

This time it unsettled her.

"I'll be right here waiting," she said.

"I won't be long," he reassured her.

He mingled easily with the crowd of people along the dock. Storm followed him with her eyes as he maneuvered his way to his ship without hesitation, walked up the gangplank, and was gone from sight.

Had she given this decision time or had she been too quick to agree to a day of fun? Did she truly wish to spend time alone with the American? Did she ache to feel a man's arms around her once again and to share intimacies without ties that bind?

She leaned her back against the crates and slid down until she sat on the hard ground, arms resting on her raised knees.

What was it that attracted her to the American? He was a man much in charge of himself and accustomed to being in charge of others. He wasn't a man who followed but who led, and he did it with honor.

She respected an honorable man, one who when he gave his word lived by it, even if it proved difficult. And Burke refused to give his word unless he felt he could keep it. Such a man was not only to be admired, but also to be trusted.

She found these qualities much more appealing in a man than his features, not that Burke wasn't attractive. He pleased her eyes well enough, but his defined character pleased her more.

"What are you doing? Stealing from my crates?"

Storm jumped at the harsh grumble and spun around to find a large barrel of a man, fingers thick as sausages, waving a coiled whip in the air.

"No, sir," she said, keeping her head respectfully bowed and his eyes distracted from her face. "Resting, that's all, sir."

"Don't lie to me," he yelled and reached out.

Storm ducked and took off past him hoping to get lost in the bustle of the busy dock.

Burke hurried to change clothes, not wanting to leave Storm alone too long. He had promised Tanin and Philip and the rest of the group that he would keep her safe, and he couldn't hold firm to his word if she wasn't with him. She'd be safe enough for a short time hidden behind the crates, but there was always a chance she'd be found.

He stripped off his clothes, washed quickly at the basin filled with water, then dressed in black trousers, white shirt, black vest, and black waistcoat. Unable to tolerate constriction of any kind around his neck, he left several fastenings undone.

Shiny leather boots followed and then a comb of his hair with a real comb and not his fingers, and he was near done.

He grabbed coins from the safe he had stocked with money, and picked up his father's diamond ring and shoved it on his pinky. It was the only finger it fit, and he wore it with pride, as had his father.

A chest of garments meant for America had been

brought to his cabin on his orders. He wished Storm to have her pick. Something was bound to fit her, and he was eager to see her dressed in fine clothes.

She would certainly be a raving beauty, but then her beauty wasn't defined by what she wore, since she was just as beautiful dressed in lad's clothing. She was striking regardless of what she wore.

He smiled, recalling her smudged face and how he had wanted so badly to kiss her when they had stood behind the crates. He had wanted to kiss her, hold her, and do much more than that, much too often of late. It was a constant thought in his mind and one he definitely wanted to see reach fruition.

Finally finished and anxious to return to Storm, he hurried out of his cabin to the deck. Much of the crew stood at the railing, their attention fixed on the dock below.

Burke hurried to the gangplank, relieved that he had been provided with a distraction to get Storm aboard without being noticed.

That is, until he saw what caught the men's attention.

The whip sliced the air so close to her ear that its crack near deafened her. Storm stood perfectly still. Her shoulder stung from where the tip of the whip had caught her when she had attempted to run. She was grateful her jacket took the brunt of the hit, though it had sliced through, and she could feel the blood dripping down her arm.

"You don't run from me," the man screamed, his full face turning red with rage.

For a second Storm gave thought to running, but the man was skilled with the whip and could do her harm. She remained where she was.

"Come over here," the man demanded.

"I've done nothing wrong, sir." She hoped to delay him until Burke arrived. It was her only chance. That they had attracted a crowd didn't help matters. Attention was the last thing she needed.

"I'll not tell you again," the man said loudly. Encouraged by the cheers of the crowd, he raised his whip.

"Strike the lad and you'll find that whip a noose around your fat neck."

The order sliced through the crowd much like the crack of the whip, silencing everyone.

Storm thanked heaven for Burke's timely arrival, and when she turned to look, she almost didn't recognize him. Clearly, his dress proclaimed him a man of wealth and station, far removed from the man she had rescued from the filthy prison, and yet he was the very same one.

He walked with that confident swagger that spoke volumes. He was a man of class and distinction, and the man with the whip realized it as quickly as Storm had, for he lowered the weapon, though he refused to relent.

"The lad stole from me and will pay for his crime," he said, shaking his meaty fist.

Storm remained where she was and Burke walked around to stand in front of her. His body completely blocked her from the view of her accuser; that he shielded her was obvious to all.

"The lad belongs to me."

Storm near shivered, his remark more a threat. Burke looked as if he wore no weapon and yet he attacked with words and a powerful stance. How did he expect to truly defend himself?

"Do I need to rescue you again?" she whispered behind him.

She heard a low chuckle.

"We'll see who rescues who."

She didn't doubt he would rescue her. His stance alone, blocking her from her accuser, clearly indicated that he didn't intend to surrender her. That he intended to protect her, save her, rescue her was evident, and the crowd cheered him on.

The realization of the attention they drew suddenly made her realize how precarious their situation could turn. If anyone should dare recognize her, question her identity, attempt to ask her name, they would be in trouble.

She reminded him of this in a rushed whisper. "Hurry."

"Agreed," he mumbled beneath his breath.

The big man finally found his voice and courage, though his quavering voice betrayed his unease. "I'll be compensated for his crime."

Burke reached into his waistcoat pocket, extracted several coins and tossed them at the man. "You'll get no more."

The man scurried after the coins that rolled and spun and scattered in different directions. It would take him a while to collect them all.

In the meantime, Burke snatched Storm by the arm

and practically dragged her up the gangplank, down the narrow steps and into a cabin, then slammed the door shut.

"How did you get yourself into that predicament?"

She was about to answer when he advanced on her. She backed away from him, his face looking as if he were in a rage.

"You're bleeding," he said and reached for her arm.

She glanced down at her shoulder, the tear made by the whip having gone clear down to her skin.

Before she could explain it was nothing, Burke began pulling off her jacket. She attempted to stop him when suddenly she wondered if she really knew this man in front of her. He was much more in command, much more at home here. And why wouldn't he be—this was his ship, his command. She was merely a visitor, an observer.

She fought to adjust to the reversal of roles, but not being fully in control did not sit well with her, and she found it difficult, if not impossible.

"It's nothing," she said and stepped away from him.

"Bullshit," he said and advanced on her once again.

She held her hand up to stop him. "Clean cloths, fresh water, and I can see to it myself."

"It isn't necessary. I'll tend to it for you," he said with a step closer.

"I'll—"

"You'll let me see to it. Then you'll search that chest for an appropriate dress, change and be introduced around the harbor as my wife, Mary," he said firmly. "We have little time and it would be foolish to waste it arguing."

She hated to admit he was right, but then he was in command here, and what choice did she really have. They did not have time to spare, not if she were to enjoy a day of freedom.

She stripped off her jacket and lowered the shirt off her shoulder. She didn't have the inclination to stand bare-chested in front of him. Things had changed since that day she had stripped her chest bare mainly to shock him. She had discovered that she liked the American's kisses and his touch.

Her glance drifted to the bed, a good size that would easily hold two people with the bedding of fine wool and thickly stuffed pillows. Would they share his bed this night? Would she taste intimacy once again? Would it prove as satisfying and loving as it had with her husband?

Too many questions waiting for answers.

"It looks worse than it is," Burke announced, cleansing her wound with a wet cloth.

"Surface wound." She glanced up into his dark eyes and for a moment was caught by his concern. He actually appeared deeply worried, and it startled her. "I'm all right," she assured him.

"He could have inflicted much more damage." He threw the cloth in the basin, sloshing water over the sides.

"You arrived in time," she reminded.

He cupped her face with his hand. "What if I hadn't?"

"I would have run,' she answered on a single breath.

"Where?"

In a heart's breath she whispered, "To you."

He shook his head slowly, growled angrily beneath his breath, and then ravished her lips as if he had never kissed her before.

That was all it took. They feasted on each other like two hungry lovers long denied. They tasted, took a breath, and tasted some more as if they could never truly satisfy each other.

His hands slipped beneath her shirt and she jumped, startled, when he took hold of her full breast, his thumb playing havoc with her hard nipple.

Good Lord, she wanted desperately to strip off her clothes and his and jump into his bed and forget the world existed for the reminder of the day. They would be two lovers lost in time.

Time.

She pulled away, feeling the loss of intimacy as his lips fell away from hers, his hand slipped reluctantly off her breast, and his warmth faded with each step that separated them.

"We have little time to spare."

He took a deep breath and nodded. "I will leave you to dress. Meet me on deck when you're finished. My crew will be aware that you are to be known as my wife. And I'll explain that the lad is recovering from his whipping."

Storm nodded, disappointed, but grateful they had tonight together.

Burke walked to the door and stopped after opening it. "You're right, Storm, we have little time to spare, and I'm going to make certain we don't waste a minute of it."

Chapter 20

Burke gripped the railing and stared down at the dock. He didn't look at anything in particular. He was too busy keeping himself from rushing back to the cabin and spending the rest of the day making love to Storm.

He should be grateful that she'd reminded him that they were here for other, more important matters, but he wasn't feeling grateful. He was annoyed that he had so little time to spend alone with Storm. They would return to the woods soon enough, and she would once again be an outlaw, but for this brief time, she was his wife. They belonged to each other, and the endearing thought stirred his soul.

"Mr. Longton."

Burke turned and shook his head. "Will you never call me Burke, Douglas?"

"When I captain the ship for you, sir, it's a title I'll be calling you by."

Douglas Mahoney had captained the ship for his father, and while his full head of hair was pure white and wrinkles covered every inch of his face, the tall, slim man was ageless. He had sailed the seas since he'd been seven and complained when his feet touched land. Burke wouldn't trust a voyage without Douglas captaining his vessel, just as his father had.

"You used to call me Burke."

"When you were a mere lad. You're not a lad anymore, sir."

No, he wasn't. He was a man on a mission of importance, and Douglas understood that, for he had made many a journey to Scotland with his father in search of Cullen.

"The crew has been informed about your wife, Mary, and her affliction."

"Good, my wife . . ." He paused, thinking the prospect of such an arrangement wasn't displeasing at all. ". . . has been of much help on my journey."

"I understand," Douglas said. "Will you and your wife be taking a meal in your cabin this evening?"

"Yes." Burke smiled and nodded. "Yes, we will."

The captain's eyes suddenly turned wide, then he smiled. "Your wife, sir, is a stunningly beautiful woman."

Burke turned to his left, as Douglas walked away, and stood there speechless.

The captain had been right; his wife was a stunningly beautiful woman.

She had chosen a deep blue velvet day dress that

made her eyes all the more blue. Her jacket fit snug at her waist, a violet, high-collared blouse lay beneath, and a bonnet the same color as her dress topped her head and was decorated with violet plumes that swayed liberally in the cold autumn air.

Her face had been scrubbed clean, her cheeks rosy, and her dark hair swept up beneath the bonnet. She truly resembled a lady of fine breeding and character, but then he had thought that of her since first they met.

Burke finally got control of himself and walked over to her, his hand extended.

She took it and moved into the crook of his arm to whisper, "This outfit suits you?"

He smiled and leaned down and brushed his lips over hers. "It suits you perfectly."

"I've never owned anything of such beauty."

"Now you do, though it is you who makes the dress beautiful."

Her cheeks turned pink, her soft blush flaring his passion, and he silently cursed the effect she had on him. Damned if he didn't enjoy feasting his eyes on her and knowing that tonight, she would be his.

He held his arm out to her. "Can I interest you in a stroll along the docks and a visit to a few of the local shops?"

Her smile pierced his heart, and surely did damage to his soul.

"I would be delighted," she said and hooked her arm with his.

The village shops sat just past the harbor. It was a quaint little place where the wealthy came to amuse themselves with purchases fresh off the arriving ships.

They were treated royally, especially once Burke began to pamper his wife with various purchases. It was obvious that the American wished to please his new bride, and how unfortunate it was that she'd been stricken with an ailment that had left her temporarily unable to speak.

Silk ribbons, sweets, and perfume were a few of the items he had indulged her with, and Burke knew Storm would object once they returned to the ship. However, for the moment she could not argue with his choices, for her supposed affliction prevented her from doing so. She could only smile and nod at her husband's generosity.

They made their way along the buildings, Storm stopping to admire lacy ribbons in the seamstress's window.

"I'll a buy you a few," Burke offered.

Storm smiled and stood on tiptoe to kiss her husband's cheek.

Burke was surprised until she whispered in his ear.

"A place of generous gossip is a pub."

Burke understood. "I think you need a few new garments to impress our friends back in America, so I shall leave you here while I have a pint or two at the local pub."

She smiled and they entered the shop.

It smelled delightful and there was color everywhere from the bolts of material stacked on shelves and draped over chairs, to the tables covered in lace and bowls of ribbons spilling out of them.

The seamstress was as petite as Storm, though her hair raged red against milk-pale skin and her wide green eyes sparkled with friendly delight. She was only too happy to oblige Burke after he explained that his wife required several garments to be made of her finest material. He hoped she wouldn't mind advising his wife on the styles of the local aristocrats, since she wanted to impress her friends back home. How unfortunate that his wife could not partake in the conversation.

The seamstress told him not to worry, she would handle everything, and shooed him out of the shop, though not before he gave his wife a peck on the cheek and whispered, "Be good and have fun."

Storm smiled sweetly and patted her husband's arm.

Burke was not reassured but took his leave. What trouble could she get into in a seamstress shop?

Plenty.

He ignored his thought and decided to keep his visit to the pub brief.

Burke entered the small pub not that different from the saloons in America, depending of course on location. The larger towns and cities had the more garish saloons, while one would find a saloon much like this in a small town. There was a bar big enough for maybe four men to stand at and three tables occupying space for two. The smell wasn't too inviting, but then once you got drinking the smell was no longer noticeable.

He went to the bar and ordered a pint, then

attempted a conversation with the skinny bartender, commenting on a range of topics including poachers, thieves, and how the Scots dealt with such crimes.

"It's Thomas Gibbons you need to talk to about such things. He's worked for some of the landlords." The bartender grinned and pointed to a lone man sitting at a table. "A pint of ale will buy you all the information you need."

"Mind if I join you?" Burke asked, placing a pint of ale in front of the man.

"Have a seat," he offered and grabbed hold of the tankard.

Burke decided to get right to the point for a good reason—the short, round man smelled as if it had been weeks since he last bathed.

"I wondered how the landlords here in Scotland deal with crimes," Burke said. "The bartender told me you were the man to talk with."

"Trouble handling your tenants in America?" Thomas asked with a laugh and took a generous swallow of ale.

Burke smiled, letting the man assume what he wished.

"The landlords tolerate no crime on their lands," Thomas said with a pound of his tankard on the table. "They deal with crimes swift and harshly. It's the only way to keep control of the tenants."

Thomas went into great detail, much of which Burke already knew thanks to Storm and his own observations since arriving.

"You should speak with the Earl of Balford," Thomas suggested. "Only a fool would steal from that man. The consequences are much too harsh."

"How harsh?"

"Prison, fines . . ." He lowered his voice. "The man knows how to get what he wants from his prisoners. Believe me, sir, no one wants to find himself in Balford's prison."

"And where can I find him?" Burke asked innocently.

"Glencurry, perhaps two days' ride from here." He kept his voice low and leaned close to Burke, who tried not to take a breath. "He's not a man to cross. Be careful dealing with him."

Burke leaned back and called out to the bartender. "Another pint for Thomas."

Thomas grinned. "Thank you, sir, you are most kind."

Burke thanked him for his time, and not wanting to leave Storm on her own too long, he took his leave. He sucked in a giant breath of fresh chilled air as soon as he left the pub, and headed for the seamstress shop.

He was a bit disappointed, since he didn't feel that he'd learned anything new. The man had simply verified what he already knew about the Earl of Balford—that the man was a bastard.

He'd dealt with bastards before, men who wanted more than their fair share, men who thought they were entitled and that the law didn't apply to them. Burke knew too that in order to deal with such men, you had to step outside the law, and as he had mentioned to Storm once, he had done so when necessary and he'd do it again.

He entered the shop ready to wait for Storm if she wasn't finished, since he wanted her to enjoy this day of freedom and fun, and came face to face with Lady Alaina.

She stood perfectly still staring at him.

She was an indescribable beauty. Whereas Storm's beauty was tangible, hers was ethereal, not like any he'd ever seen before or expected to see again.

Burke decided that fate had thrown them together, and he intended to take advantage of the situation. He approached her. "Pardon me, but do we know each other?"

She lowered her eyes. "Forgive me, I thought for a moment, but lately—" She shook her head. "You remind me of someone."

"Perhaps I know him."

"That's not possible. You're an American, he's a Scotsman."

"There's a Scotsman that looks like me? Poor fellow."

Lady Alaina laughed. "That is where you are different since he fancies himself a handsome man."

"Then he's a wise one too."

"You have his humor."

No, he and Cullen had their father's humor. He was anxious to know if they spoke of the same man so he asked, "What is this charming fellow's name?"

She whispered it so softly that he didn't hear it.

"What was that you said?"

"Lady Alaina, I am almost ready for you. Oh good, Mr. Longton, you've returned. Your wife is just about finished," the seamstress said after stepping from behind the curtain. "Excuse me a moment, Lady Alaina, while I finish with Mrs. Longton."

Lady Alaina drifted off to sit in a silk-draped chair near the window and Burke almost swore aloud. One second more and he would have had a name. He'd be damned if he was going to leave the shop without a name. If she knew Cullen, then she would know if the prisoner they followed was his brother.

Storm stepped from behind the curtain fastening the last clasp on her jacket and averted her eyes when she caught sight of Lady Alaina.

"Sweetheart," he said, walking over to Storm. "You'll never guess. I have a double here in Scotland and this lovely woman knows him."

He walked over to Lady Alaina, Storm on his arm. "May I introduce myself? Burke Longton from the Dakota Territory in America and my wife, Mary, who I'm sorry to say has lost her voice temporarily from an illness suffered during our voyage here."

"Lady Alaina of Glencurry, the Earl of Balford's daughter," she offered in return.

"A pleasure," Burke said, and noticed how Alaina stared oddly at Storm.

"How rude of me for staring, but you also look familiar."

Storm's smile was congenial.

"Perhaps our ancestors roamed this area," Burke suggested, though he wondered if there could be a reason for Lady Alaina to recognize Storm. If so, they couldn't remain in her presence for long. "This fellow you mentioned that I resembled, perhaps if I spoke with him—"

"He's no longer in the area," Lady Alaina said, clearly upset.

"I'm ready for you, Lady Alaina," the seamstress said, walking over to her.

Burke noticed she looked relieved, as if the tiny woman had rescued her.

"It was a pleasure meeting both of you. I hope you enjoy your visit to Scotland."

Burke could have sworn he caught the start of tears forming in her eyes as she bid him farewell and walked past him.

"Lady Alaina," he called out softly, but loud enough for her to hear and turn around.

He caught a glisten in the corner of her eye and knew he had been right, she was on the verge of tears, and he felt guilty having upset her.

"The name," he said. "I didn't catch the fellow's name whom I resemble."

"Cullen," she said, and quickly turned away.

Chapter 21

"It's Cullen!" Burke exclaimed once they entered his cabin.

Storm took off her bonnet and jacket and placed them on the chest. "It doesn't make sense."

"What do you mean?"

"How would Lady Alaina have made an acquaintance of a prisoner?" Storm shook her head. "The earl would never allow his daughter access to the prison. We could very well be chasing the wrong man."

"Then I need to question her some more and find out what she knows of Cullen."

Storm shoved her hand out to stop him. "That would definitely cause suspicion, and I wouldn't be surprised if she is already suspicious of us. With gossip a livelihood on the docks there'll be many tongues wagging about the American who asks so many questions. And if Thomas could be bought with a pint or two of ale, what makes you think one of your crew can't be bought as cheaply?"

Burke didn't look too happy. "What you're suggesting is that we'll need to leave here by tomorrow the latest if we're not to take chances."

"We'll need to leave before dawn's first light."

"You don't think we should be seen again?"

"I think enough people have seen us already, any more and we'd be asking for trouble," she said. "And besides, between what we learned from Lady Alaina and the information we can find out from the man we pay, it may be enough to piece the puzzle together."

"If not?"

"Then we'll have no choice but to speak with Lady Alaina again."

Burke paced the room. "Then why not just question her now and save us time?"

"We need more information," she advised, attempting to calm his agitation while understanding it. He was a man who took decisive action, but more thought was called for in this situation, and besides, she didn't want to see him imprisoned, especially not by the Earl of Balford.

"Which we can learn from her," he said with a wave of his hand.

"I don't think that is a wise course of action. Foreigners asking too many questions aren't well received. What we need to do is piece together what we already know and add to it. Then we can make a better judgment call."

Burke stripped off his waistcoat and rolled up his sleeves. "What do we have?"

Storm's glance gently fell over Burke. He was so very different from her Daniel in features, but alike when it came to protecting her. Burke had certainly taken a firm stance on that when he had stepped in front of the man with the whip. He had made it clear that no one would hurt her and he had done so with confidence.

At that very moment when he had stepped around her, blocked her from harm, she realized that he would do anything to keep her safe, even placing his own life in jeopardy.

"Storm?"

She stared up at him as he stroked her arms.

"Are you all right? You looked to have drifted away."

His tender touch sent a tingle through her. It spread a warm heat throughout every part of her body, warning that passion was close behind.

She stepped away from him. "I'm fine. Lost in thought is all."

"Good thoughts?"

His crooked smile warned that her answer could prove to sidetrack them from their present conversation. While her body alerted her to its readiness, her mind cautioned that the matter of his brother needed attention now.

"Your brother's name was finally mentioned, so it tells us that he has been or may still be in the area."

"You're right. This is the first time someone

actually has mentioned him by name." Burke rubbed his chin. "Peter mentioned that I resembled the prisoner and Lady Alaina spoke of my resemblance to Cullen. That means the two very well could be one. Cullen must be the man being held prisoner by the Earl of Balford."

"Did you notice the tears in Lady Alaina's eyes when she spoke Cullen's name?"

"Yes, I did," Burke admitted anxiously. "She's obviously upset by his imprisonment. Perhaps they were friends."

Storm shook her head slowly. "There's only one reason a woman would shed tears when speaking of a man."

"And that is?"

"Love."

Burke dropped down into the chair. "Something invaluable was stolen from the earl, isn't that what we were told?"

Storm sat on the cushioned stool beside Burke. "His daughter's heart was stolen. She must have fallen in love with Cullen, a man beneath her station."

"But why imprison him? Why not just ship him off to another country?"

"I don't know, but keep your distance from the Earl of Balford until we can figure this out."

"Why?" Burke asked. "I could offer to take Cullen back to America with me and his problem would be solved."

"Would you leave the woman you loved if presented with such an offer?"

Storm grew uneasy with the way his dark eyes rested on her, holding firm as if they refused to let go.

"Never!"

"Then I think we can safely assume that your brother would have an identical response. If he and Lady Alaina truly love each other, one is not going to let the other go. They will fight for their love, and the only victor in this battle will be the Earl of Balford."

"You're sure of that?"

"Believe me. I know the earl well."

Burke's eyes narrowed. "Lady Alaina thought you looked familiar as well. Why is that?"

Storm clenched her hands as that storm-ravaged night came back to her in full force. Before she could find her voice, Burke stood, took her hands in his, and gently guided her to the chair. Then he sat on a stool he pulled in front of her.

"Tell me, Storm."

He squeezed her hand, offering comfort and courage, and she began her story.

"My husband, Daniel, and I had a small plot of land. We were happy, content in our own world, with ourselves. Then one day the landlord claimed that half of our land did not belong to us. The land he proposed to rob us of was ready for harvest and would have provided us with sufficient food for the coming winter and enough to pay our tenant rent."

She took a breath, and she was relieved that Burke kept hold of her hands. His touch was warm and so very comforting.

"Naturally, Daniel protested, but the landlord

had him imprisoned for a ridiculous charge. Fees for his imprisonment mounted, and without the harvest to sell at market, I was penniless."

She choked on her words and the memories they evoked.

"Take your time," Burke encouraged.

"The landlord took pleasure in making his prisoners suffer and more so if the family did not provide him with extra coins." Tears welled in her eyes and she sniffed them back. She had cried endlessly then; she didn't want to cry anymore. It did her no good, served no purpose, and hadn't brought her husband back to her.

"I watched my Daniel grow thinner and thinner from hunger, the little food I snuck to him not sufficient to maintain his abused body."

"Was there no one who could help you?"

"Tanin," she said on a tear and wiped it away. "His Ellie had been imprisoned simply because the landlord had taken a fancy to her, and he was not about to let her spend one night in that cell."

"He helped you?"

"I found out his intentions to free his wife and asked if I could join him." She choked on her laughter. "He thought me a fool. What could a pint-sized woman do?"

"I guess he found out fast enough," Burke said with a grin.

"I did surprise him, freeing his Ellie with ease and then . . ." She swallowed the lump in her throat and tried without success to quell the vivid memories that rushed through her mind. "Daniel took his last breath in my arms." Storm bit at her lip to stop it from quivering. "His—" She choked back the sobs that wanted to rip from her throat. "His last words to me were—" She paused to regain control. " 'I knew you'd come for me. I knew you wouldn't let me die here.' "

Tears flooded her eyes but she contained them. "Tanin carried Daniel out of the prison and into the woods. He carried Daniel all the way to the ruins of the old church and he helped me bury him there. A fitting place to say good-bye, since it was our second anniversary."

"I'm so very sorry," Burke said.

"If I had been a day or two sooner, perhaps I could have saved him. I would have tended him day and night until he was well. I would have never left his side. I would have—"

"Shhh, Storm," Burke said, placing his hand gently on her cheek. "You did what you could."

"I didn't do enough. I let my husband die." Tears rolled down her cheek, and before she could wipe them away, Burke stopped her and gently eased them off her face with his thumb.

"You did all that you possibly could and Daniel knew that. He told you so himself before he died."

"He didn't have to die."

"No, he didn't, but it wasn't your fault that he did. It was the landlord's greed and brutality that killed Daniel," Burke said.

"Tanin has told me as much many times and though I know it is so, it doesn't help ease the pain in my heart."

A knock at the cabin door broke them apart, and Burke bid the caller to enter.

"Supper will be ready shortly, sir," Douglas said. "May I see to preparing the cabin?"

"I could use some fresh air," Storm said and grabbed her bonnet and jacket.

Twilight was claiming the horizon as Storm emerged on the deck of the ship. She wanted a brief distance between her and Burke, but he would have none of that, reaching out and hooking her arm in his.

"You don't run from me, Storm. It's your memories that chase you."

She grew annoyed and tried to yank her arm free, but his grip was too strong.

"Get mad if you wish, but you're not going anywhere. You'll stay here beside me."

"Is that a command?"

"Must it be? I offer my friendship, my concern, my empathy for your plight. I do not wish to see you go off alone to suffer your memories. Share them with me so that your pain is eased."

No one had so bluntly offered such friendship to her. Her men cared for and respected her, but none dared speak so boldly to her. Burke spoke his mind and made no excuses for it. He wore his honesty as boldly as he spoke it, and, strangely enough, his direct manner comforted her.

"I have not shared memories of my husband with anyone since his death."

"Then I say it is about time you do. It is good for the soul to release its burden now and again, and I daresay your burden has been a heavy one to bear."

The twilight glistened off his dark brown eyes and highlighted the few wrinkles that fanned the corners of his eyes. She favored the thin lines, for they spoke of a man who had weathered the elements and survived, a man strong in nature and conviction.

"Daniel would have liked you." Her remark surprised her for it was the truth.

"I believe I would have liked Daniel. Tell me more of him."

Storm had shared laughter and tears with Burke by the time they returned to the cabin for supper. He had been right—speaking of her husband had served as a catharsis for her, finally allowing her to shed some of her pent-up pain.

She was enthralled by the lavish display that had been prepared. Pewter plates and goblets dressed a table draped in fine white linen while a white china tureen was the centerpiece of the table. The smell of fresh fish stew permeated the air along with freshly baked bread, and an array of cheeses and fruits.

It was enough food to feed her entire camp for a whole day.

She shed her bonnet and jacket and took the seat Burke held out for her.

"I know your thoughts and I will see that your camp is adequately supplied with food for the coming winter. Tonight, however, you will enjoy this meal without guilt."

She smiled. "You know me well, Mr. Longton."

"Of course I do, Mrs. Longton."

Her hand squeezed the linen napkin in her lap, the title sending a quiver racing through her stomach. Today she had had a small taste of what it would be like to be Burke's wife and she found it too much to her liking.

"There is one thing I've wanted to ask you, though I think I have my answer."

"What is that?" she asked as he emptied a ladle of stew into her bowl.

"We had started talking of Lady Alaina and how she might know you when you began to speak of your husband. I can only assume—"

Storm interrupted. "Lady Alaina saw me now and again when I visited with my husband. It was mostly from a distance, though once up close when I was leaving after a visit and crying terribly. She attempted to console me, but I wanted nothing to do with her and brushed past her."

"I don't blame you. How could you when her father was responsible for imprisoning your husband."

"Now you understand why I do not want you going to the Earl of Balford to bargain for your brother's release. I will not lose another man I care for."

Chapter 22

⟡⟡

Silence ensued, and Burke admired Storm's courage. After sharing the heart-wrenching story of how she lost her husband, she had the courage to admit that she cared for another man.

Cared enough that she would not see him suffer the same fate.

"I have given thought to *us*, Mr. Longton," she said calmly.

He had done the same, but he hadn't admitted that he cared for her as well, or that his caring might go deeper than he had expected. A strange thought but one that plagued him lately.

"What about us?"

She pushed the spoon around in her bowl. "I am an outlaw. I have no future to offer a man. There can be no future for us since you will return to

America and I will remain in Scotland and fight for the rights of the less fortunate."

"Which means?"

"We have a brief moment in time to enjoy each other. I propose that we do just that until it is time for you to leave."

"What if I want more?" he asked, finding himself annoyed that she would think that a quick roll in the hay was all he wanted from her. But hadn't he? At first, possibly, but now? He wasn't certain what he wanted from her, and that irritated him even more.

She gave a soft laugh and shook her head. "There is no *more* for us. There is only now and good-byes."

"And I am to accept this?" Why he suddenly thought her idea ludicrous astounded him since he had thought the same as she. They would share a brief interlude and then he'd be gone. Now, however, the idea disturbed him.

"It is all we have."

Her sadness showed in her deep blue eyes that normally stormed like a raging sea but now appeared serene and ever so beautiful.

"Not so," Burke said, tossing down his napkin and pushing away the bowl of stew that he had barely touched. "We have what we choose to have."

"We have what life has dealt us," she corrected. "We were brought together for a brief time and then we will part. Do we share this time provided us or do we waste it and always regret the opportunity?"

Her remark caused his heart to ache like hell.

How did he love her and leave her? And did he love? Had he suddenly discovered he had feelings for the wisp of a woman who had entered his life in a flash and planned to leave the same way?

"I will never love as I did my Daniel, but I must admit, Mr. Longton, that I have feelings for you, else I would never propose such an interlude."

"I daresay I feel the same," he admitted, perturbed at his own questionable feelings.

"Then we have nothing to lose, do we?"

Burke feared they had more to lose than they bargained for, but then how would he discover that if he didn't pursue his interest in her? Then and only then would he know for sure if he could truly walk away from her.

"Are you willing to find that out?" he asked.

"I have my answer. There is nothing for me to discover, only to enjoy."

"Why do you refuse to allow yourself to love again?"

She placed her spoon to the side, not having tasted a mouthful. "I don't refuse. I just know that I could never love as strongly as I did Daniel."

"As I mentioned once before, first love can never be replaced, but love can still flourish and be even stronger than before."

"Oh no," Storm said adamantly. "I'd never love with the strength that I loved Daniel."

"Then you aren't being fair to Daniel."

Storm looked affronted. "Why do you say that?"

"If your husband loved you, truly loved you, then he wouldn't want to see you alone. He'd want you to love again, and with the same if not more courage and strength than you did him. Would you not want that for Daniel, if it were you who had died?"

Storm didn't hesitate. "I would want Daniel to be happy."

"Then what makes you think he wouldn't want the same for you?"

Storm placed her napkin on the table. "It doesn't really matter what Daniel would want for me. My fate was sealed the day I rescued him from the Earl of Balford's prison. The man is determined to see me caught and paid to suffer for the humiliation I caused him. I've stayed several steps ahead of him but he will catch up sooner or later. It is inevitable."

Burke stood, walked around the table to her, and yanked her out of her seat by her arms. "There is no way in hell I would let you be captured and imprisoned."

"You will not decide my fate, Mr. Longton."

He pulled her up against his chest. "I am your fate, *Mrs. Longton.*"

He claimed her mouth with a feverish kiss that had their passion soaring in seconds.

He held her close, running his hand up to her hair and freeing it of the combs that held it in place so that he could run his fingers through the silky black strands. He wrapped his hand in the long waves and tugged her head back to expose her neck to his lips, and he feasted on her smooth flesh.

She moaned her pleasure and it stirred his own. With quick fingers he opened her blouse and moved his lips to her hard nipples and continued to feast.

She tasted exquisite, and he couldn't get enough of her, nor she him, since her hand cupped the back of his head.

He took a moment to free her completely of her blouse and himself of his shirt and once again pulled her up against him.

She gasped as their naked bodies made contact, and he swallowed the staggering moan that rose in his throat.

Lord, but she felt good against him. She was warm and soft and fit perfectly to his chest, as if they were made for each other. Her hard nipples dug into him and the full mounds of her breasts snuggled against him as if they had come home and were content.

She belonged there, melded with him as if they were one, and the thought startled and excited him as he leaned down and took her lips once again.

He kept his arms firmly around her as he walked her over to the bed and lowered them down on it, continuing to kiss her as they descended into the soft bedding.

He near shivered when her hand explored his chest, her fingers playing with his nipples before they slipped down to rub the hard length of him through his trousers.

He wanted to feast his eyes over every inch of her, become familiar with every little detail until he knew her as no one had ever known her before him.

He whispered in her ear, "I want to kiss every part of you, claim every nook and cranny and make you mine."

He moved his lips to her mouth, and the palm of her hand greeted him.

He didn't like the sadness he saw in her eyes. "What's wrong?"

"I thought I made it clear that I could never be yours. This is but a brief interlude, no more."

Why did the idea disturb him? He had had interludes before, and it had never bothered him to say good-bye to the women. Why did the thought of bidding Storm farewell weigh so heavily on his mind?

He could tell her he had meant just for this night, for this time they would spend together, and yet he couldn't bring himself to say it.

"I can't give you more, Burke."

He thought, or perhaps he imagined it because he wanted to, that she sounded regretful, almost as if she were on the verge of tears. Did she want more herself but know it wasn't possible? Did it hurt her to believe so?

"Nothing has to be decided tonight," he assured her, leaving possibilities open to them both.

"Yes, yes it does," she said, pushing him gently off her.

He reluctantly moved away and she reached for a pillow to shield her naked breasts as she sat up.

"Why?" he demanded a bit more forcefully than he had intended.

"Because it is the way of things, and nothing will change that. You will return to America and I will remain in Scotland."

"What if we fell in love?"

Storm's blue eyes widened considerably. "We cannot."

"What if we did?" he asked, the force of his query remaining adamant.

"It's not a possibility. We barely know each other."

"If I remember correctly, you and Daniel hadn't known each other long before you fell in love."

"That was different," she said.

"Why?"

She looked puzzled, as if the answer hadn't come as easily as she had expected.

"No answer, Storm? That's because there is no answer. Love is love, and it comes in its own good time to unsuspecting people."

She bounced off the bed holding the pillow to her chest. "Are you claiming to love me?"

"No," he said, though the thought plagued him. Why fight her on this if he wasn't in love? "I just feel we should leave fate to deal with it, not throw obstacles in its path."

"I know my fate and I know my feelings. I will not love again."

"You are a stubborn one," he said on a laugh and shook his head.

"Much like you," Storm said with a toss of her chin.

He folded his arms across his chest. "So where does this leave us?"

Storm sighed softly, and Burke could see her shoulders droop along with her guard.

"You look for something I cannot give."

Burke raked his fingers through his hair and came close to muttering an oath. "I don't know what I look for, but . . ." He paused and stepped closer to her. "I'd like to find out."

"I don't know, perhaps . . ."

He pressed a finger to her lips, preventing her from objecting. "We owe it to ourselves."

She gently pushed his finger aside. "Why?"

"We're attracted to each other and have a small time frame of opportunity here, *which*"—he emphasized—"if we ignore, we will live to regret."

"You can't be sure of that."

"You can't be sure we won't, so why take the chance? Why not see what awaits us? Why not delve into the unknown and let fate deal with us? But then you know your fate," he said. "So what have you got to lose?"

He didn't wait for an answer. Instead he walked over to the chest near the chair and pulled out a white silk nightgown and handed it to Storm.

"Here, for you. Tonight I want nothing more than to hold you in my arms as we sleep. Can you give me that much?"

She looked bewildered and took a moment to answer him. "I would like to sleep in your arms tonight."

"Good, then change while I disrobe and join me beneath the blankets." He turned his back to give her privacy, and then shed his clothes and climbed beneath the covers naked.

It took only a few minutes for Storm to join him. He held back the blankets for her to slip beneath, and when she did, he took her in his arms and rested her body against his.

She cushioned her head on his chest and rested her arm across his midriff.

He rested his chin on top of her head and held her snugly against him and whispered, "Good night, Mrs. Longton."

Chapter 23

⟡

S torm led the way through the woods, the sky overcast and the air chilled. She and Burke had left the ship before dawn and had traveled by horseback until late morning, when they once again returned to journeying by foot.

They had maintained silence throughout most of their travel, though not due to necessity. It seemed they both favored their thoughts, for which Storm was grateful.

Her day of rescue and fun had turned out upsetting. Not only had she tasted a day of freedom, but for a brief time she had experienced the joy of being Mrs. Longton, and she had liked it.

She had discovered Burke was a considerate husband, catering to her, wanting to make her happy, and placing her needs above his own. That he had simply held her in his arms and not attempted to make love with her surprised her and touched her heart.

She had woken on and off during the night and always found him wrapped around her or she around him. It was as if each of them needed to keep hold of the other. He had kissed her awake, informing her that dawn would soon greet them and they had best be on their way.

She hadn't wanted to leave the safety of his arms, the warmth of his bed, the solitude of his cabin, but she had had no choice; she left them all.

It was time to return to who she was and who she would always be—an outlaw.

It was crazy to think she could be anything else. This was her life, and all she could do was accept it. After all, she had chosen it and she had no one to blame but herself.

She had to start thinking of Burke as simply a man who hired her to help find his brother. Once done, he would be gone for good. The fee would provide handsomely for her small band of people. They would have sufficient food for some time and warm clothes to guard against the winter, not to mention the necessary bribes that helped secure rescues.

As far as sharing intimacy with Burke was concerned, she would need to give it more thought. At first, it had just been a way of appeasing her loneliness, but now she wondered if perhaps her emotions were becoming entangled in ways she had not thought possible. Until she could make more sense of her feelings, she thought it best to keep her distance.

"You can't run away from me."

Storm skidded to a halt and spun around, for a moment believing he had read her mind. She reined in her nonsensical thought and said, "We need to keep a good pace to arrive at our destination on time."

"I'd say we're going to arrive early at the rate we're going. Can't we take a brief reprieve? Enjoy the food."

"I suppose a brief repose won't hurt," she agreed reluctantly.

They found a secluded spot, though one that gave them the advantage of seeing if anyone approached, and settled down to enjoy bread, cheese, and apples.

Storm had thought Burke's attire yesterday had defined him, but she had been wrong. The way he looked today truly defined the man. He wore dark brown trousers, tan shirt, black jacket, and a long black coat he called a duster. He explained that it kept the dust off the cowboys when they traveled the range in America.

The image it evoked of a faraway land made her realize just how different Burke and she were and made her even more determined to remain aloof until she could sort through her feelings.

"You can't avoid *us*, Storm. Why try?"

Why did he have to be so astute? She took a bite of an apple, hoping to do just as he warned and avoid the issue.

Burke laughed. "Nice try, but eventually your mouth won't be full and you'll be able to answer."

She could explain there was no *us*, but that wasn't truthful. She could be honest and tell him she was concerned about her feelings, but that could prove dangerous. She could attempt to ignore him, but he would be persistent.

She decided to buy herself time. "Now isn't a good time to discuss this."

"It's the best time. There's no one around, just the two of us. We couldn't ask for a more perfect time."

"Tonight," she let slip and bit her bottom lip too late.

Burke laughed. "Afraid?"

Yes! Yes! she wanted to scream, but instead she smiled. "Not at all."

"Then why not just talk now? We've discussed endlessly what we have learned so far about my brother, so there is no more to be said where that is concerned. There is, however, the matter of *us* that does need further discussion."

"There really is no *us*," she argued.

"I tried believing that too." He shook his head. "It didn't work."

"Mr. Longton—"

"I love when you address me that way, so formal and yet so intimate. It gives me the shivers." He shook his body to demonstrate.

Storm couldn't keep from smiling. The man was a charmer, a delightful charmer who managed to make her smile even when they disagreed.

He took hold of her hand. "Give us a chance, that's all I ask of you."

The snap of a branch had them both bolting up on their feet and searching the area. A deer stood poised not far from them, and once it caught their scent, it took off in a rustle of leaves and snapping twigs.

"We shouldn't linger," Storm said, wrapping up the food and returning it to the pouch. "The sky promises rain, and if we pick up our pace we can make it to a small farm that has long been abandoned but will provide sufficient shelter."

They hurried off, Storm grateful Burke didn't pursue the issue of them. With so much to consider, Burke and she should be the last thing on her mind. She reminded herself of that each and every time Burke popped into her thoughts and she chased him away, only to have him return again and again.

They made it to what remained of the farmhouse, though the old lean-to that looked to have sheltered the animals was in better shape, so they decided to seek refuge there.

They found a dry corner without leaks, and with the space being small, they had no choice but to huddle together to remain dry and warm.

"This is cozy," Burke said, wrapping his arm around Storm.

Storm made herself comfortable in the crook of his arm. It wasn't hard. Actually, it was quite natural since she had done it many times and found the fit perfect.

"I've been meaning to tell you how much I enjoyed spending the day with you," Burke said.

"You've spent days with me," she reminded, not wanting to talk about them but knowing that he probably wasn't going to give her a choice.

"Not as my wife. I must say I did enjoy showing you off."

"Showing me off?" she asked, startled.

"Of course. With you on my arm, men looked at me with envy."

She laughed.

"You think I jest?" he asked seriously.

She glanced up at him, her eyes shining a brilliant blue.

His brow narrowed. "You don't realize how beautiful you are, do you?" His finger began to trace along her face. "Your stunning features can rob a man of his breath and turn him senseless."

She giggled.

He tapped her nose. "You shall not make fun of the truth. I gave many men a warning glance when their glimpse settled too long on you."

"Or a more rational reason would be that someone recognized me."

He shook his head. "Not possible. No one would expect Storm the outlaw to disguise herself as the wife of an American and parade along the streets of St. Andrew."

He was right about that. It would be the last place anyone would look for her, which was why she had agreed to his plan in the first place.

"Accept it. You're beautiful."

He sounded as if he made a declaration that everyone would pay heed to.

"For a day I was," she admitted, having felt different when she dressed in the fine garments he provided for her. For a brief time she felt like a true lady and was stunned at the difference in the way she was treated. Merchants catered to her, men tipped their hats, women of distinction exchanged smiles with her, and suddenly she had become a woman of worth and importance.

She had become the opposite of herself and all she stood for.

"I am who I am, a peasant who fights to survive."

"You're no peasant, Storm," he said softly. "You're a courageous, remarkable woman."

She stared up at him, unsure how to respond.

"You continue to look at me with those gorgeous blue eyes of yours, and I'm going to have no choice but to kiss you."

"You need a reason to kiss me?" she found herself teasing and, not surprisingly, eager for his kiss. His lips were much too inviting to ignore, and surely, she had to do something about that arrogant shine in his dark eyes that announced he was in command.

He grinned. "You really do challenge me, and damned if I don't enjoy it."

He took her lips gently at first, almost teasingly, before he laid claim completely.

That she ached for the taste of him, she didn't realize until he had kissed her. She thanked the heavens for this moment, for this small space, for the rain, but most of all for Burke and his exquisite kisses.

A clap of thunder broke them apart and allowed them to draw breath.

She settled back in the crook of his arm but did not return to the kiss. He hugged her against him, and she rested her head on his chest.

"Don't deny what we have together, Storm."

How could she, but then how could she not?

Would she complicate her life even more by becoming involved with the American even for a short time? Was it better not to have memories? The memories of Daniel, while wonderful, were also heartwrenching. But then she had loved Daniel; she didn't love Burke.

Why, then, did all this disturb her so much? If she just cared for the man and nothing more, then why didn't she just go ahead and share a brief interlude with him? Why did the thought of him eventually saying good-bye to her hurt her heart?

She fell asleep nestled against him, hoping her answer would come easily.

By late afternoon the next day, they met up with William and Philip in the woods.

"We found the fellow," Philip informed them. "He claims he has the information we need for a price."

Storm nodded. "I imagine it will verify what Burke and I have learned."

Philip and William listened to Storm and Burke detail their findings about Lady Alaina and Cullen.

"It would make sense," Philip said.

William scratched his head. "Wouldn't it be easier if Burke just offered to settle an amount on the earl and take his brother back to America?"

"I thought the same," Burke said. "But Storm suggested that if Cullen is in love with Lady Alaina, he would refuse to leave Scotland, even on threat of his life."

"Foolish," William said with a shake of his head.

Burke slapped the man on the back. "You've never been in love, have you?"

"Thank the heavens," William declared.

Once the laughter settled down, Philip asked, "What else can this man tell us?"

"If we're lucky, where to find Cullen," Storm said.

"Did it seem that he might possess such information?" Burke asked.

"He was hesitant," Philip said.

"Hesitant or cautious?" Storm queried.

William nodded. "Cautious, definitely cautious. The fellow kept in the shadows, his back to the building so no one could sneak up behind him, and he kept his voice low. We had to strain to hear what he said."

"It's curious that there should be so much secrecy involved in it all," Philip said.

"The earl isn't going to want the world to know that his daughter fell in love with a common man of no title or importance and that he loves her," Storm said. "It just would not be acceptable."

Storm noticed that Burke had remained silent listening to the exchange. His eyes narrowed and he appeared to drift off in thought. Something weighed on his mind, and she couldn't help but wonder what it was.

"When do we meet this man?" Storm asked, her question bringing Burke out of his musing.

"Tomorrow at dawn at the fork in the river," Philip said.

"A safe place?" Storm asked.

"Secure enough," Philip said. "William and I

have already found the vantage points. I thought it
best if William and Burke take points while you
and I speak with the man."

"I want to be there," Burke insisted.

"I think you should," Storm said to everyone's
surprise. "This man sells information for a price. If
he meets with me and recognizes my identity, then
he will certainly tell, for a goodly sum, my general
location. Burke offers no such appeal to him, so
therefore Burke and Philip would be the logical
men to meet with him. William and I will take the
points."

"You are a wise leader," Burke said with a smile.

"You're just discovering that, Mr. Longton?"

"Admitting it, Storm, for all to know."

Storm ordered that they make camp near the
meeting place. She wanted to be sure that the fellow
arrived alone. It took a couple of hours to cover the
area and make certain all was in readiness for tomorrow's meeting.

Food taken from the ship provided supper for the
evening. Storm wanted no campfire or scents to
drift in the air and attract unwanted visitors or alert
anyone to their location.

It would be a cold night for the four, but tomorrow they would have what they had come for and
be on their way home.

As usual, Storm took the first watch, and Burke
joined her.

"You should get some sleep. Your watch will
come fast enough," Storm warned when he plopped
down beside her on the ground. It wasn't that she

didn't want his company. It was just that she didn't favor discussing their relationship right now, and that was all he seemed to want to talk about when they were alone.

"Don't worry, I'm not going to mention us. I just want to spend some time with you."

"We've spent a lot of time together of late."

He shrugged. "Somehow it never seems enough."

"Are you being romantic, Mr. Longton?" she asked with a smile.

"You know . . ." He paused and nodded slowly. "I think I might be."

She laughed softly. "You can be amusing."

"You find my efforts at romance amusing?" He shook his head. "That's not a good sign."

"At least you try," she encouraged. "And I do appreciate the effort."

He leaned over and stole a quick kiss. "I'm glad to hear that, but it's no effort. I simply speak the truth."

He stunned her silent.

He kissed her again, only this time his kiss was filled with passion. It consumed her much too quickly and just as quickly heightened her desire for him. It had to stop, but she didn't want it to; Lord, she didn't want it to.

"I'll leave you now," he said after releasing her lips. "Reluctantly."

She watched the darkness swallow him and raised her fingers to faintly touch her pulsating lips. She hadn't really wanted their kiss to end and hadn't wanted him to leave.

If she chose to have an interlude with him, would she be able to release him easily or would her heart ache?

She seriously needed to consider the question, or perhaps it was the answer that disturbed her.

Chapter 24

⌒◯◯⌒

The skinny little fellow reminded Burke of a weasel. He didn't trust him from when first he laid eyes on him. He had dark, beady eyes and barely any hair, and he acted as if he expected someone to pounce on the scene at any moment.

"What are you afraid of?" Burke asked after being in his company for only a few minutes.

"Nothing, nothing," the man said quickly, and kept turning his head from Burke to Philip.

"You have a name?"

"Names aren't necessary," the man said.

"But the coins are," Burke confirmed.

"No coins, no information," the man said with quivering bravery.

Burke withdrew several gold coins from his pocket and held them out in his palm.

The man went to grab them with thin, grimy fingers; Burke was faster and closed his fist.

"First the information and then you get paid. The prisoner's name."

"Cullen, a big fool of a man."

"Why do you say that?" Burke asked.

The man gave a gruff laugh. "He was stupid to think that Lady Alaina could love him. He's nothing but a peasant, not fit to be in her presence."

"Lady Alaina didn't return his love?" Burke asked, curious, since the tears that had welled in Lady Alaina's eyes had told Burke a different story.

"Of course not. The earl has special plans for his daughter and it don't involve the likes of a peasant."

"So the reason this Cullen has been imprisoned is because he fell in love with the earl's daughter?"

"And pay he will for his foolishness," the man said with a sharp nod.

"And what price will that be?" Burke asked, intending full well that his brother would not suffer simply because he had fallen in love.

The man turned his head, his beady eyes searching the area, then whispered, "He's being sent to Weighton."

"That's a harsh punishment for simply falling in love," Philip said. "Why not just send him away or sell him into slavery in a far-off port?"

The man shrugged. "Don't know. Only know that the earl is furious and intends for the man to pay for what he's done."

"Make him pay for falling in love?" Philip said with a shake of his head. "Makes no sense."

The man shoved his hand out, palm open. "Don't care if it does or it doesn't. I told you what I know and now I want my money."

"Is Cullen in Weighton now?" Burke asked.

"Arrived yesterday," the man confirmed.

"How did you learn all this information?" Burke asked.

The man turned defensive. "What difference does that make?"

"Curious." Burke shrugged.

"Curious can get you killed," the man snapped.

"Not answering my question could get you penniless," Burke said sternly.

The man kicked at the ground and answered reluctantly. "Me sister works at the earl's manor house and accidentally overheard the earl talking with a man."

"What man?" Burke asked.

He shook his head. "She don't know, never saw him before, but soon after, the fellow Cullen was thrown in the earl's prison. That's it, that's all I know. Now me coins."

Burke held his closed hand over the man's open palm. "One more thing. What does this Cullen look like?"

The man stared at him for a minute. "Like you, a lot like you."

Burke dumped the coins into the man's hand, and he greedily swallowed them up with a taut fist.

Burke watched the skinny man sprint off into the woods. He had a feeling the fellow wouldn't stop running until he reached his destination.

"This isn't good," Philip said, shaking his head. "Come on, we need to meet up with Storm and William as planned.

Burke followed Philip and silently agreed it wasn't good. Not if what he had been told about Weighton was true. If it was impregnable, then what chance did he have of getting his brother out of there?

He'd be damned if he had come this far to see his brother rot in a prison for the rest of his life. There had to be something he could do, and he had a feeling that buying his brother's freedom was the only option left to him.

It didn't take long for them to meet up with Storm and William.

"We need to keep moving," Storm advised. "We don't want to take any chances. We'll talk when we stop for the night."

All agreed with a nod and set a good pace through the woods. Burke was growing familiar with the area and knew that by tomorrow midday they'd reach the camp.

He would do anything to free Cullen. He had made a promise to his father, and he intended to keep it no matter what it took. He often wondered if his father had amassed his wealth just in case he would need it someday to help Cullen. And if that was necessary, he'd spend his last coin to see his brother free.

They found shelter for the night behind a large rock formation, and Storm deemed it safe for a small fire. William and Philip went to see if they could catch a fish or two from the nearby creek while dusk still provided a trace of light, and Burke and Storm got the fire going.

The dry, broken twigs had the fire burning fast enough, and it wasn't long before Burke and Storm sat beside it warming their hands.

"The air holds an extra crispness tonight," Storm said.

Burke nodded and rubbed his hands. "Don't avoid it, Storm, tell me about Weighton."

"It's not penetrable," she said.

He didn't like the sound of defeat in her voice and he wasn't ready to accept defeat. "There must be another way."

"Possibly, but we'll have to give it thought."

"I've given it thought and look where it's gotten my brother," he argued and released a gruff sigh. "I want Cullen safe and in front of me. I want to claim him as my brother and tell him all about our father and how hard he had searched for him all these years. I want him to know he has a home in America and money enough to ease his life. I want—" He shook his head. "I want this all to be done with."

Storm reached out and covered his hand with hers. "I know how you feel."

He was about to snap that she didn't, how could she? Then he remembered her husband and knew that she understood exactly how he felt. Suddenly he was grateful she sat beside him.

"What do I do?" he asked, not only needing her help but *wanting* her help as well.

"I don't know, but we'll find a way to get Cullen out. I promise."

"You can't mean that," Philip said, he and William joining them.

They held two fish cleaned and speared with sticks for roasting, which they set to the flames, and sat on the opposite side of the fire from Burke and Storm.

"Aye, you can't," William agreed. "It's foolishness to think we can rescue anyone from Weighton."

"You yourself insisted that if you were ever captured and taken to Weighton, no one was to attempt a rescue," Philip said. "The American should know the truth. There is no escape from Weighton. His brother's fate has been sealed."

"I can't accept that," Burke said adamantly. "There must be something that can be done, even if I have to go to the Earl of Balford and buy my brother's freedom."

"That might work," William said, turning the fish over the flames. "Maybe if you can convince the earl that your brother has some fancy title back in America, he might consider letting his daughter marry him."

"That's a good point, William," Burke said. It just might prove to be the solution to his problem.

"You can't be serious," Storm said. "And besides, you told me there were no titled people in America."

"I am a land baron," Burke said with a grin.

"Baron Longton." William smiled. "Sounds like a title to me."

"I don't know," Philip said, shaking his head. "That fellow mentioned something about the earl having plans for his daughter."

"Plans change all the time," William said. "Just

think of all the times Storm changed rescue plans."

"Necessary changes," Storm argued.

"I'd say these were necessary changes," Burke said. "And there's only one way to find out if it will work. I need to talk with the Earl of Balford."

He had expected a resounding no from Storm, so her silence surprised him.

"It might be worth a try," Philip said.

Still Storm said nothing, and he wondered what she thought. "What's your opinion, Storm?"

"The Earl of Balford is not a man to be trusted," she said. "I would feel better knowing what plans he intends for his daughter before rushing into this. But I can understand your reluctance to wait any longer in securing your brother's release. Weighton is not known for its hospitality."

Burke respected her opinion. She had proven time and again to be right in her approach to difficult situations, and given enough time, he wouldn't be surprised if she devised a rescue plan for his brother. Time, however, was limited, and so was his patience.

"If that weasel of a fellow whose sister works at the Balford manor house didn't know the earl's plans for his daughter, how will we find out?" Burke asked.

Silence answered him.

"That's what I thought," Burke confirmed with a nod. "I have no other choice."

"Perhaps you do," Storm said, and all eyes stared at her.

"I'm listening," Burke said, focusing on her deep blue eyes. He could tell much from the shifting blue colors of her eyes, and right now the deep color told him she was concerned for his plight.

"You have the advantage of having already met Lady Alaina. If there was some way you could speak with her privately and tell her that you're Cullen's brother, perhaps she would then confide in you. She could also possibly tell you whether her father would be agreeable to your offer."

"That is an excellent suggestion," Burke said, suddenly feeling that Cullen's rescue could be closer at hand than he had thought.

"Storm's a wise leader," William boasted, and Philip agreed with an affirmative nod.

Later that evening, with William and Philip retired, Burke sat with Storm on her watch.

"You're not upset with me?" Storm asked, leaning against him.

He slipped his arm around her, knowing she had to be chilled from the cold night air and pleased that she sought warmth from him without hesitation. He had intended to wrap his arms around her anyway. He had grown accustomed to holding her and missed her when she was gone too long from his arms.

"Why would I be upset with you?"

"I thought perhaps you felt that you wasted time by not speaking further with Lady Alaina when you had the opportunity."

"No, it's better this way. I'm now armed with more information that will probably prove helpful when I meet with her. I would have never known to ask of her father's plans. I would have focused entirely on my brother and possibly ruined my chances of securing his release."

"I do hope this proves successful for you and especially for your brother."

"You don't sound hopeful," Burke said.

She gave a sad laugh. "Don't mind me. My encounter with the Earl of Balford has left a bitter taste in my mouth. Perhaps it will be different for you."

He snuggled her closer to him, wanting to protect her from her own painful memories. "You know what I wish?"

"That all goes well and you free your brother," she said with a smile.

He shook his head before faintly brushing his lips across hers. "No, I wish you and I were on my ship in my cabin making love."

He felt her reaction; her body startled in his arms.

"I want to make love to you, Storm. Actually, I ache to make love to you. The choice of course is yours, but I had hoped you would not delay your decision or deny your desire."

"I won't deny that I want you," she admitted softly.

"Then there is no reason to delay." He kissed her quick and sharp, stinging both their senses.

She shivered. "That you excite me is undeniable. It is the consequences I give thought to."

"What consequences?"

She hesitated for more than a moment. "What if I fall in love with you?"

Her words were a direct hit to his gut and if he

239

wasn't sitting, he'd have fallen over from the sharp impact.

"You told me you would never love again."

"You said that I might not love the same way but love was still possible," she reminded him.

"I also said that fate would have the deciding hand in it."

"My fate has been sealed," she said sadly.

"If you are so certain, then why worry about falling in love with me?"

Her blue eyes glazed over with tears he was certain she would not shed. Her slight cough to clear her throat confirmed for him her battle to contain them.

"Because . . ." She hesitated and looked away from Burke. "Because if I did fall in love with you, I fear the pain of bidding you farewell when all of this is over."

Chapter 25

Storm pushed away from Burke and fought back the tears that threatened to ravish her. She would not cry in front of this man. Tears only served to demonstrate weakness, and she didn't intend to have Burke see her as weak.

Burke leaned forward and took hold of her shoulders, turning her to face him. "If we should, by chance, by fate, fall in love, why do you think I would ever bid farewell to you?"

"What choice would you have?" she asked bravely and maybe with an ounce of hope. Would he possibly consider remaining in Scotland and making his home there with her?

"I want to take you home to America with me where you'd be safe."

Hope vanished in a flash and she made herself clear once again. "I will never leave Scotland."

"You are an outlaw here with no hope of a normal life."

"Exactly," she said, his words confirming her future.

"In America you wouldn't be an outlaw. You'd be a free woman with no fear of being hunted, imprisoned, and executed."

"You forgot torture," she reminded caustically.

"No, I didn't. I couldn't bring myself to even consider such a heinous fate for you. However, it would be all the more reason for you to leave Scotland and make a new home in America."

"My home is and always will be Scotland." She didn't bother to suggest he remain in Scotland with her. He would just continue to argue that America offered her freedom. If she chose to have an interlude with him, she would have no choice but to keep her heart out of it. Could she do that? Of late, it was a question that haunted her.

He cupped her face in his hands. "When you love, home is where that love resides."

"It's not that easy."

"It is. America is a safer place for you, and therefore the wisest choice."

Reluctantly she pulled away from him, his hands falling away from her face. "The wisest choice would be for me not to fall in love with you."

"Love, my dear stubborn Storm, is not left to us mere mortals."

"We shall see about that," she challenged.

Burke grinned. "I wouldn't tempt fate if I were you. It's my experience that fate is always the victor."

Storm didn't respond. She simply resumed her position against the rock, Burke joining her. Without preamble he took her in his arms once again. She didn't object. She settled against him as before, comfortable in his embrace.

Only this time she silently warned herself repeatedly that their time together would be brief and he soon would be out of her life forever. She intended to prepare herself for the inevitable, burn it into her heart and soul so that she wouldn't feel the pain of his farewell.

They arrived at camp the next day with storm clouds close on their tails. Everyone dispersed to his respective home, reuniting with family and friends for a short time.

Not one to waste valuable time, Storm issued orders to her men that they would meet in two hours at Angus's place. With rain likely, she didn't want their meeting interrupted, and Angus's quarters, though one room, was sufficient to hold them.

Storm made her rounds of the camp, making certain they all had what they needed and assuring them that winter would not pose a problem. The look of relief on their faces reinforced Storm's stubbornness about remaining in Scotland. There was no way she could leave these people to fend for themselves. They had become a family, relying on one another, and you didn't walk away from family.

Peter was doing much better, as was Henry, who, Janelle informed Storm, had been a great help to her.

She also told Storm that Henry was worried that he would have to leave the camp. Janelle had tried to alleviate his fears and assure him that he was welcome to reside with the group, but the lad seemed not to believe her.

Storm found Henry huddled against a tree, staring up at the racing storm clouds. The chilled wind had picked up, and soon raindrops would fall. In a few weeks, snow could fall, and there was much to do before then.

"Feeling better, Henry?" she asked on approach.

Henry stood upright, away from the support of the tree. "Much better."

"Janelle says that you have been of help to her."

"Whatever help I can be to anyone. I will pull my weight while here."

His last words were barely audible but Storm caught them. "While here? Are you leaving us?"

"There are many mouths to feed here and I am not a good hunter." He lowered his head, his chin near to his chest. "I have no skills."

"Of course you do."

He raised his head, shaking it. "No, really I don't. I have drifted around trying to survive and I have learned little along the way."

Storm placed her hand on his shoulder. "You learned to survive or else we would not be having this conversation. You would be dead."

He focused startled eyes on her.

"There is much you can offer us and much we can teach you. This is your home now. You have a family to look after you and for you to look after, so worry not. You will reside with Angus and he will teach you the skills you need to know."

"Or," interrupted Burke, who walked out from behind Storm to stand beside Henry, "you could go to America with me and start a new life with much promise and possibility."

"Truly?" Henry asked like a child who was just presented with a gift. "I heard there are riches for all in America."

"Riches aren't handed to you. It takes hard work and determination, which I have no doubt you possess."

Henry stuck out his chest. "I'm not afraid of hard work."

"Then there's a place for you on my ranch in America and the chance of owning your own land someday."

The lad's eyes blazed like round full moons. "Own my own land? Are you certain?"

"Do not fill the lad's head with nonsense," Storm snapped.

"It's not nonsense," Burke said. "Anyone can own land in America. Of course it's wilderness and requires much work, but many are doing it and successfully. My father was one of them. He amassed a small empire for himself with the sweat of his own hands and a lot of backbreaking labor."

Henry stepped forward. "I'd work hard to have a chance to own my own land." He looked to Storm. "I don't have a chance of owning land here. There's no future in Scotland for me."

Storm shot Burke a heated glare, but spoke softly to

Henry. "The choice is yours, Henry. You are welcome to stay here with us or go with Burke to America."

He gave a huge smile, then suddenly threw his arms around Storm and hugged her tight before stepping away. "You have not only saved my life, you've now given me a chance at a future." He walked over to Burke. "I gratefully accept your offer."

Burke shook his hand, and Henry hurried off to share his news.

"Do you know what you've done?" she asked accusingly.

"Given the lad a shot at a decent future?"

"And put the same thoughts in others' heads."

Burke shook his head. "What's wrong with people wanting a good future?"

"Dreams, you offer nothing but dreams."

"My father started with a dream. He wanted a better life for his wife and young son so he sailed far away and worked night and day until finally he owned a plot of land and started to build a home. He wanted more for his family than just working hard only to have someone else reap the benefits. He wasn't afraid; he took a chance. Henry's not afraid; he's willing to take a chance."

"Are you accusing me of being afraid?"

"You have courage and you have taken endless risks for others. When do you finally take a risk for yourself? When do you finally stop punishing yourself for not rescuing your husband soon enough?"

Storm fisted her hands at her sides so as not to reach up and slap his face.

Burke stepped closer to her, and Storm couldn't determine if he was brave or just plain foolish.

He kept his voice to a whisper. "You tell me you will never love again. You tell me you refuse to leave a land that deems you an outlaw. You tell me you will not take a chance on making love with me for fear it could lead to love. You tell me your fate has already been decided. What you truly tell me, Storm, is that you're afraid to live."

Burke turned and Storm watched him walk away—rather, stomp away, for his strides demonstrated irritation.

His accusation swirled in her head, and while it had sparked her anger, it had also sparked awareness. Could he be right? Had life been too difficult to bear after she had lost her husband? Had she been rescuing others all this time in the slim hope of rescuing herself?

There were days she wished for a normal life. She wanted to wake up beside a man she loved, tend a garden, cook a good meal, and see to her children.

Then she would think of all the ones she had rescued and their tears of joy over being free. So hadn't fate decided things for her? Had she a choice?

Did she have a choice now?

Tanin waved to her from Angus's open door. They were all there waiting for her, waiting for her to lead, to help, to provide, to follow what fate had dealt her.

She threw her shoulders back and her head up and marched forward because there certainly was no going back.

Angus offered his chair to her by the fire when she entered. She took it knowing he was paying her respect by offering her the best seat in his home, one he had made with his own hands. Tanin sat at the small table with Philip, while William, Malcolm, and Burke stood near the door. Angus sat on a sturdy bench opposite Storm.

"I've given this idea some thought," she said, sitting forward in the chair. "We need to find a way to get Burke alone with Lady Alaina, and the only way to accomplish that is to find out her routine. Does she take a daily ride, a daily walk? Is she planning a trip? A carriage ride?"

"I will provide coins so that it will be worthwhile for anyone to divulge the information," Burke offered.

"I also think it's imperative that we do this with haste," Storm said. "We are all well aware of how deadly Weighton is, and the longer Cullen spends there, the greater risk of death."

"Perhaps that weasel of a man could help us again," Burke suggested. "He did mention that his sister worked at the manor house."

"We could find out who his sister is and go straight to her," Philip said.

They talked for the next hour, formulating a plan that would be implemented with haste. If all went accordingly, Burke would find himself speaking with Lady Alaina very soon.

Angus offered supper to the lot of them, a hearty rabbit stew bubbling in the pot over the hearth's flames. Tanin declined, eager to spend time with his wife. Malcolm had promised a pretty lass he'd sup with her, while Philip had plans he refused to share. William and Burke accepted the invitation while Storm declined, though made no excuse for it.

She hurried along the rain-soaked ground, her feet splashing through the puddles formed by the heavy, pelting rain. She was relieved when she closed the door of her small quarters behind her, shutting out everyone, or rather, shutting herself in.

She yearned for this time alone, this solitude where she could think and make sense of her suddenly senseless world.

Everything had been clear to her before Burke arrived. Now nothing seemed as it was or had ever been. He made her question her own motives for the rescues she made and for the life fate dealt her.

She slipped out of her wet clothes and into the lone linen nightgown she possessed. She gave a brief thought to the silk one she had worn while on Burke's ship. It had been so soft and comfortable, as had been his bed and his arms.

She shook her head. Why was she even considering having an interlude with Burke? Was she crazy?

Lonely.

That was her problem. She was lonely and she found Burke attractive. She simply thought of sharing a few moments of intimacy with the stranger and then he'd be gone. How had that thought escalated to fear of falling in love with him?

It was nonsense, pure nonsense.

She would never love again so why worry about it?

Burke could be persuasive, or was it that she just plain enjoyed his company? She hadn't found that in a man since Daniel. And she enjoyed his quick wit, which often made her smile. He had courage and strength and he was honest, which she respected above all else. He was a man a woman could easily love.

She shook her wet clothes and draped them over the chair near the fireplace.

She had no time for love and it would be dangerous if she did allow herself to love. In the end she would suffer, for she would have to let him go, return to America.

Besides, who was to say that he would love her?

She released an exasperated sigh.

Why was she questioning herself so much? Why didn't she just go and share a night of intimacy and be done with it? Forget love, forget Burke leaving, forget everything for one single, solitary night and love as if nothing else mattered in the world.

She was who she was—an outlaw. She was not going to change, and she was not running off to America, whether she fell in love or not. Her life was here in Scotland, and here was where she would stay.

For one night, she could simply be a woman.

For one night, she could simply love.

She stood before the fire staring at the flames, feeling her heartbeat, feeling her body ache for intimacy, feeling the need to love.

Finally she heard Burke's footsteps along the walkway and his door close.

She ran her fingers through her hair, smoothed her nightgown with nervous hands, and walked out the door.

Chapter 26

❧

Storm rapped lightly at his door, and for a moment she thought perhaps that he had already fallen asleep. Then the door opened.

They stared at each other while thunder rumbled overhead.

"Cross my doorstep and you seal your fate, Storm," Burke warned and stepped back, opening the door wide.

Storm didn't hesitate. She stepped across the threshold and right into Burke's arms.

He lifted her up against him and she wrapped her arms around his neck while her mouth met his in a kiss that ignited their passion in a flash.

She wrapped her legs around his waist as he walked with her across the room, and they fell on the bed still locked together. Still, they refused to relinquish their kiss. They fed off each other with a hunger that apparently could not be satisfied.

Clothes were shed in haste and eagerness until they were spread out naked beside each other. Then hands began to wander.

Storm ached to touch him, all of him, just as he did her.

It was as if they had always known each other, familiar with every valley and mound.

"God, you're beautiful," he said, surfacing from feasting at her breast.

"You make me feel beautiful," she admitted, running her small hands over his hard-muscled chest and loving the feel of him. His lean muscle stimulated her senses, as did the heat of his flesh.

He claimed her lips again, and she joined in the kiss until they finally nibbled along each other's lips.

"I can't get enough of you," Burke said.

"I feel the same."

"I intend to make love to you all night."

"Promise?" she asked, fearing that this would be the only time they would have together and wanting to make the most of it.

Burke ran his hand down the length of her, settling faintly between her legs. "I promise."

Storm moaned with pleasure when his fingers intimately explored her, and she was soon lost in a haze of passion that she wanted to linger in forever.

When his playfulness became too much she reached down and took hold of him. "I'll have you now."

Burke grazed his lips over hers. "Are you sure?"

"Do not tease," she protested. "I know what I want and I want you."

He nibbled at her bottom lip and then down along her neck to settle on her hard nipple. Then he rose over her like a majestic bird about to take flight and entered her with a tenderness that startled her more than if he had plunged into her.

"We fit," he whispered in her ear before he settled into a steady rhythm that grew with each mounting thrust.

She grabbed hold of his shoulders and threw back her head, enjoying the cadence they set together. It flooded her body and soul, and she rode the rhythm until it peaked.

"Burke!" she breathed hard in his ear. "Oh God, Burke," she exclaimed as she climaxed as she had never thought possible, the ripples of pleasure going on and on and on.

He collapsed on her almost simultaneously and she hugged him to her, wanting to keep him as close to her as possible.

She regretted when he rolled off her though he kept his body beside her. He took her hand in his to kiss it before laying their clasped hands on his chest.

Their encounter had been far from brief and yet she felt it was far too short. She wanted more, much more, and the thought concerned her, though for now she chose not to think about it.

"Damn, woman, but you're a great lover," he said with bated breath.

She smiled. "You're not bad yourself."

"We're a match then." He kissed her hand again.

A thunderclap startled her, and she jumped.

Burke turned and took her in his arms. "No need to worry. I'll keep you safe and warm, since, of course, you'll be staying the night."

"I'm not going anywhere until dawn."

He grinned. "That's good because I planned on holding you hostage if you had thought otherwise."

She laughed. "You think you could have held me prisoner?"

Burke shook his head, his grin wide. "Oh, sweetheart, I know exactly how to keep you prisoner."

She giggled and snuggled against him. "You'll have to show me how."

"All night. I'll show you all night."

They laughed and kissed and teased until once again, their passion flared and they were lost in a haze of lovemaking. It continued all night, and when dawn finally peeked over the horizon, Storm fell soundly asleep in Burke's loving arms.

Storm was the first to stir, then Burke, and they greeted each other with smiles.

"What a lovely night, with a lovely woman," Burke said.

"Such romantic words," Storm said, trying to keep reality away for just a while longer.

"You haven't seen anything yet."

She laughed softly and knew that she'd be wise to leave his bed right away, but she foolishly lingered.

He traced her breast with his finger and nuzzled her neck. "I love the feel and taste of you.

Thank God he kept his nibbles to her neck, or else

she'd be lost. As it was she was on the verge of attacking him, and that she couldn't do. She had surrendered to one night of passion; there could be no more, or else she would be in danger of losing her heart.

The thought jolted some sense into her and she bolted up in bed. "There's things I must see to."

Burke tried to coax her back into his arms. "Nothing is as important as us at this moment."

Storm threw the covers off her and hopped out of bed, grabbing her nightgown from the floor and slipping it on hastily. It tangled around her, being she had it on backward, and the next thing she knew, Burke was helping to untangle her.

His hands were gentle, smoothing the gown down and lingering in just the right places that sparked her passion with each intentional touch.

Storm backed away. "I need to go."

"Can't you spare a few more minutes?"

Storm kept her eyes on his face, if not she probably would have surrendered to her passion and his obviously growing passion.

"Now," she said with the shake of her head. "I must go now."

His outstretched arm stopped her when she tried to pass, and he shook his head. "I don't think so." He hoisted her up and had her on the bed in a split second, and in another, he had her nightgown up and him inside her.

It was a fast and furious mating that she thoroughly enjoyed. There was no preamble, no fussing, no playfulness, just fast, hard lovemaking that felt wonderfully delicious.

When it was over and their breathing returned to normal, he helped her off the bed and walked her to the door. "Now you can leave, but be warned, I'll be looking for you tonight."

Storm scurried out the door and didn't take a breath until she was safely in her quarters. It was to be one night, no more. If she continued to make love with him, she was bound to fall in love with him. Besides, she already had feelings for the American.

She couldn't exactly define them, or perhaps she didn't want to. She made haste to dress, trying without success to avoid thoughts of the American. However, did she expect not to think about him after having made love with him?

She smiled and sighed, thinking how wonderful it had been and feeling a little guilty that she had enjoyed it so very much. Her climaxes had gone on forever with a little help from Burke. It was something she had not experienced with her husband, but then they had been young and inexperienced.

She finished dressing and warned herself to keep her distance from the American. It would do no good to get deeply involved with him.

But wasn't she already?

She wanted to free Burke's brother just as badly as he did. Cullen needed to learn he had a brother, and Burke needed to finally meet his brother. It was necessary for both parties, necessary for family to be reunited.

That was her priority, not intimacy with Burke. She had to keep that in mind or else she would find herself lost with no chance of finding her way back again.

It was decided that William and Philip would go and gather the information on Lady Alaina since they were familiar with the man who had last supplied it. In the meantime, Burke scribbled a note to Douglas, the ship's captain, and Malcolm and Angus were sent to collect more clothes and coins in case needed.

That left Storm, Tanin, and Burke to wait for their return.

By afternoon the camp had turned quiet; clouds still claimed the sky, though the rain had stopped.

Storm liked times like this when there were no pressing matters that needed her attention. She could just drift through the remainder of the day without worry. Such days were far and few between, so she took advantage when she could.

She made her way to the old church ruins. She didn't know why, but she felt drawn there, and so she went and sat on the crumbled stone wall.

Had guilt brought her here?

The night Daniel had died in her arms, she had sworn she would never love again, never be with another man again, and never forgive herself for not saving her husband.

Now here she was, fresh from making love with another man and wondering if she could possibly fall in love again or even dare give it thought.

"Where is he buried?"

Storm didn't startle; she had heard someone follow

her, and since Burke's tracking skills were excellent, he had meant to let her know that he trailed her.

"I left his grave unmarked," she said as he walked over to her. "I didn't want anyone disturbing him. Sometimes graves are robbed for clothes or boots and I wanted Daniel to rest in peace."

"Would you prefer to be alone?"

"No, I don't feel the need to be alone," she said, glad that he had joined her though she couldn't say why. He looked handsome in his duster—it defined his character, wild and rugged and in command.

"What brought you here?" he asked.

She hesitated. She still hadn't determined the answer to that question. She only knew it was the place she presently wanted to be.

"I'm not sure," she answered honestly.

He reached out and took her hands in his. "No regrets, Storm?"

She smiled. "Not a one."

"Good. I feel the same, and I wouldn't want to think you came here to your husband's final resting place out of guilt."

"The thought had crossed my mind," she admitted, retaining her smile. "But I can honestly say I don't feel guilty." She wondered why it didn't disturb her but actually provided her with a sense of freedom.

"I'm glad for you; perhaps then you've finally let your husband rest in peace."

Was that what she had done? Was that why she felt such a glowing sense of peace within her? Did she not only free herself, but Daniel of the burden she had placed on them both when she refused to let him go, let him rest in peace?

"Sometimes, Mr. Longton, you make sense."

"I thought I did all the time," he said on a laugh and squeezed her hands.

She returned the squeeze, his humor and thoughtfulness appreciated, as well as his touch. His hands were warm, and she felt safe. How long had it been since she felt safe?

He drifted closer to her, slow and easy, and she thought to stop him. If he came any closer, she would kiss him, and she couldn't chance that. She'd certainly want more from him—he was simply addictive, and that was not good for her.

Last night was their first and last time together.

It had to be, or else she risked losing her heart to him.

He was standing directly in front her before she realized it. His hand reached out until his fingers slowly stroked her face.

"Your skin is so soft. I love to touch you," he said on a whisper.

She near shivered but instead grabbed hold of her passion and attempted to divert it, ignore it, and do whatever she could not to respond.

Burke, however, obviously had a different plan in mind, and she silently cursed his persistence. He took hold of her neck with one hand while his lips found hers and teased them with nibbles and kisses.

That he attempted to seduce her was obvious; that it was working was just as obvious.

"I think we should return to my quarters," he whispered near her ear as he nibbled at her lobe.

Storm could do no more than sigh.

"My sentiments exactly," Burke said and grabbed her around the waist and hoisted her off the crumbled stone wall.

She thought to deny him, deny herself, but somehow she couldn't find the words. Before she knew it, she was naked in his bed and he was touching her everywhere, exploring every nook and cranny with his fingers and his lips.

She bit her lower lip so as not to make a sound, yet she wanted to scream out her pleasure. He moved over her and in her with ease and agility. Before she knew it, she was holding on to him for dear life as they simultaneously rode wave after wave of pleasure together.

When finally spent, they lay beside each other, hands clasped, breathing heavily, their passion fulfilled. And that was how the remainder of the day continued since neither of them seemed to be able to get enough of each other.

Only when night finally claimed the sky and the camp peacefully slept did Storm and Burke surrender to much-needed rest.

Chapter 27

B urke sat on the edge of the bed and knew he was in trouble. He and Storm hadn't been able to keep their hands off each other since they'd fallen into bed together fours days ago.

The more they made love, the more he enjoyed it and the more he wanted to make love to her—and the more he feared he was falling in love with her.

But then he had feared that before becoming intimate with her. She had, to his surprise, worked her way into his heart. He couldn't say when he first realized how he felt about her. It had just happened. All of a sudden, it was there.

Love.

It must have sneaked in when he wasn't looking. When he wasn't aware of it, never even considering it, and yet it had made itself known. He didn't mind. He rather liked the idea of loving Storm. She wasn't your ordinary woman, which meant he'd never have an ordinary life with her. He wouldn't be surprised if, once she arrived in America, she would find a cause to fight for and pursue it with gusto.

There was, however, one problem: How would he convince her to go with him to America?

He'd propose marriage.

That was a simple solution to his dilemma. But would she agree to marry him? She had been adamant about staying in Scotland. What made him think she would ever agree to leave her homeland?

Love.

There was that word again.

Would love prove to be the deciding factor in this difficult situation? Love would certainly not allow him to leave her behind. Someway, somehow, he would need to convince her that she had to return to America with him, preferably as his wife.

He ran his fingers through his tousled hair, having woken only a short time ago to find Storm gone from his bed. He didn't like when she wasn't there. He had fast grown accustomed to her sharing his bed, and he damned well favored her beside him.

She slept naked nestled against him so that anytime he woke in the middle of the night or early morning, he could touch or stroke her soft skin. He didn't know how he'd ever sleep without her. She had in a very short time become a necessary part of him that he had no intention of relinquishing.

As far as he was concerned, she belonged to him. They committed to each other each and every time they made love and she was going to have to accept that whether she wanted to or not.

She was his and that's all there was to it.

Unfortunately, he didn't think she'd see it that way.

He'd have to convince her, and if he wasn't able to do that, then he'd have to take charge and make a decision—one he wasn't sure she'd be too happy with.

He dressed quickly and went in search of Storm. They really needed to discuss their situation. William and Philip would probably return any day now and then what time would they have? This needed to be addressed and settled now.

Burke glided to the ground on the rope and found that he was too late. William and Philip sat at the campfire with Storm. The sun had barely risen, and no doubt Storm had sensed the men's return, which was what probably had her leaving his bed so early. She had an uncanny sense that made her a good leader and proved advantageous for her time and again.

He wasn't happy about postponing their discussion until this evening, but he had no choice. Right now, his brother Cullen's situation needed discussing.

"Good news I hope," Burke said upon joining them at the campfire.

Philip nodded. "Gratefully, Lady Alaina is a woman of habit."

"Then there is a way for me to meet with her without her father knowing it?" Burke asked.

"She takes a stroll through the huge garden every day," Philip explained.

William grinned. "Better yet, she's by herself."

"Her father prides himself on the safety of his land," Philip said. "He would never suspect or even think one would dare approach his daughter on his property."

"She's not watched?" Burke asked.

"The property is watched," William informed him.

"You will need to go in without being seen," Storm said. "That will prove more dangerous than meeting with Lady Alaina."

"Not a problem, watchful eyes can be diverted or misled," Burke said with assurance. "I'd like to see to this as soon as possible."

"You should wait for Malcolm and Angus to return," Storm advised. "This way, if your meeting with Lady Alaina goes well, you'll have all you need to approach her father."

Burke nodded, knowing she was right, but anxious to get started. "When are they due to return?"

"Any day now," Storm said and looked to William and Philip. "Get some rest, Burke, and I will formulate a plan and discuss it with you later."

The two men looked grateful to be dismissed and walked with weary strides to their respective homes.

Burke moved to sit beside Storm. "What do you think?"

"It seems too easy, and that worries me."

He wrapped his arm around hers and locked her

fingers with his. "The earl probably feels safe with my brother in custody."

"Or could it be a trap?"

"For whom?" he asked.

"I don't know. I only know that something doesn't seem right and I believe you should be extremely careful when meeting with Lady Alaina."

"Care about me, do you?" he asked with a grin, attempting to tease, yet hoping her answer did anything but.

She squeezed his hand. "You know I care for you."

Her response disappointed him. What was he expecting? Did he think she would proclaim her love for him? Did he assume because love had struck him, it had also struck her?

"I want you safe," she insisted. "I don't want to have to rescue you, though I would if necessary. You can count on it."

He stared at her for a moment. Was she trying to tell him the way she truly felt the only way she knew how? That she would risk her life for him as she had for her husband? Did he dare ask? Did he want to know?

"You'll need to do this alone," Storm informed him. "We risk detection if too many men are present. We'll wait on the outskirts of Balford land. If you don't return within an agreed-upon time, then I will send one man in after you."

"Sounds reasonable," he said.

"Reasonable or not, anything can happen, and we need to be prepared for any and all upsets."

"Are you planning on going?" he asked, and wasn't surprised when she shot him a startled look.

"Why wouldn't I?"

He shrugged, as if it didn't seem important, when it was of the utmost importance to him. "Could be dangerous."

"Every mission is dangerous."

"True enough, but this one even more so since the Earl of Balford would certainly claim a feather in his cap if he caught the infamous outlaw Storm."

"Don't worry about me. I can take care of myself."

He brought their clenched hands to his mouth and kissed her hand. "I want to take care of you."

Her eyes widened, their blue color softening momentarily before sparkling to a brilliant blue. He loved the shifting color. It made him feel as if he were either in the middle of a raging tempest or staring at a tranquil blue sky.

She stumbled over her words. "There is—is no need—no need at all for that."

He kissed her hand again. "Do you really think I could repeatedly make love with you these last few days and not—"

She yanked her hand free and moved away from him. "We've enjoyed some time together, that's all. It doesn't make you responsible for me."

He arched a brow. "Afraid I might have fallen in love with you?"

"That's nonsense."

"Why? You're a beautiful, interesting, courageous woman and I love spending time with you. I love making love with you, love going on missions with you, love holding, kissing—damn if that doesn't sound like I'm falling in love with you."

"Don't," she scolded, shaking a finger at him.

He grabbed hold of her finger. "You can't tell me that I can't love you."

She pulled her finger free. "You can't love me. It would never work."

"Because you're stubborn?"

Storm shook her head. "We're two different people from two different worlds."

Burke wanted to move closer, wrap his arms around her and ease her doubt, but he knew it was better to give her distance and let her savor his words until finally she took a taste and found them to her liking.

"We are more alike than you want to admit," he said.

"We are nothing alike and our worlds are far different. You have wealth, land, security, and a future. I have nothing, least of all a future."

He tapped his chest. "I am your future."

Her startled expression told him he had struck a chord. She felt something for him and probably was afraid to acknowledge it, for then she would need to confront it and make a decision that would either change many lives or hurt one man.

Storm shook her head. "No, there can never be a future for us."

"I don't see it that way. Love is a commitment to me."

"There is no *love*," she snapped.

"You can't command love and you can't fight it. Love is always the victor, just like fate."

"I don't love you," she said emphatically.

Burke laughed. "I think otherwise."

She threw her hands up and shook her head.

His manner turned serious, his voice low. "I don't believe you would make love with me the way you do if you didn't love me. I can feel the ache in your body for me, the need to be close, to join together, to commit. It's in every kiss, every touch, every embrace. It's a pleading tremble in your body, heart, and soul that only I can satisfy. You know it as well as I do." Burke caught the way she attempted to still the quiver that rushed over her body. "See, it speaks to you now, agreeing with me."

She shook her head. "No."

"You can't deny the truth. It will surface eventually."

She stood. "This discussion is over."

"Not really, Storm," Burke warned. "It's only just begun."

Malcolm and Angus returned by late afternoon, with Malcolm singing the praises of Burke's ship and sharing stories the sailors had told him of America. Young Henry sat enthralled while others joined the small group gathered around the campfire. Burke knew without a doubt that he would be asked many questions about his home and that a few brave souls would soon be asking if they could sail with him.

It was human nature to want to make a better life

for oneself, and all it took was some hope and promise. America provided both.

"I'll be working on Burke's ranch," Henry boasted proudly. "Then someday I'll have my own land."

The older men snickered and Burke jumped to Henry's defense. "That you will, Henry. I know of a nice piece of land that one day just may suit you."

"What kind of land?" Tanin asked, standing behind Henry, his arm around his wife, Ellie.

"Grazing land for cows and cattle and land for planting. I harvest enough food and then some to supply my ranch."

"What of your tenants?" Tanin asked.

"I have no tenants," Burke explained. "Men work for me and receive a decent wage and live in the bunkhouse."

He could see by their expressions that they didn't understand about a bunkhouse. "The men share a common shelter with beds for each."

"What of the wives?" Ellie asked.

"Most cowboys aren't wed, though the man who oversees the cowboys for me is and he's provided with a house."

"Besides wages?" Tanin asked.

Burke nodded and noticed that Ellie whispered in her husband's ear. That there was promise of a future in America was too much to ignore. He was certain Ellie was probably suggesting the very same. What did they have here? What could they hope to have here?

He had watched Tanin. He was curious, a quick learner, and not afraid of hard work—all were ingredients for success. Burke decided to put the thought in his head.

"You'd do well in America and would have your own land soon enough."

Ellie smiled and squeezed her husband's arm. "It's something to think about."

"My mother—"

"Could go with us," Ellie finished. "I'm sure her healing skills would be welcomed."

Tanin shook his head slowly. "Storm—"

"Will not stop you."

All eyes turned to their pint-sized leader who entered the circle around the campfire.

"You are free men and women. The choice is yours."

Silence followed her declaration, and Burke knew what they thought. The tiny, brave woman had saved their lives and provided them with shelter and a family of sorts. How could they desert her?

There was only one answer to that.

Storm had to go to America, and it was up to him to get her there.

Chapter 28

S torm was one of the last to retire for the night. Burke had left the campfire hours earlier, and she had no doubt he hoped she'd do the same. She couldn't. She was upset.

Burke's vivid description of America painted a desirable picture and had set many minds to thinking. Why not? There was no promise of owning land in Scotland. They would struggle their entire lives and have nothing in the end. At least America provided them with a chance for a decent life, and even if they struggled, it would be for their own land.

How could she deny them that? They couldn't go on living in treetops in the woods forever. She knew how eager Tanin and Ellie were to have a family, and yet at the same time, they both feared it. How could they raise children when Tanin constantly kept two steps ahead of the law?

America seemed the answer to many of their prayers and Storm had the feeling that a few of them would take the opportunity offered and set sail with Burke.

Was she being foolish in not considering the same?

She paced the small confines of her quarters, the questions haunting her mind.

She hadn't expected to feel as tied to Burke as she had these last few days. They spent endless time together and made love every night. Her days had suddenly become more joyous. She smiled more, laughed more, enjoyed life more. Burke had a good sense of humor and he was a man of intelligence. Their discussions always stirred and challenged her mind.

She had actually panicked when she suddenly realized that he would leave and she would once again be on her own. She had admonished herself to keep her distance, to only enjoy his company but not let herself *feel*.

She had, however, *felt* from the very first time he had touched her, kissed her, and that was what started it all. She had experienced emotion for the first time since her husband's death and it had felt so very good.

Suddenly her emptiness was gone and life once again seemed worthwhile.

It actually wasn't a sudden realization. It somehow just happened without her knowing it. She hadn't wanted to feel for the American. She hadn't believed she could. He was not the type of man she ever imagined herself interested in.

She had never expected to be interested in a man again. This attraction was a complete surprise and confused her, but then Daniel had told her once that love never made sense.

Love.

It wasn't possible that she could love the American. Or did she refuse to acknowledge her feelings? Did she really think she could be intimate with the man and not feel?

She plopped down on the bed, annoyed.

Answers certainly weren't forthcoming and she was growing tired of fighting with herself. A simple interlude had turned complicated in so many ways, and she didn't have the slightest idea how to uncomplicate matters.

She was grateful for the distraction of the rap at her door—until she saw who it was.

"Burke," she said on a sigh.

"Don't sound so happy to see me."

If only he could feel the catch in her stomach and the flutter in her heart, he'd know exactly how she felt on seeing him.

"You're angry with me," he said, approaching her.

She stood and moved away from the bed. "No, how can I be when you offer a future to many who thought they had none. It is kind of you."

She sensed his next words would be that he offered her the same, but she didn't want to hear that, not now.

"I'm tired," she said, moving farther away from him. "I will see you in the morning. Remember we leave at dawn."

He nodded and turned to leave, then swerved around and walked over to her.

She braced for the kiss she knew he'd deliver and steeled herself against responding. She couldn't fall into bed with him again, she couldn't. She lost herself completely to him when she did and she couldn't allow herself to do that anymore.

He reached for her face, cupped it in his warm hands, and kissed her until she thought she would go insane from the want of him.

She kept her hands fisted at her sides, her back rigid and her heart cold.

He brushed his lips across hers. "Is it a challenge you want?"

She opened her mouth to answer and he plunged in, his tongue taking complete charge and sending spears of passion stabbing pinpricks of pleasure over every inch of her body.

He scooped her up in his arms and had her on the bed in no time. His hands worked magic beneath her clothes, not once attempting to remove her garments or his.

"Only if you want me, Storm," he whispered in her ear. "I will love you only if you want me to."

She thought to push him off her. Her hands went to his chest and rested against hard muscle. One push, one simple push, and he'd be gone.

He waited, his arms supporting his strength as he hovered over her. And there in his dark eyes where his hunger for her was always obvious, she caught a spark of intense love.

It jolted her heart and soared her passion and she

wrapped her arms around his neck and pulled him down on top of her.

Their passion was much too heated to waste time in removing clothes, so garments were shifted out of the way, bodies entwined, and movement fast and furious.

She feared her cries must have surely echoed out into the night, for the pleasure he brought her was so great, she could not control her moans. He must have thought the same for he captured as many as he could with kisses.

She savored the aftermath of their lovemaking and wanted nothing more than to fall asleep in his arms and not think of tomorrow or the future, just this time here and now spent with him.

As if he read her mind, he saw to undressing both of them and getting them settled beneath the blanket where they snuggled against each other, as had been their way since first they made love.

They didn't talk. It wasn't necessary. Their bodies had done the talking for them, and now Storm had a lot to consider, but not this moment. This moment was to enjoy.

They fell asleep wrapped around each other, and she woke in the middle of the night aroused by his intimate touches, and they made love again.

In the morning, before dawn touched the horizon, they rose and dressed and spoke not a word. Soon they would, but for now, it would wait.

Five of them, Storm, Burke, Tannin, William, and Philip, had spent two days observing the activities and routine of the guards along Balford land. It was easily determined what route Burke could take to reach the gardens and where the most secluded spot was for him to approach Lady Alaina.

Storm advised him that Lady Alaina's daily stroll usually lasted thirty to forty minutes, and given the time it would take Burke to reach the location, it would leave him with no more then twenty minutes to speak with her. Otherwise, he ran the risk of guards breathing down his neck.

In the early morning of the day of the meeting, Storm found Burke standing on the edge of the forest that bordered Balford land.

"You are getting closer to rescuing your brother," she encouraged as she approached.

He held his hand out to her. "Thanks to you."

She took it and he pulled her into his arms and hugged her tight. She loved that he was so generous with his affection, for it made her feel wanted.

"I hope this goes well for you today," she said, snuggled in the crook of his arm.

"If nothing else, I will discover more than I already know about my brother, and that is bound to help me."

"Yes, Lady Alaina would know much about your brother, being in love with him."

"I am eager to hear it all, for then I can reach a reasonable conclusion that will allow me to take the next step."

"Attempting to purchase your brother's freedom," Storm said softly.

"You don't think it a viable option."

She laid a gentle hand on his chest. "Lady Alaina would be the best one to answer that."

"I value your opinion."

"Something tells me that you need to be cautious. The Earl of Balford is a deceitful man and that means a dangerous man."

"I will keep your warning in mind at all times."

"You'd better," she said with a poke to his ribs. "I don't want anything happening to you."

He pulled her in front of him with his hands resting at her waist. "Why is that?"

She stared into his dark eyes and knew what he wanted to hear from her, felt it in his touch, heard it in his voice, but was she ready to tell him? Did she know for sure herself?

"Time to leave," Tanin said from behind them.

She shivered, Burke's dark eyes warning along with his whisper: "I will have my answer soon."

Chapter 29

Burke waited at the end of a row of box hedges. According to Philip, Lady Alaina's routine was to enter the garden, walk to the edge of the forest until she came to a row of box hedges, then stroll around them and retrace her trail.

The high hedges would afford them privacy, and the length it took to walk them would provide him with the needed twenty minutes.

He was anxious to speak with her, anxious to learn all he could about his brother, anxious to be one step closer to freeing Cullen.

He heard the rustle of footsteps and the swish of material along the ground and stilled, waiting for Lady Alaina to turn the corner of the hedges.

She did and startled to a stop.

"Forgive my intrusion," Burke said and offered his arm to her and quickly refreshed her memory of him. "We met at the seamstress shop in St. Andrew. Burke Longton from America."

Her tense stance eased and she accepted his arm. "Forgive me, I did not know you visited with my father."

"I haven't visited with your father. It is you I wished to see."

Her steps faltered and he was quick to reassure her.

"I mean you no harm, Lady Alaina. I seek information about my brother—Cullen."

She stopped and glanced over his face with loving eyes. "I wondered how two men with an uncanny resemblance could not be related."

"Let me explain," Burke offered, and proceeded to tell her his story in detail and how Cullen had no idea that he had a brother.

Tears threatened her eyes. "Cullen would be so happy to learn of this. He always wondered about his father. He would be pleased to know how much his father loved him."

"Tell me of my brother, please."

"He is a wonderful man with a good sense of humor."

Burke grinned. "Like our father."

"He's taller than you and broader in the shoulders and chest. He is so very gentle and loving."

"You fell in love with him?"

She nodded.

"How is that possible?"

"Cullen is an easy man to love."

"No, I mean how did you two meet? How was it

possible for you to even get a chance to fall in love?"

"Cullen is a master with a bow and arrow. My father hired him to school the guards in his techniques. My friends and I expressed interest in learning and my father, after objecting and then realizing we simply thought of it as entertainment, agreed."

She turned silent, and Burke could see her eyes clouding with tears. It was obvious the memories caused her pain, and he felt compelled to offer comfort while learning what he could of his brother.

"I am sorry to upset you. I know this must hurt terribly, but it is very important for me to find out whatever I can of Cullen if I'm to free him."

Her hand flew to her chest and she gasped. "You will free Cullen?"

"I don't intend on leaving Scotland without my brother."

Her eyes turned sad and her shoulders sagged. "You will take him away."

"Along with you if you so choose," he offered and smiled. "I have a lady of my own I wish to return with to America. We can all be family together."

"That sounds delightful, but my father would never permit it. I am to wed a titled man of my father's choosing, one who will financially benefit my family."

"If my brother is anything like me, he'd never allow that to happen."

She smiled and wiped at a single tear that spilled down her cheek. "You are right, which is what caused Cullen's plight."

"Tell me," Burke urged, time running out.

"Cullen and I decided to run off together once we realized how much we loved each other. We planned to forge a life high up in the Highlands where no one would find us. As long as we were together, nothing else mattered to me. Before we could implement our plan, I took ill." She paused and fought back tears. "My father sent me away and Cullen searched for me, though it was my father who found him and imprisoned him."

"How long has he been imprisoned?"

"About six months. My father has moved Cullen from prison to prison in an attempt to keep me from him, but I have found ways to visit with him. Now my father has sent him someplace I dare not visit."

"Weighton."

Alaina nodded slowly. "My father does not realize that he not only condemns Cullen to death but his daughter as well, for I will die a little each day along with Cullen."

"That's not necessary," Burke informed her emphatically. "I intend to free my brother and you will both come to America with me. Cullen is a rich man and will provide you with a good life."

"As long as I am with Cullen nothing else matters, but I don't see how you'll be able to free him from Weighton. It is impregnable."

"So I've heard, but what if I made your father a substantial offer for my brother's freedom and guaranteed he'd never set foot on Scottish soil again?"

Alaina sighed. "I don't know. He's adamant about making Cullen suffer."

"I could offer him a sizable amount of money."

"I would hope that he would accept it, but knowing my father's arrogance and pride, he might just enjoy refusing your offer and seeing that you suffer, as he feels he was made to do."

"You are here alive and well. He suffers no loss."

Alaina glanced to the ground and spoke in a near whisper. "I gave to your brother what belonged to my future husband."

Burke raised her chin with his finger. "You gave my brother your love and he gave his in return. There is no shame in that. The shame is that your father refuses to allow his daughter happiness."

Alaina smiled. "Yes, you are much like your brother."

Burke was pleased to hear that he and Cullen shared identical traits, and it made him even more determined to free him and meet him for himself. They had many years to catch up on and the rest of their lives to finally do it.

"Since Weighton seems impregnable, my only choice is to speak with your father and make him an offer."

"If he refuses?"

Alaina's shudder informed Burke of her expectations of the plan, and while it concerned him, it was his only option for the moment. Which meant he had no choice; he had to give it a try.

"Could you arrange a meeting with your father tomorrow for me? Tell him I'm only in the area for the day and would like to discuss business with him."

She nodded. "I will explain how I met you and your request for a meeting."

"Will he ask what it is in regard to?"

"No, business is left to men and he would not expect you to have discussed it with me."

"I must go," Burke said, regretful he couldn't spend more time with her and learn more about his brother. "One more thing. When did you last see Cullen, and how was he?"

"Before he was moved from Mewers—" She stopped suddenly. "I saw you at Mewers. I had learned that Cullen was to be moved and hoped to see him before then, but he was already gone when I got there. You were there in search of him that day?"

"My group freed the young lad hoping he'd provide us with information. I had wondered why you stared at me."

She smiled. "When I first saw you I thought my eyes played tricks on me and that Cullen walked free. Then I realized it was my heart that had played tricks on me."

Burke took her hand and squeezed gently. "Cullen will walk free, and perhaps I can be persuasive enough to convince your father that I'm a land baron, which makes Cullen one. Would he consider agreeing to his daughter marrying a land baron?"

Alaina crossed her arms over her heart. "With all my heart I pray he would, but my father is a stubborn and vindictive man, and the man he wishes me to wed is a very powerful duke."

"It's worth a try," Burke said. "I will see you tomorrow at—"

"Just before noon. I will convince my father of the importance of the meeting, telling him how wealthy you are."

"I'm glad my brother found love with you and glad I'll have you as family."

Alaina squeezed his hand before releasing it. "I'm so very glad you're here to help your brother. Until tomorrow."

She hurried off, and Burke made his way back into the forest where Storm and Tanin waited for him while William and Philip continued to keep watch.

"Lady Alaina was receptive to my questions," Burke explained once they returned to their campsite. "She and Cullen fell in love and planned to run off together. She took ill and her father found Cullen and now makes him pay for loving his daughter while the earl intends to wed her off to a duke."

Storm shook her head while pacing in front of Burke. "He's looking to make powerful connections through marriage. I wouldn't be surprised if the duke helped him to get Cullen imprisoned in Weighton."

"I'm meeting with the earl tomorrow," Burke said, standing firm in anticipation of Storm's objection.

"It will be a waste of time," Storm said and sank to the ground to sit.

"I agree," Tanin said, resting against an old rotting stump.

Burke sat beside Storm, the blue of her eyes swirling like an impending storm and warning of her concern. "Why?"

"The earl is looking for power and the only way

of obtaining it is through the marriage of his daughter. No amount of money will match that."

"She's right," Tanin said. "I fear you waste your time."

"What other choice do I have?" Burke asked, and watched as Tanin sat straight up and stared with wide eyes at Storm.

"Don't even tell me you're considering it," Tanin warned, his eyes fixed on Storm.

Burke looked over at her, and in the depths of her blue eyes he could see a plan brewing like a storm that was about to rage and consume everything in its path.

"You know as well as I do, this meeting will go badly," Storm said and turned to Burke. "You can't meet with the earl. We must find a way into Weighton to free Cullen. It is the only logical solution."

"I can be persuasive," Burke argued.

"It's not about persuasion," she argued. "Besides, I still lead this group and my decision is final, and I say there'll be no meeting between you and the earl."

"It's my choice," Burke said firmly.

Storm shook her head. "No, it's not. Your foolish move could not only cost my group dearly but it could cost your brother as well."

He'd hear her out since he respected her opinion, but he'd be damned if the final choice would be hers. "How so?"

Storm looked to Tanin and he answered.

"The earl is a vindictive man—"

"Lady Alaina said the same."

"Then listen to her for she speaks the truth," Tanin said. "He has been the cause of suffering and countless deaths, and even of ones he claims to love. He had Lady Alaina's mother confined to an institution, claiming she was insane. She killed herself after there only a month. He then married again and found a way to get rid of her when he insisted she was barren. He has gone through four wives and now looks for a fifth to give him the son he so desperately wants."

"The earl intends to use his daughter to benefit his thirst for power. Otherwise she is useless to him," Storm said. "While you may be able to convince him that your brother holds a title of land baron, that title does him little good here in Scotland. You are wasting your time and I will not allow it."

"It's not your decision," Burke snapped.

"Think again, Mr. Longton," she warned calmly.

Burke sent Tanin a look that begged for privacy and the man walked off, though not before making sure Burke understood that he agreed with Storm.

He wasn't surprised when Storm stood and took a firm stance, her hands on her hips, her head held high. He was glad she didn't wear the stocking cap that portrayed her as a young lad. He loved her wavy black hair that shouted she was a woman and a beautiful one at that.

She just wasn't any woman—she was his woman. And though the thought melted his heart, he knew he needed to shield himself for he was about to go into battle with the infamous Storm.

He came to his feet, easing his back and shoulders

until he stood tall and firm. "I've made my decision, Storm. You can't change my mind."

"It's not about changing your mind. It's about obeying me, which I recall you had a problem with from the beginning."

Burke opened his mouth to speak, and Storm was quick to still him with a warning.

"Think wisely, Mr. Longton, your response will affect many lives."

Burke remained silent, though it wasn't because he intended to change his mind. He merely wondered how he would convince her that this was his choice, something he had to do. Suddenly he realized the perfect solution. He'd sidetrack her.

"I told Lady Alaina she could come to America with us."

Storm glared at him, and damn if he didn't see the tempest rising in the blue of her eyes. He wished he had a storm coat to protect him from the squall that was about to hit.

"There is no us. Worse, you gave Lady Alaina hope."

"There certainly is an us, and what is wrong with hope?"

"Hope always disappoints. It does so right now since you are so hopeful about us."

"Hope does not always disappoint," Burke argued. "Whether you want to admit it or not, there is an us and there will continue to be an us all the way to America."

"See, you hope, and your hope will soon be dashed, and then what?"

"Let me reiterate. Hope does not disappoint. It offers encouragement and urges one to pursue his dream and see it to fruition. I intend to free my brother and have him live with me in America. We will watch our children be born and grow together. We will be family."

"Senseless dreams," she scoffed.

He stomped over to her and grabbed hold of her arms. "A dream perhaps, but a dream I will see to fruition."

"Believe what nonsense you will, but unless you listen to me you will never free your brother and return with him and Lady Alaina to America where you will live this idyllic life."

"I will have it," Burke said adamantly. "And there will be an us."

"That's not possible," she assured him.

He took hold of her shoulders and yanked her up against him. "Yes, it is possible, Storm, for I am determined that you will be my wife."

Chapter 30

~~~~~~~~~~~~~~

William and Philip entered the camp, forcing Burke to release Storm, for which she was grateful. For an instant, though, she thought perhaps it would have been best for him to continue to hold on to her, since she feared her trembling legs might fail her and she'd collapse, so weak did she feel.

Burke's remark had hit her hard. Did he really presume that she would wed him? He had yet to claim to love her, and here he stated that she would be his wife. The man certainly was a fool, or was he hopeful?

He was an idiot.

She spoke with William and Philip and spent a few moments with Tanin before she wandered off to find a secluded spot in the forest. She needed time alone to think.

Burke was making a mistake that he would surely

regret, and yet she could not convince him of it. He was so intent on rescuing his brother that he couldn't see that he was making the wrong choice.

How did she convince him not to keep that meeting tomorrow?

How did she make him realize that he was about to do his brother more harm than good?

How did she let him know that she would never be his wife and that she would never go to America with him? And why did the thought upset her?

Hope.

There was no hope for the likes of her. Burke did not understand that and foolishly wasted time and thought on an impossible notion. She, however, was practical, and already a plan had begun to form in her mind. It was a dangerous one for sure, but if it proved successful, Cullen would be free, and she wanted that for Burke. She wanted to see him set sail for America with his brother at his side.

It would break her heart to say good-bye to him, but she had no other choice. Whether she loved him or not didn't matter.

Love.

Lord, she didn't think she'd ever love again. She really didn't think it was possible. Yet Burke had made her feel things long buried, not to mention new feelings that crept in and confused her even more.

She smiled and hugged herself. She so enjoyed making love with him. He was so very attentive and so gentle and so . . .

Her smile faded and her arms fell from around her. She couldn't dwell on Burke, couldn't even consider that she loved him. It would only make their parting more difficult.

"You forever try to run away from me."

Storm startled and shook her head at Burke. "You should have warned me of your approach, and I don't run from you. I seek solitude."

"You run out of fear," he argued.

"Fear of what?" she asked, and then thought it too late to retract her answer for she was sure of his response.

"Fear of my love, fear of being my wife."

She threw her hands out in front of her. "This cannot be and I will not discuss it."

"Why? Because it might make sense?" he asked and eased closer to her. "Because the very reason we enjoy making love is that we are in love?"

"There are more important matters to discuss," she insisted, attempting to dissuade him.

"Nothing is more important than love," he said adamantly. "Which means nothing is more important than you."

"Your brother?"

"Would my brother put me before Alaina? I know he would not. His love for her would come first, and rightfully so."

She held her hand in front of her to guard against him, or was she guarding against herself? Was she preventing her own feelings from surfacing?

"There is too much to presently consider. This must wait for another time," she said.

"No! Why do you refuse to acknowledge what you feel?"

"You do not know what I feel," she accused.

Burke stared speechless at her until finally he spoke. "How can you believe that, when every time we make love we feel each other's need, each other's love? It is there in our touch, in our kiss, and when we join. It cannot be denied, ignored, or dismissed. You will have to face it eventually. You love me, Storm, and you fight it. I, however, do not fight my love for you. I cherish it, embrace it, and welcome it. I love you, Storm, and there's no changing it or denying it. I love you!"

"Don't love me," she shouted at him.

He laughed. "You can't command my love."

"It can never be," she said, shaking her head.

"It is," he said, reaching out and drawing her into his arms.

She didn't have the strength or the will to fight him. For the moment, his arms seemed like the perfect place to be, for she knew they offered comfort and security, and she presently needed both.

She drifted gratefully into his embrace, and when he wrapped his strong arms around her, she near sighed with relief. She rested her head on his chest and listened to his steady heartbeat. It always reassured her, though she couldn't say why. She only knew that the strong beat gave her strength and comfort.

She would allow herself this short reprieve before having to return as a leader. For now, she was simply a woman who cared deeply for a man. As far as love, she couldn't consider that. She wouldn't. It would only worsen matters.

It would only serve to break her heart—and his.

They remained in an embrace for several minutes until finally Storm realized that it could go on no more. The situation had to be faced, decisions finalized, and hopefully commands obeyed.

She eased out of his arms reluctantly and stepped away from him. "Tell me you will not go meet with the earl tomorrow."

His hesitation warned her of his response and her body grew taut, prepared to battle.

"I must take the chance, even if it is a slim one, and meet with the earl."

"And if I command you not to do this?" she asked with an ache in her heart, for she feared she knew the answer.

Burke shook his head. "You know I must do this. You know you would do the same in my place."

"I'm not in your place. I lead this group, so the decisions are mine."

"That's right. The decisions are yours, which means you can respect my choice, even though you disagree, and allow me this."

He had replied with respect to her position and asked the same of her. He could have simply told her he'd do what he wanted but he hadn't. He left the decision to her as to whether this would cause a problem.

"I think you're making a mistake, but—" She stared at him, concern for his safety welling up inside her and squeezing at her heart. "It is your mistake to make."

"That's encouraging," he said.

"I should encourage you to be a fool?"

"I have no other choice," he argued.

"Perhaps there is."

"I don't agree and neither do the others," Tanin said sharply, causing them both to turn and face him.

"What's going on?" Burke asked, looking from one to the other.

"Tell him," Tanin said accusingly.

"It could work but plans would need to be strictly adhered to," Storm said calmly.

Tanin shook his head. "She wants to attempt to rescue Cullen from Weighton."

Burke looked to Storm. "I thought you said Weighton was impregnable?"

"It is," Tanin said.

"It might not be," Storm advised, and both men shot wide eyes at her.

"How so?" Burke asked.

"I have an idea that might work, but I need to give it more thought before sharing it with you."

"I don't like it," Tanin said.

"It may not matter one way or the other," Burke said. "If the earl accepts my proposal, then this is a moot point. I don't think we should worry about it until then."

"She won't stop thinking about it," Tanin argued, pointing to Storm.

"It may be necessary for me to think about it. If I don't, valuable time can be lost and a man's life may be forfeited. I prefer being prepared just in case."

"It's unthinkable," Tanin warned. "There's no way it can be done. It's certain death."

"For Cullen," Storm confirmed.

Burke stepped between the pair. "At the moment it is merely a consideration that tomorrow may prove nothing. There's no point in arguing over something that may never see fruition."

"Tell him, Storm, or I will," Tanin threatened.

"I gave you an order to keep what we discussed to yourself," Storm said.

"Not this time," Tanin said, shaking his head. "Not what you proposed. It's damned foolish and can mean death."

Burke turned an anxious glance on Storm. "What's Tanin talking about?"

"I told you, it's an idea that needs further investigation and preparation."

"It needs no consideration. It needs ignoring, forgetting, burying," Tanin insisted.

"Storm," Burke said firmly. "Tell me now."

Storm thought to ignore them both. She was the leader and her word was law, though it seemed Tanin had chosen to ignore her order. She couldn't, however, carry out her plan if she didn't have the support and determination of her men. It would take a concentrated effort from all of them to succeed.

"Keep in mind that it is a fermenting thought that needs further consideration," she advised before continuing. "The one reason it is so hard to rescue anyone from Weighton is because no one knows the inner workings of the place. Every prison rescue we're made was successful largely due to the knowledge we obtained about the prison itself."

Burke nodded. "When you rescued me I remember that you knew of the cells at the end of the corridor."

Storm nodded. "We learned of that from people who had been held prisoner there and had been released. Then there were the greedy guards who were willing to exchange information for coins."

"So we find ourselves some greedy guards," Burke said.

Tanin shook his head. "The man who tried now rots in Weighton. No guard there would dare take such a chance. He's only too aware of his fate, and no amount of coins would be worth the chance of being condemned to Weighton."

"The only other way is for someone to enter Weighton as a prisoner, learn what they could for a few days, and be prepared when the others make the rescue attempt," Storm said.

"That's not a bad idea," Burke said. "The fellow could learn the workings of the place and possibly even locate Cullen's cell. He can even see if there's a good escape route."

Tanin rubbed the back of his neck. "Yes, this *fellow* could do all that in between being tortured, beaten, and starved."

"It's a gamble, and the fellow would need to volunteer. I could do it. I wouldn't expect someone to place his life on the line for my brother."

"Wouldn't work," Tanin said. "Weighton is for special prisoners, mainly ones who have committed crimes against king and country. You're a foreigner, and it would take time to make a case against you, and until then you would be held in another prison."

Burke shrugged. "Then there is no one—"

Tanin nodded. "Now you understand."

Storm kept her chin high and her stance firm while Burke rushed at her.

"You will not—*will not*—be a pawn to save my brother."

Chapter 31

Burke turned to Tanin. "Leave us, and rest assured this plan will never see fruition."

"I'm relieved to hear that," Tanin said and walked away.

Burke had to calm himself or else he would grab Storm and shake the foolishness out of her. The idea that she would surrender herself to free his brother, while heroic, was simply foolhardy.

He turned with a shake of his head to face her. "You didn't really believe that I would let you do this, did you?"

"*Let* me? Since when did you become the leader of this group?"

"Since the leader lost her mind." He spit out a frustrated sigh. "It's inconceivable to me that you would think I would allow you to purposely place your life in danger."

Storm tapped her chin. "Let me think. You presently made a decision that I think is foolish but I do not stop you. I, however, devise a plan that could very well work and what do you do?"

"It is far different and you know it," he said, not believing this conversation could even be taking place. There was no way in the world that he would ever allow her to be taken prisoner. He'd die defending her.

He grabbed hold of her, his grip strong as if he feared losing her. "Promise me you will think no more on this."

"It is a viable plan that may prove necessary."

"Never," he near shouted. "Never would I allow it."

"*Never* is a strong word," Storm advised softly.

The blue of her eyes was as calm as the sky on a beautiful summer's day, and that worried him. She wasn't taking him seriously, and he wanted her to take him very seriously and know for certain her plan ended right here, right now.

"Get this plan out of your head and keep it out of your head," he insisted. "It will not be discussed again."

"You will see your brother die rather than consider a feasible plan?"

"A feasible plan does not trade one life for another," he argued. "I will not chance losing you to save my brother."

She eased his hands off her and placed a gentle hand to his face. "This really is my choice."

Burke took her hand and kissed her palm. "No, it isn't."

"I'm the leader—"

"No. You're the woman I love, who I want to marry, have children with, and grow old with. We'll find another way to rescue my brother."

"If there is none?"

"Your plan is not an option," he said firmly, then wrapped her in his arms. "I can't lose you, Storm. I love you too much."

He felt her tense and understood. To her way of thinking, they had no future. He would return to America and she would remain behind in Scotland. But she wasn't aware of his tenacity, especially when it came to protecting the people he loved. And damn if he didn't love her with all his heart.

"We'll work this out, don't worry," he said, hoping to ease her concern and his own, for he worried that Storm was just as tenacious as he.

Burke often wondered how Storm secured some of the things she needed, and now, seeing the horse and carriage waiting on the road when he emerged from the forest, he wondered even more.

"Don't ask," she cautioned before he could question her. "Don't worry, it isn't stolen."

He liked when she fussed with his shirt or jacket, as she did now, her tiny hands smoothing down his collar and toying with his buttons, until finally coming to rest on his chest. It was as if she wanted to touch him but needed to take a roundabout way of doing it.

"Be careful," she ordered. "And remember the earl is a deceitful man. Do not trust him. Keep to business. Do not waste pleasantries on him, get right to the heart of the matter."

"Do I look presentable?" he teased, wanting to see her smile. He had already changed into suitable garments that Philip had retrieved from his cabin.

She shook her head and smiled, and he felt a stab to his gut. Stocking cap, smudges, and all, she still was beautiful and her smile confirmed it.

"Your tailored black wool suit speaks of wealth as does that diamond ring on your finger."

"It was my father's," he said, holding his hand up. "I hope to give it to Cullen."

"I'm sure he will treasure it."

He leaned down and stole a quick kiss. "I will free my brother. I am sure of it."

"I am too," she encouraged, though it gave him a start.

He feared she kept her plan in mind, even worked on it, allowing it to grow, and he'd be damned if he'd see it given birth.

"You be good," he ordered teasingly.

She grinned. "I'm very good."

He nuzzled near her ear. "That you are, my love."

"Tanin and I will wait here for you to return. The others will spread out around the manor house in case you should need assistance. Remember someone is close by at all times."

"I am grateful and I am confident," he said and

gave her a hug before climbing into the single horse-drawn carriage.

She reached out and took hold of his hand that held the reins. "Take no chances. I don't want anything to happen to you."

He leaned down close and whispered, "Love me, do you?"

She laughed softly. "How can I help it?"

Her words reverberated in his head as the carriage bounced down the rutted road. In her own way, she had admitted she loved him, and the joy of it overwhelmed him. He was going to make everything work—from freeing his brother, to reuniting Cullen with Lady Alaina, to marrying Storm, to taking them all back to America with him.

They'd be family, all of them, and his father and mother would have been pleased knowing that the ranch they had worked so hard to build would see family grow and prosper on it.

Burke entered the Earl of Balford's manor house with strength and determination, ready to do what he had to, to protect the people he loved.

He had expected Lady Alaina to greet him, but a manservant escorted him to an ornately decorated parlor, where he was told the earl would be with him shortly.

The room's garish furnishings shouted wealth and gave Burke hope. Since the earl favored money, he just might favor releasing Cullen for a goodly amount that would fatten his coffers considerably.

"Mr. Longton."

Burke turned from admiring a painting of a young

lass with a small dog on her lap to greet the Earl of Balford.

"My lord," he said with a respectful bow of his head. He had no idea if he was addressing him correctly but instinct told him it wouldn't hurt. And the way the tall, slim man held himself so rigid and with his garments matching the style of the room, he could tell the earl was a man who deemed himself important.

The earl walked over to a white, ornately designed chair trimmed in gold and sat, then pointed to a less garish chair and with a careless wave ordered Burke to sit.

Burke sat on the edge of the chair.

"My daughter mentioned something about a business proposition," the earl said as if not at all interested.

Burke couldn't help but notice that there was no resemblance between the earl and his daughter, not even the slightest. Their natures even seemed opposite since Lady Alaina appeared a caring soul and the earl . . .

Burke took a good look at him and knew right away he was a cold-hearted bastard.

"I have a proposition that would award you substantial financial gain," Burke said.

"I'm listening."

Burke didn't waste a minute; he did as Storm had advised. He got right to the point. "You hold my brother prisoner and I wish to pay for his release."

The earl's posture grew even more rigid and his

face brightened with interest. And why not? Releasing a prisoner was an easy way for him to make money and an easy way for Burke to gain his brother's freedom.

"Your brother's name?" the earl asked casually.

"Cullen."

The earl's demeanor changed in a flash, his eyes narrowed, his lips pinched tight, and his slim hands gripped the arms of the chair. "That man is charged with a grievous crime and must suffer his punishment."

"What was my brother's crime?" Burke asked, knowing full well it was forbidden love that had imprisoned Cullen, but knowing he could never acknowledge that to the irate man.

"Treason!"

Burke tensed. Treason wasn't dealt with lightly in any country, but money had opened prison doors before and he hoped it would now.

"I can promise you more than sufficient restitution for my brother's bad judgment."

"Nothing, absolutely nothing, could redeem your brother's foolish actions."

Burke remained calm. "True, foolishness can brand a man forever, but why let him rot in a jail cell when you can exchange him for a sizable amount of money and a guarantee that the man will never set foot in Scotland again."

"Money cannot make right the horrendous wrong that this man did."

Burke could have sworn the man hissed like a

snake getting ready to attack, and he knew he had to tread very lightly. If he wasn't able to secure Cullen's release, what alternative was there?

Storm's capture.

He didn't want to give it thought. He had to make this work.

"Of course not," Burke agreed. "But exiling him from his homeland is a death sentence in itself."

"This man would never leave Scotland," the earl argued.

"What choice would he have? He'd be tied and secured in a cabin and not released until far enough out at sea, where he could do nothing about it." Burke knew this was the time to make the proposition too appealing to turn down. "Besides, I'm willing to offer you full ownership of a gold mine in America in exchange for my brother's freedom."

The earl couldn't hide his surprise or pleasure. "A producing gold mine?"

"A powerfully producing gold mine," Burke confirmed.

"That is an interesting proposition," the earl said and eased back in his chair.

"I can have the papers drawn up immediately, and by the end of the week we can make the exchange."

The earl gave it thought, and Burke waited anxiously for his answer. He didn't believe he'd be turned down; few if any men could refuse a gold mine dropped in their lap. To Burke it was a small price to pay for his brother's freedom.

"I think we could work this out," the earl said. "See to the paperwork and we'll meet at Weighton in two weeks to make the exchange. I have business that will take me away and I won't be available until then."

Burke wasn't happy with the delay, but he had little choice but to agree. "Agreed, I will meet you at Weighton two weeks to the day to make the exchange."

"Joseph will see you out," he said, pointing to the door where the manservant stood.

The earl never even stood or shook hands with Burke. Burke did not trust a man who did not shake on an agreement, and he wasn't pleased with being dismissed like a peasant who had annoyed the mighty lord.

He also wasn't pleased with the two-week delay, but there was nothing he could do to change that. He had waited this long to find his brother, so another two weeks shouldn't matter. He hoped.

Storm had been right that the earl couldn't be trusted, but then Burke would sign no papers until his brother stood in front of him, a free man.

Storm and Tanin stepped out of the woods, signaling Burke to their position. Malcolm appeared when he brought the horse to a stop, and took the reins from him.

"He accepted," Burke said, jumping down from the carriage.

Tanin and Malcolm smiled and nodded. Storm remained silent.

"I'll see to the carriage with Malcolm," Tanin said and walked off with the other man.

Storm walked into the forest and Burke followed. He knew she wanted to talk with him and he knew she would caution him. However, it was over and done. His brother would be free, and now all that was left for him to do was to convince her to go to America with him.

He reached out, took hold of her arm, spun her around, and hugged her close before kissing her as if he'd just returned from a long journey.

When he finished, he rested his forehead against hers. "I missed you."

"You weren't gone that long." She sighed and brushed her lips over his.

"You missed me too." He laughed knowingly, then kissed her again.

She playfully pushed at his chest. "You are foolish."

He hugged her tighter and rocked back and forth with her secure in his arms. "Foolishly in love."

She laughed and shook her head. "This is no time to be talking of us. We—"

"Aha, you admit there is an *us*."

He let her wiggle out of his arms.

"I want to hear about the earl. Did he accept easily or did you need to convince him?"

Soon she would need to face the fact there was an us. For now she was right. This needed to be discussed and Storm put at ease. He didn't want her wasting another minute on a plan that no longer proved necessary.

"He wasn't receptive at first, but the gold mine changed his mind."

"Gold mine?" Storm asked, stunned. "You offered him a gold mine?"

Burke shrugged. "It had to be an offer he couldn't refuse, and I can't think of a soul who would refuse a gold mine."

Storm shook her head and paced in front of Burke. "This isn't good."

"Why? The earl gets more than he should in exchange for my brother's freedom."

Storm stopped and glared at him. "Only a fool would refuse a gold mine and the earl is no fool. But he is also a man determined to have his revenge. I do not trust this arrangement he has made with you."

"I don't either. I know the earl is deceitful, so no papers will be signed until my brother is standing in front of me. I also do not intend to arrive alone at the meeting. I shall have the captain of my ship with me and several sailors."

Storm shook her head. "I still don't like it. I don't believe the earl will release Cullen. He wants him dead and he will see him dead."

Burke tried to ease her trepidation. "It will go well. We will plan and see that it does." He reached out and stroked her arm. "I know you were unable to save your husband from the earl, but we will save Cullen."

Storm stepped away from him. "You think I worry that your brother faces the same fate as Daniel?"

"It's all right that you do," Burke said. "I appreciate your concern."

"My concern has nothing to do with my husband. It has to do with a man who deceives people and will always deceive people. The earl cannot now or ever be trusted. He sets a trap and will see your brother dead before turning him over to you, though after taking ownership of your gold mine."

"Now you wound my intelligence," Burke said annoyed. "I'd never let that happen."

"You won't see it coming."

"I'm a cautious person—"

"Not cautious enough when it comes to the earl," Storm warned.

"You managed to break into his prison and free your husband and he never saw it coming. I think I can manage the same."

Storm rubbed her forehead and leaned against a thick tree trunk. "He didn't expect me, a mere woman, to make such a foolish attempt. I had the element of surprise on my side."

"And Tanin to help."

Storm sighed. "Tanin wasn't with me in the prison."

"You told me that Tanin had plans to free his wife and you asked to join him."

"Yes, but I changed his plan since I knew it was doomed to fail and we executed my plan instead."

"You had a plan all along? You intended to free your husband on your own?" He shook his head. "Something happened that night with the earl, didn't it? That's why he is so determined to catch you and make you pay. What happened, Storm? What did you do to the earl?"

Chapter 32

Storm wasn't interested in reliving the night her husband died, but she wanted Burke to understand the Earl of Balford's true nature. He was a man who cared for no one but himself and would do anything to get what he wanted, at any cost.

She couldn't let that cost be Burke. She had foolishly allowed the American to steal her heart, and she realized just how much when she caught sight of him in the carriage safely returning to her.

She had barely taken a breath while he was gone. She had worried every minute of his absence and had already had a rescue plan formulated in case it became necessary.

Under no circumstances would she allow Burke to remain a prisoner of the earl for even one day and chance his being carted off to Weighton like his brother.

"Storm," Burke said softly.

She stared at him for a moment. She loved looking upon his face. His features defined a man of strength and honor, while his quick smile warned of his humor, and his dark eyes betrayed the depth of his feelings.

He was a man easy to love and one who loved her with the same ease. Love had found them both or as Burke would remind her—it was fate.

Storm cleared her head with a shake. "I had a rescue plan ready when I approached Tanin. Naturally, he thought his plan better until he heard mine and then he realized mine was the one more likely to succeed."

"It involved the earl, didn't it?" Burke accused.

"It couldn't help but involve him," Storm admitted. "If the earl's life was in danger, then the guards wouldn't dare stop a rescue."

"How did you manage to get hold of the earl?"

"I didn't have to. I knew my husband was close to death and I knew the earl would offer to release him if I submitted to him."

Burke shook his head. "What? He would free your husband in exchange for sex?"

"Only when he knew the prisoner lay close to death. He wasn't about to really let him free, regardless of what money he had collected or promises he had made. He had done it many times before to other prisoners' wives, so I knew I could count on him to do it again, especially since he was casting overtures in that direction the last few times he had spoken with me."

"I'm going to kill the bastard," Burke snarled.

"I wish I had, but I needed him to free my husband in hopes that I was not too late. The earl was shocked when I pulled a knife on him."

"How did you ever get him from the manor house down to the prison without anyone seeing you?"

"We were already in the prison," Storm said. "You see, the earl liked to take a prisoner's wife in front of him."

"Damn, now the man really has to die."

"I made the guard free Ellie and she trussed up the two guards, and then with me pressing the point of the knife to the earl's neck and drawing enough blood to frighten him to remain still, Ellie tied him up. We secured them, and Tanin saw to the guard outside and was waiting for us when we came out. He helped me with Daniel and we all took off."

Storm took a breath and fought back tears. She would not cry and she would not linger on the sad memories. She told Burke this story for a reason and she hoped it served the purpose she intended.

"You understand now why you should not trust the earl?"

"I understand even more, and believe me, I don't trust him. Once the papers are signed, Cullen and I will leave Weighton immediately—"

"Weighton? The earl wants the exchange to take place at Weighton?" she asked, shaking her head. "The earl doesn't intend for your brother or you to leave the prison."

"My captain and several sailors will be with me."

"He won't let them in the prison. Rules, he will

313

claim, and in your zeal to free your brother you will imprison yourself."

"Not so, I know what I do."

"Didn't you hear what I just told you? The earl will have his way. He will have your gold mine, your brother, and you. This will never work. We need another plan."

"There is no other plan," Burke warned.

Storm walked up to him and jabbed him in the chest. "You're a stubborn American."

"And you're not a stubborn Scot?" he said and grabbed her finger, spun her around, his arms closing around her middle, and leaned his face over her shoulder to press his cheek to hers.

She struggled for a moment, then leaned back against him, resting her hands on his arms wrapped around her. "It serves no purpose to battle each other."

"Then surrender and the problem is solved," he advised with a kiss to her cheek.

"I cannot. This plan is doomed to fail."

"We will plan it together so that there is no room for failure," he offered.

"It will not work, Burke," she said, wishing she was wrong, yet knowing she was right.

"It will. We will make it work."

He truly believed in the plan's success and she hated to discourage him, but how did she make him see the truth?

Then an idea occurred to her. "I think Lady Alaina could again prove helpful," Storm said, drifting out of his arms to turn and face him. She would

314

know or could learn of her father's intentions. She would be able to convince Burke of the folly of his plan. Then Storm herself would need to convince him that the only way out of Weighton for his brother was for her to go in.

"I don't think her father would discuss his plans with her."

"Probably not, but I believe Lady Alaina would have a way of finding out. She has known of Cullen's whereabouts each time he was moved."

Burke seemed hesitant.

"If we are to make this plan work, we need to make certain we consider all the variables and be prepared, or else we are guaranteeing our failure."

"There you go making sense again," he teasingly accused.

"I try," she said and drifted back into his arms. He welcomed her as he always did, his arms going around her, protecting, comforting, loving her.

"Can we get a message to her?" Burke asked.

"I'll see that one is sent right away. We'll let her know of her father's plan and ask that she keep us apprised of any changes."

"Tell her also that we'll let her know when to be ready."

Storm nestled in the crook of his arm to glance up at him. "Ready?"

"She's going with us to America."

There was no point in addressing this subject again. Burke had his opinion on the matter and she had hers and they would never agree. She would let him believe what he wished to believe. It would make the next couple of weeks easier. Then he would be gone and it would be done. She would never see him again.

The pain in her heart nearly brought her to her knees and she cursed herself for falling in love with Burke. But it was done and she could do nothing about it but bid him farewell.

"No disagreement?' he asked with a smile. "Do I dare hope we've made progress?"

"We have much to plan. We can't waste time on a trivial matter."

"Trivial?" His smile faded and he dropped his arms from around her. "My love for you is not trivial. My wanting us to wed and have a life together in America is not trivial. My—"

His sudden pause had her eyes turning wide. He looked about to say something and she had a feeling that, whatever it was, she wasn't going to like it.

"You're coming to America with me and that's the end of it."

She broke into a smile, and she gave a little cough to clear her giggles before she spoke. "You are amusing."

He crossed his arms over his chest. "Feel amused if you like but you are going with me."

Storm turned blazing blue eyes on him. "I don't take orders—"

Burke marched right up to her. "You're going with me and that's that."

Storm took a step away from him. "We'll discuss this at another time." She turned and walked away.

"Put it off all you like, Storm," Burke called out.

"It doesn't change the fact that you're going with me to America."

They packed up and were soon on their way home. Storm didn't want to waste a minute of their precious time. Philip remained behind as a contact for Lady Alaina. He would bring them news when it became available and he would inform her of when to be ready to join Cullen.

They would have little time once they returned to camp. It would take three days to get to Weighton, and with only two weeks left, that didn't give them much time to plan and execute a solid rescue.

Time was running out fast for everyone, and Storm wasn't sure if success was possible. That didn't, however, prevent her from trying. The journey home was spent wisely. She formulated a plan in her head, making changes, perfecting it, and praying it would succeed.

She kept Burke out of her head as much as possible—not that he didn't force his way in. She was reminded of his intentions every time she caught sight of his determination. It was etched in every line and curve of his rugged face and in the glint of his dark eyes.

Of course, when her glance happened to stray to his lips, that was an altogether different thought. She would lick her own lips and be reminded of his taste, so pungent and powerful. His kisses never failed to awaken her passion. Even the mere thought of them could heat her desire, and it took much willpower to refocus her thoughts.

"Lick your lips one more time," Burke warned

from alongside her, "and you'll find yourself being dragged off into the bushes for a rousing bout of lovemaking."

"Promises, promises," she teased.

"Don't challenge me, Storm," he cautioned, his dark eyes stirring with repressed passion.

Her own urges stirred like molten heat, and for a moment she was tempted to take his challenge. How much time was really left to them? Shouldn't she make the most of the time left to her? Shouldn't she taste his love as many times as possible before he bid her good-bye?

His love.

Wasn't that what she would miss? His love, being loved, having someone to love?

"I won't," she said sadly and walked ahead of him.

He caught up with her and kept pace alongside her. "But you want to."

"I won't deny that I do. It's just not the time or place."

"Making love requires no specific time or place."

She smiled softly, recalling the many times they had made love, and that none had been planned or expected. They made love simply because they felt the need and the desire to mate.

"You agree," he said with his own smile.

"How can I not?" she asked, her smile spreading. "You have left me with wonderful memories."

Burke reached for her hand and took firm hold. "We have many more memories to make together."

She wished that were so. She wished things were

different and that she could love this man freely, without any complications. Unfortunately, that wasn't so, and she could not continue to think on such a dream. She had to let go.

Malcolm suddenly joined them and signaled Storm that someone approached.

Everyone dispersed in directions away from the approaching footfalls. Burke naturally went with her, since he rarely left her side whenever they were on a mission. It was as if he had proclaimed himself her chief protector.

No one seemed to mind, but then her men knew that if their leader had not wanted the American near her, she would have seen to it.

She and Burke took cover behind the trunk of a giant spruce. It was wide enough to shield them both, and the bushes that grew around it offered further concealment.

Malcolm and Angus had hurriedly climbed two big spruces and perched on branches in order to see who trailed them.

Both men signaled Storm that they had yet to determine who approached, so silence reigned, as did patience.

Malcolm was the first to signal that all was well, and soon they all gathered around once again.

"It's Philip," Malcolm said.

"He has Lady Alaina with him," Angus added.

Gooseflesh rushed over Storm. Something had to have happened for her to come this distance with Philip. And it couldn't be good.

It took only a few moments for Philip and Lady

Alaina to finally appear. She seemed a bit out of breath, and Philip was quick to help her sit on a fallen log, while Malcolm graciously offered her water from the pouch he carried.

Lady Alaina accepted it gratefully and took a few minutes to collect herself.

"Lady Alaina has learned vital information concerning Burke's agreement," Philip offered as an explanation.

"So soon?" Burke asked, surprised.

Lady Alaina nodded, then took another swallow of water.

"Tell us, Philip," Storm said.

"Lady Alaina did not share the news with me. She insisted that I bring her directly to Burke."

Lady Alaina finally regained her composure. "I had to speak with you myself, Mr. Longton."

"Please call me Burke. After all, you will soon be my sister-in-law."

Lady Alaina pressed both hands to her chest. "How I wish that were true. Unfortunately, my father intends to see Cullen and you dead."

"He never planned to honor our agreement?" Burke asked.

Lady Alaina shook her head. "After you left I made certain to remain near my father, though he didn't know I lurked about. I learned when I was very young to become invisible to my father while watching his every move. It kept me safe."

She paused a moment and stared at Storm. "I know you and yet . . ."

"My wife," Burke reminded.

Lady Alaina shook her head. "No, you're the infamous Storm. If I remember correctly, my father was instrumental in starting your career."

"He was," Storm said and, wanting to spare the woman any more obvious discomfort, added, "but it is the news you have we wish to hear."

Lady Alaina nodded. "Yes. Yes, it is important. My father has no intentions of releasing Cullen and no intentions of giving up the gold mine you offer him. He intends for neither of you to live."

Chapter 33

Burke maintained his composure though he would have much preferred to repeatedly punch something. He was a fool for even thinking the earl would play fair. Now what choice was left to him?

"That leaves us only one choice," Storm said.

"Absolutely not. You're not going into Weighton," Burke said sternly, and the other men nodded in agreement.

Lady Alaina hurried to Storm's side, grabbing hold of her hand. "Do you think it could work? Do you think you can really rescue Cullen?"

"I believe that we'd have a fair chance with someone on the inside. Once contact could be made with Cullen, there'd be two who could work together on the escape. The others could secure the outside area so that when we made our break, there'd be no one to stop us."

"It sounds as if it could work," Lady Alaina said hopefully.

"It's too much of a risk," Burke said, refusing to even give the idea thought and yet knowing that there was no other choice. But how could he condone sending the woman he loved into harm's way?

"It may be the only way," Tanin agreed reluctantly.

"Finally, someone who realizes the dire straits of our situation," Storm said.

"Sending you into Weighton could mean sending you to your death," Burke said angrily. He couldn't help it. He was so frustrated with the circumstances. He couldn't see how he would find the strength to stand by and let Storm be captured and dragged off to prison. He'd want to kill any man who dared lay a hand on her.

"Your brother faces certain death if we don't. At least with me going in he has a chance, which is more than he has now."

Reason certainly was her forte, not that the plan made sense, or made it any easier for him.

Burke suddenly got an idea. "There's no need for you to go into Weighton. I'll be going in to ransom my brother and that will put me right where I need to be to help expedite the escape."

Lady Alaina shook her head. "No, my father does not plan for you to ever reach Weighton. He actually took great pleasure in knowing he'd prevent a re-union between you and Cullen."

"That's it. I go in," Storm said emphatically.

"What can I do to help?" Lady Alaina asked eagerly.

Burke stood silent, though he felt the urge to shout out his anger. He didn't want this. He didn't want to chance losing the woman he loved to save his brother, and yet he knew without a doubt that Storm would advise him that it wasn't his choice. It was hers.

"Keep listening," Storm advised. "Let us know of anything you think is of importance. Philip will remain nearby and stay in contact with you. He will also let you know when it is time to join us. You need to make certain your father believes that you are going away to visit friends or something so that he does not become suspicious."

"I will make a plausible excuse that he will not doubt since he keeps a watchful eye on me, which is why I must return now before he suspects something. Good luck to you all," Lady Alaina said and walked over to Burke. "I cannot wait to see the look on Cullen's face when he lays eyes on his brother for the first time."

"I daresay the look in his eyes when he knows that you will be going to America with him will far exceed it."

She smiled and kissed his cheek. "Thank you. Thank you for a chance at happiness."

Once Philip and Alaina were gone, the group continued discussing the plan in relative silence until near dusk, when they stopped for the night. It wasn't until later, when all but Burke and Storm were asleep, she taking the first guard as usual, that Burke got a chance alone with her.

"You know I don't like this," he said, sitting beside her on a slight rise that allowed a good view of the forest from various angles.

"I know," Storm said, and slipped her arm around his.

He asked a question he knew the answer to, but he had to voice his concern. "Tell me why I should let you do this."

"You don't have a choice."

"What if I said I love you too much to chance losing you?"

She hesitated, then answered. "I would think I am lucky to have someone who loves me so much, but it would change nothing."

He took strong hold of her hand. "I will be relieved when this is over and we are sailing home to America."

Storm sighed. "Burke, you know I cannot go with you."

He would settle this dilemma once and for all. Actually, she had settled it once she had made the choice to go into the prison to free Cullen. "Do you love me?"

She glanced at him with the most serene blue eyes he had ever seen, and he knew then and there just how much she loved him, though he wished to hear the words.

"I love you very much, Mr. Longton."

He smiled. "Then it is settled."

"Burke, please understand my—"

"No," he snapped. "You understand that now you have no choice in the matter as I have no choice in deciding if you go into Weighton or not."

"What do you mean?" Storm asked confused.

"You are the infamous outlaw Storm. What do you think will happen once you pull off a successful escape from Weighton? Not only will you have doubled the earl's wrath, you will most likely have incurred the king's wrath, and the bounty on your head will surely double, possibly triple. There will be no safe place for you to hide. You will have no choice but to leave Scotland. You sealed your fate, my love, once you made the decision to enter Weighton."

Her silence told him that she weighed the impact of his words and knew them to be the truth.

"In my zeal to free your brother, I had not given the consequences thought. You are right. I will be hunted viciously, as will anyone associated with me. No place will be safe."

"Give it thought now," he said. "And while you're thinking on that, think on this." He brought her hand to his mouth for a kiss. "Storm, will you do me the great honor of becoming my wife?"

She stared at him.

"The choice is yours. I do not want you to feel that you must marry me in order to go to America. If you don't wish to marry me, I will see you safely to America and I will provide for you until you get on your own feet. However, you do love me, so it would seem reasonable that you would want to marry me. Would you? Marry me, that is."

She smiled.

"A smile is a good sign. Let me remind you again of how very wealthy I am, how much you adore my sense of humor and how deeply I am in love with you."

Her smile grew. "You forgot your leadership qualities."

"See what a good catch I am." He grinned.

"There is only one thing that matters," she said softly.

"What is that?" he asked and leaned his face down near hers.

"Love, that you love me and I love you. Nothing, absolutely nothing else matters. Foolishly, I thought it did." She shook her head. "I thought rescuing people was my fate, but I realize it's not forever. Life changes. It always does whether we're ready for it or not. I admit I'm not ready. I don't believe I ever would be, but it looks like fate has decided that my life is about to change." She kissed him.

The kiss was gentle and Burke favored it for it sealed their future, their fate.

She rested her cheek against his. "I can't believe I am agreeing to this. What will happen to my men, my group of people who depend on me? There's so much to consider. Is this really a wise choice?"

"I will offer passage to America for all those who choose to go, and for those who do not, I will give them sufficient coin to go elsewhere."

"You would do that?"

"I would do that for you, for I know you would worry over their fate and I want you to leave

Scotland free of worry for those who choose to remain behind."

She shivered, and he took her in his arms.

"This has been the only home I've known. I had never thought to leave it. It will not be easy."

"There is nothing left for you here. We will build a new life together in America and you will have friends there to share it with. I would bet that most all of your men and people would go with you to America. In a way, you will be taking part of Scotland with you. I have no doubt Tanin would go."

"I agree," Storm said, snuggling against him. "I know he and Ellie yearn for a real home, land to work, children to raise, and of course Janelle would go with them. They are her only family."

"All of your group is family, and I doubt if any want to be left behind."

Storm poked his chest. "I never intended to fall in love with you."

"You couldn't help yourself. I'm just too wonderful."

She laughed. "I will not lack laughter being married to you."

He took hold of her hand and kissed it. "You will never lack love, for I will love you always."

"You are generous with people and you are generous with your love. I truly am a lucky woman."

"I keep telling you that."

She giggled and poked him with her free hand. "Modest you are not."

"No, I am not," he said and took hold of her other

hand, holding them both together. "You can always count on me speaking the truth, always count on me admiring you, respecting you, and loving you. And always, always being there for you, no matter the circumstances." He gave her shoulder a gentle shove with his. "We can always discuss your faults in private."

She laughed again. "What of your faults?"

"It's rare that I'm wrong."

She continued laughing as she pulled her hands free of his and slipped them around his neck.

Burke wrapped his arms around her, kissing her with an intense passion that let her know just how very much he loved her, wanted her, ached for her.

"I wish we were in my cabin on my ship sailing home," he whispered in her ear.

"We will be soon enough."

He brushed his lips faintly across hers. "You don't know how relieved I am to hear you say that. I didn't know how I was going to convince you. I only knew that I couldn't—wouldn't—leave Scotland without you."

"I seemed to have made it easy for you."

He nodded. "You certainly have. You've finally admitted you love me. That was all I needed to hear."

"And if I hadn't?"

He laughed solid and strong. "I knew you loved me. I was just waiting for you to realize it."

"You are incorrigible."

"But I'm right."

"That's right, you're rarely wrong," she said teasingly.

He patted her hand. "You know your future husband already."

"Do you know your future wife?" she challenged.

"I know her very well," he murmured and nuzzled her neck.

She giggled softly and scrunched her neck. "Tell me what you know."

"She is an extraordinarily brave warrior." He nibbled at her ear. "A skilled swordsman." He tickled her neck with his lips. "A woman of deep conviction." He brushed his lips along her warm cheek. "A woman of honor." He kissed her lips lightly. "A beautiful, loving woman whom I shall cherish forever."

A tear lingered in the corner of her eye and Burke caught it on his finger.

"I had hoped for a smile, not tears."

She smiled while another tear slipped out. "I have never heard love spoken of so eloquently."

"I promise you will hear it often from me. Not a day will go by that I won't express how I feel about you or show you. Who knows, you may even grow tired of hearing it."

"Never," she said. "Never will I grow tired of hearing it."

He rested his forehead on hers. "How lucky I am to have found you. I never would have suspected from our first meeting that a pint-sized woman dressed as a lad and wielding a sword would work her way into my heart. I do believe fate had a heavy hand in it."

"It had to have been fate for I would never have thought that I could fall in love with a brash, stubborn American, let alone marry him. And go to America?" She shook her head. "That was simply impossible and it was the furthest thought from my mind."

"I warned you about fate," Burke reminded with a smile.

"I stubbornly refused to listen, but what difference does it make," she said with a shrug. "Fate won out as you warned me it would. Let us hope fate once again is on our side when we enter Weighton prison."

"It has to be," Burke said, drawing her close in his arms. "Fate couldn't possibly bring us together only to tear us apart."

Storm cuddled closer in Burke's arms, and he knew her thoughts, for he was certain they mirrored his. Fate couldn't be that cruel.

This time Burke did not intend to leave anything to fate. This time he would be the one in charge. He would determine the outcome. He would make certain the escape plan was foolproof, that nothing would go wrong, and most importantly, that no harm would come to Storm.

He would do anything to keep her safe.

"You've traveled all the way from America to fulfill your father's dream. Don't let anything stand in the way of freeing your brother," Storm said, her head resting against his chest.

Burke remained silent. He knew what she meant and he refused to acknowledge it. He would not trade her life for Cullen's. He would make certain both she and his brother were freed, if he had to die doing it.

Chapter 34

Camp was a bustle of activity once the news of the rescue plan had spread and the fact that each and every one of them was free to make a choice of going to America to start a new life or remaining behind with funds to help them survive for a while.

Time was of the essence, so it was necessary that everyone make a choice quickly, for soon their home would exist no more. Those going to America would be escorted to Burke's ship to await departure, while those choosing to remain in Scotland would be provided with funds and be on their way.

Storm stared up at the homes they had fashioned in the treetops and the various shelters on the ground that had served them well. She thought of the months of hard work constructing the homes and the camaraderie that had gone into it all. They truly were a family.

By late afternoon, she wasn't surprised to learn that the young ones wished to adventure to America while several of the older people preferred to remain in their homeland. Out of the twenty-five people who comprised the camp, only four had chosen to remain in Scotland.

All her men had chosen to join her in America.

There was joyfulness in the camp that she had never seen or felt, but then there was finally hope, and hope brought joy.

Janelle walked over to her. "Do I interrupt a moment of solitude?"

"A moment of memories," Storm said with a smile, and hooked arms with the older woman to walk.

"I wanted to tell you that I am glad you have finally allowed yourself to love again. It is long past time for you to release your hurt and pain and begin to live, and to allow the others to live," Janelle said.

Storm stopped and looked at her strangely. "Allow the others to live?"

"No one here would have ever deserted you even if they grew tired of such a confining life. They are all loyal to you and would have it no other way."

"Do you tell me some wished to leave?"

Janelle patted her arm. "Weren't there times you wished to leave?"

Ellie's anxious call for help had Janelle running off but not before saying, "Ellie is so excited about a chance for a new life for her and Tanin. Thank you for being unselfish and allowing my son, his wife, me, and all the others to take this chance."

Storm stood staring after her. She had never

considered how the others had felt. She assumed this life had been their lot, but had it? Had she pursued it with a vengeance without thought of others? Had she carried her revenge beyond the necessary?

"What's wrong?"

Storm went easily into Burke's arms as he spun her gently around and embraced her as if she had been gone too long from his arms.

"I have been wrong," she said softly.

"Wait," he said and paused. "I want to savor this moment, for I doubt I will hear those words from your lips again."

Storm gave a short laugh and shook her head. "Incorrigible."

"No, I'm honest," he whispered and kissed her cheek. "Now tell me what you were wrong about."

She realized at that moment just how much she loved her future husband. He had caused her to laugh and feel at ease before addressing her problem. Her feelings were of the utmost importance to him, and what a wonderful thought that was.

"I was wrong to think that my life consisted only of rescuing people. There comes a time to live life as these people have proven, embracing the opportunity with joy and eagerness and not a bit of regret."

"Sometimes it takes others to open our eyes for us," Burke said.

"I certainly had blinders on. I not only prevented myself from living, but others as well."

"You did what you believed necessary. One last rescue and it will no longer be necessary. Life changes."

She smiled at him and placed her small, cool hand to his warm cheek. He felt so very good, so solid, and so strong, and he belonged to her. The feeling overwhelmed her and she nearly shivered. She moved closer against him, not wanting to think of the last rescue, not wanting to believe that it could fail and that she could lose everything. Just as she had nearly lost him because she was too stubborn to see that there was more to life than only thinking of herself and revenge.

"I will be glad when it is over," she said.

He hugged her close. "I won't let anything happen to you."

"I know, but there will be two days I will be a prisoner before the rescue can be attempted."

"Remember what we discussed," Burke said, gently pushing a strand of dark hair away from her eye with his finger. "If you cannot locate Cullen within that time you will leave on your own."

"So you have reminded me several times," Storm said, stepping away from him.

"Which means you have no intention of following my orders."

"This is my rescue plan, therefore my decisions rule," she said firmly.

"Tanin warned that they might not wait to torture you. If that is so, you will have no chance to find Cullen, you will be too busy suffering."

Storm began to pace in front of him. They had gone over this repeatedly, and repeatedly Burke had protested her remaining in the prison more than a few hours. It had taken much discussion among the men to convince him that wouldn't work. It was two days or nothing.

"It is rare that torture is immediate. It is much preferred that the prisoners be left in their cells for a few days to grow fearful of what awaits them," Storm said.

"You can't be sure of that," Burke protested. "Having the infamous Storm in their clutches might give them itchy fingers and have them eager to begin torturing you immediately."

"That's not likely, but it is a chance I must take."

"I don't like it and I'm going to want to kill the man who dares make you suffer," he snarled.

She stopped pacing and shook a finger at him. "You are not to enter the prison. You will stick to our plan."

"As long as you come out of the prison at the agreed-upon time. Otherwise I go in."

"Don't make me worry about you," she warned. The idea that he would endanger his life by charging into a fortified fortress upset her beyond reason.

"You worry about me?" he asked incredulously and shook his head before reaching out and grabbing hold of her. "How do you think I'm going to be able to keep hold of my sanity while you're in Weighton? I'll constantly fear that you're suffering horrible torture while I sit by and do nothing. I don't know how I will do it."

"Our plan is a good one and it will work if we all work together as agreed," she said. She understood his concern, for she would feel the same. She would find it impossible to sit idly by while Burke attempted such a feat.

"It's easy for you to say. You're not the one waiting. You're the one doing something. I still wish there was another way."

"We either go in and get your brother out or he dies," Storm said, not meaning to sound harsh but reminding him what he already knew. This was their only chance.

Burke wrapped her in his arms, and she knew by the way he held her he feared ever letting her go. His arms were strong around her, his muscles taut and his heartbeat fast.

"Two days and we set you up for capture," he whispered in her ear. "Those two days are mine."

How she wanted that to be so.

"There is much to do before we leave—"

"The days will be busy enough, but the nights belong to us." He squeezed her tightly. "I will have it no other way."

She wouldn't either. If their plan should falter, at least she would have this time with him to always remember and to keep her strong.

"Neither will I," she murmured.

They hugged, holding on tightly to each other, both afraid, both determined to protect the other, and both knowing they'd give their life if necessary to save the other.

Storm sat by the campfire wrapped in a wool blanket, enjoying the broth Janelle had prepared. She hugged the warm tankard in her hands and sipped at the steaming liquid, grateful for its warmth.

The chill of winter reminded her that autumn was near to ending. A good portion of the day had been spent on the rescue plans, while other plans were made to get those going to America to the ship.

She finally had a chance to sit and take a breath and not think. She didn't want to think anymore tonight. Burke was busy with Malcolm and Angus trying to determine what weapons would best serve their purpose.

Then soon, very soon, she and Burke would be alone for the night, and the thought tingled her skin, running gooseflesh over it.

"Mind if I join you?" Tanin asked.

She patted the ground beside her. "Have a seat."

He plopped down beside her.

"I thought you and Ellie were busy gathering your belongings. From what Janelle told me, Ellie is thrilled to be going to America."

"Truth be told, Storm, so am I."

"Don't sound so guilty," she said. "It is I who should feel guilty for not considering that you and Ellie might want more than a life of crime."

"It was forced on us."

"But we didn't need to pursue it. We could have stopped along the way and attempted to live an ordinary life. I unfortunately never gave it a thought. I believed myself a savior—"

"You are," Tanin argued.

"For a few perhaps, but in the end what did I really accomplish? Landlords continue to treat their tenants badly. There is no justice for the poor and the starving, and few if any truly care. Better that I had lived a normal life and fought to improve conditions than fight the law. Or perhaps I should have been adventurous and left Scotland for distant shores."

"This is your home."

Storm shook her head. "I believed it was, but really my home is with the man I love, just like you and Ellie. Your love is your home and always will be."

Tanin grinned. "You speak of love as one who is in love."

She laughed and hugged the tankard more tightly in her hands. "It took a stubborn American to convince a stubborn Scotswoman that she could love again."

"Burke is good for you," Tanin said with a nod.

"When did you determine that?"

"From the very first day he argued with you. I knew he was a man you would respect and admire and one who would be able to penetrate the shield you kept so firm around your heart."

"He certainly did that."

"You let him, otherwise he would have never succeeded," Tanin said. "You wanted to love him as much as he wanted to love you."

Had she wanted that from the beginning? Had she been searching for someone to challenge her stubbornness? Her pain? Her hurt? And prove that she could truly love again?

"I am glad we rescued the American that fateful day, for he now rescues us."

"He certainly does," Storm agreed with a smile.

Tanin left Storm with her thoughts, and it didn't take long before various people joined her for a few moments to express their appreciation for all she had done for them and the opportunity that they had been given.

By the time Burke joined her she had tears in her eyes.

He reached down and eased her to her feet.

"Your people are grateful," he said.

"It is you they should be grateful to."

He slipped his arm around her slim waist, and they walked from the campfire. "Not really. If it wasn't for your courage and persistence none of this would have been possible. It is because of you that they have a chance at a new life."

"I refuse to take all the credit."

"Too bad, it's yours," he teased and hurried her along. "But if you feel you owe me something, then I suggest—" He leaned down and nuzzled her neck.

"How romantic." She giggled and scrunched her neck, trying to prevent his sensual tickles.

"You want romance?" he whispered, and suddenly scooped her up, flinging her over his shoulder. He grabbed hold of the rope and they were up to the tree house before Storm could protest.

She sighed and rested her head on his chest while he carried her into her small quarters. Then slowly he began to undress her piece by piece while gently kissing every exposed part of her.

Her passion lit like an ignited flame, bursting

with a quivering heat. She melted under his kisses, his touches, and was aching with the want of him by the time he stripped naked and took her to bed.

"Lord, I'd love to take my time with you but I want you so badly I don't think I can wait."

"I feel the same," she urged, her hands reaching down to feel his readiness.

He groaned. "Damn, but I love when you touch me."

"I love the feel of you, especially inside me."

He took her lips in a frantic kiss before saying, "Then let me give you what you love."

She grabbed hold of his arms, strong and taut as he eased himself inside her slowly and gently, until she swung her hips up and took him in her with a solid push.

They both groaned and set a rhythm that had the bed rocking, their hearts pounding, and their bodies sweating.

Afterward they lay beside each other, hands clasped, while their breathing eased and their satisfied bodies completely relaxed.

"Promise me you'll take no unnecessary risks," Burke said softly.

Strange that he should say that since she was thinking the same herself. This would be one rescue mission that she wanted desperately to survive. The others never mattered to her, but then she didn't have anything to live for. Now she did.

Now she had Burke.

"I promise," she said, and meant it with all her heart.

"I don't know what I would do if I lost you."

The tremor in his voice told her just how sincere he was, and it touched her heart and quivered her stomach. Lord, but she wanted a chance at a life with this man.

"I feel the same about you. I never believed I could feel that way again; perhaps I feared feeling that way again. Now, however, I'm glad I have you to love. I forgot how truly wonderful loving and being loved feels."

He leaned on his side and ran his finger gently over her lips. "I want you to keep my love strong in your heart while on this mission. Know I am with you at all times and know I will not let anything happen to you."

Storm kissed his finger and attempted to ease his concern and possibly her own. "My stubbornness will not allow me to remain captured."

"And my stubbornness will make certain that you return to America with me."

"Which has been your plan from the beginning, to take me to America," she accused teasingly.

He kissed her softly and grinned. "And my plans always succeed."

Storm silently prayed it would be so. It had to be so. She loved him too much to lose him.

Chapter 35

Burke didn't want to let Storm out of his sight but he knew that in a few minutes she would walk off and be captured.

It had all been planned. William had scouted an area near Weighton where Storm, Tanin, and Angus would be spotted. While the two men would be able to escape, Storm would be imprisoned. Burke and her men would wait in an area where they could remain undetected until the time came to carry out the remaining part of the plan.

They had made certain the capture would take place near Weighton so she would be incarcerated there immediately. News of her capture would spread fast enough, which was why two days was the maximum time she could remain behind the prison walls. After that, there was no telling what orders would be given and what fate she would meet.

"Almost time," Tanin informed Storm and walked away, leaving the couple alone.

Burke tugged her stocking cap down on her head. "You have the knife I fashioned for you tucked in your boot?"

"Yes. I don't think anyone will find it between the strips of leather. It is concealed quite well."

He grabbed hold of her. "I hate sending you off like this."

She placed a gentle hand on his arm. "I know, but soon I will return with your brother and we will all set sail safely for America."

"Promise," he urged. "Promise me you'll be careful and take no chances."

"I have promised you time and again, but I will promise you this one last time," she said quietly and squeezed his arm. "I promise you I will be careful, and I promise you I will return safely."

He kissed her hard and long, fearful that it might be their last kiss.

Their hands held tight for a moment and then drifted reluctantly apart, and she walked away from him, taking one last glance back before the dense woods swallowed her from his view.

He continued to stare at the trees and bushes, thinking for a split second that he should go after her and stop this madness. But then he would insult her with his lack of confidence in her.

He had thought about simply sailing off to America with her and leaving his brother behind. It wasn't something he could do. He had promised his father, and he could not break that promise. Besides,

Cullen was his brother, and he could never leave him to die. He was also reminded of the look of love in Lady Alaina's eyes when she spoke of his brother. They loved as strongly as Storm and he.

He could not desert them. It would be like failing Storm and himself.

There was no easy choice in this matter and little time to make one. Once his attempt failed, there was no other option left to him, though he tormented his brain trying to find one.

Time had run out, and now he had until tomorrow evening to wait and pray that Storm and his brother made it out of Weighton alive.

Storm ached from the punches and kicks the guards had taken delight in delivering to her. Once they had discovered who she was they had pranced and strutted like braggarts, claiming they had captured the uncatchable Storm.

What they hadn't realized was that the whole time they had been praising themselves they had paid little attention to the way she had watched every twist and turn and noticed every guard post and key hook along the way to her cell.

She now had a good notion of how to make her escape and how many guards would stand in her way, not to mention which ones she felt wouldn't present much of a problem.

Burke had entered her mind a few times during capture, but she had chased him away. She'd had to; she couldn't allow her thoughts to be diverted at such an important time. Her only concern now was to find Cullen and somehow manage to get them out of there by tomorrow night.

The buffoons who had captured her never bothered to search her boot for weapons. They were satisfied as well as surprised by the sizable sword she carried, and assumed it was her only weapon.

She now sat chained to a wall in a cell that held another prisoner who was not Cullen. He was older, thin, and white-haired.

"The angel's wings have been clipped."

Storm looked over at the man, who could barely lift his head. "What did you say?"

"You're the angel who rescues prisoners. You must be, for only the infamous angel would be brought to the likes of Weighton. Who have you come to rescue?"

Here was her chance. "Cullen. I look for a man named Cullen."

The man managed to keep his head up straight. "If I tell you where this man is, will you take me with you?"

He looked as if he could barely stand on his own, and Storm knew then and there she would not see him die in prison.

"I give you my word." He smiled, though Storm saw that it pained him to do so.

"The word of an angel is a good thing." He coughed, and again pain was visible on his thin face. "You will find Cullen in the torture chamber. The guards seem to delight in punishing the man."

She sighed and shook her head.

"You have no choice?" the man asked.

She knew what he meant. In order for her to free Cullen, she would have to be sent to the torture chamber. By morning at the latest, though tonight might be better, but then she took the chance of being tortured to the point of being useless.

"They like to torture at night," the man advised. "It would be best if you waited to be sent there tomorrow."

"Tomorrow night is the escape."

"I will be ready."

She laughed along with the man, since how ready could he be?

"When you free me, I will walk on my own. I give you my word," the man assured her.

"Do not worry. Regardless of whether you can walk or not, you will come with Cullen and me. I will not leave you behind."

"Bless you," he said, and Storm caught the glisten of a tear in his eye.

She had a decision to make. Did she take a chance and be sent to the torture chamber tonight, giving her time to see to Cullen's condition and to determine their escape? Or would tomorrow provide her with enough time?

"Don't go tonight," the man cautioned. "Anger them tomorrow and they will take you and leave you there to think about your fate. It will give you the time you need and spare you the torture."

"You are wise in their ways."

"I have been here many months. I know their ways and how they think. Many of them like to gather at night to watch the tortures."

"Which leaves the other guard posts empty," she said, happy to learn that bit of information.

"The guards believe themselves safe since there are many guards that patrol the outside."

"I need not worry about the outside."

He nodded. "You have help."

"Plenty of it once we leave here," she assured him.

"Then it's up to you, me, and that Cullen fellow."

The night proved difficult for Storm. Sleep eluded her, her thoughts on Burke and her aches painful, not to mention that the guards took great delight in coming into the cell throughout the night to deliver a few more blows to her body.

She wasn't sure when morning came since the cell had no window, so there was perpetual darkness, but her fellow inmate alerted her to sunrise.

"It is the workings of the prison that keeps me informed of time. Wait a few hours and cause a commotion that will irritate them. They will remove you fast enough."

"How do I determine nightfall?" she asked.

"The guards gather at sunset to fill themselves with food and drink before torture."

Storm nodded. "I will return for you."

He nodded. "Be careful. You are a wee wisp of a thing."

"An observation that usually proves fatal to many," she informed him with a smile and began to make a commotion.

It was spitting at the guards and calling them cowards that got her yanked from the cell, but not before she sent the white-haired man a wink.

349

The revolting smell in the torture chamber nearly had her heaving. She didn't want to think of the many things that produced such a repugnant odor or that she could very well be the cause of one of the odors if she remained too long.

Luck was on her side when the guards placed her in a cage that hung from a rafter in the ceiling.

"Good place for you to watch the show tonight and know you'll be next," one guard jeered.

She spit at him again, and he gave the cage a whack with a heavy stick and sent it swirling around and around and around.

The two guards laughed as they left the chamber.

Storm held firm to the bars of the cage until it finally slowed. She had to focus her eyes since the spinning in her head had yet to stop. When she was finally able to see clearly she looked around the room.

She cringed at the various torture devices—metal pinchers, a stretching rack, prodding irons set hot with fire from the cauldron hanging over flames, and others whose uses eluded her. She refused to linger too long on them. Just the idea of what pain they could cause made her wince. She finally spotted a man chained to the wall, his head hanging down to his chest and his body slumped. He wore only a plaid kilt too soiled to determine the colors. He had long dark hair that was matted with blood.

That he had suffered endlessly was obvious.

"Cullen," she called out, having heard the guards' footsteps fade in the distance and feeling safe that no one would hear her.

The man didn't move.

"Cullen," she said more strongly.

He lifted his head, though barely, before it sagged again.

Storm knew what would get his attention. "Cullen, Alaina sent me to free you."

His head shot up and she winced. One eye was almost swollen shut, and dried blood caked at the corner of his swollen lip.

"Alaina?" he asked, looking around.

"Over here," she said, working to slip the knife out of her boot and get started on the lock.

Cullen looked about until he finally saw Storm. "Who are you?"

"A friend of Alaina. She waits for you near St. Andrew where a ship will take you both to America."

"How can this be so?"

The lock was easy, and before she knew it, she was free and standing beside Cullen. Looking past his bruises, she could see the resemblance to Burke. She wished there was time to speak with him, but she had to make the escape plan clear. Between the two of them, they could incapacitate the men and make a swift departure.

"Your brother has come for you."

"Brother?"

"There is no time to explain about your brother. Just rest assured you have one. This is what we must do," she said, and outlined her plan of escape. "Are you strong enough?"

He looked her up and down. "Are you?"

She smiled. "You're just like your brother."

"We shall see," he said skeptically. "Tell me of Alaina. Is she well?"

"She waits impatiently for you."

"As I do for her." He shook his head. "I do not see how you will be able to get the keys from the guard. You are but a wee thing."

She grinned. "I've done this before. Trust me."

Less than an hour later Cullen was shaking his head while chaining the gagged guards to the wall. "I can't believe you overpowered him."

"Believe it, and know we have little time to get out of here."

His movement was remarkably agile for a man who had suffered such torture, but then Storm had seen men in worse condition respond with strength. The promise of freedom could give the weakest man courage.

It didn't take long to free the older man, and though he stumbled, he made his way along with them.

Cullen saw to two other guards and Storm took care of another one herself. They were almost home free. Another twist, one more turn, and they would be out of the prison where Burke and her men waited to help them.

The older man faltered, and Cullen was quick to support him and keep him moving. Storm followed behind, ever ready for the unexpected.

Suddenly a guard came out of nowhere, charging at them.

"Get out of here," she yelled at Cullen. "I'll be right behind you."

He nodded and took off.

* * *

Burke and Tanin stood behind the open door, waiting.

"They should have been here by now," Burke said, his fear near to bursting.

"Give her time. Storm knows what she's doing and we have time yet," Tanin said.

Clouds scurried across the night sky as if running away from something just as Storm was surely doing. He couldn't help but worry that the plan had failed and she was now being tortured.

A shuffle of footsteps interrupted his worries, and he and Tanin braced for attack.

Cullen flew out the door and looked around.

Burke and Tanin were on him in a second.

"You must be my brother," Cullen said, shoving the older man at Burke. "We'll talk later. I need to go back and rescue the woman that came for me."

Burke handed the old man off to Tanin and grabbed Cullen's arm. "I'll get her."

"Not without me. I owe her," Cullen said, and charged back into the prison.

Chapter 36

Storm felt her life slipping away. The guard, even though he had suffered a knife wound, had overcome her and now held her up by the neck, braced against the cold stone wall. Dampness from the stone seeped into her garments, sticking them to her body while she labored for breath and knew that death was near.

Could this be her end? By a simple squeeze of a hand? Her vision blurred, and then she thought of Burke and how he waited just a short distance away. He had promised he would keep her safe. He would come for her. He would save her.

He would be her avenging angel as she had been for so many.

He would not fail her.

She only needed to survive until then.

She found her last ounce of strength and struggled

with the man, beating at his neck. His fingers faltered just enough for her to catch a much-needed breath. Then his meaty hand closed around her slender neck once again.

She pummeled him with her small fists and lashed out with her feet, delivering blow after blow to every part of his body she could reach.

She was feeling faint, feeling life slipping away again, and all she could think about was Burke. If she could have spoken, she would have screamed his name.

Instead, she let loose in her head, hoping somehow Burke would hear her.

Burke.

"Not that way," Burke said, Cullen in the lead.

"Are you sure?" his brother asked, stopping short.

"Absolutely." Burke charged to his right with a force that propelled him like a battling ram. He could almost hear Storm calling out to him.

Over and over and over in his head, he heard her frantic calls and he was desperate to reach her.

He turned the corner with Cullen on his heels, and what he saw turned his worry to rage. He charged at the man who dared to put his hands on the woman he loved.

His fist connected with the man's lower back and took him down in one blow. To make certain he stayed there, he delivered several more and then hurried to scoop up Storm.

She coughed and choked. "Out of here."

"You can barely speak and still you give orders," Burke said, hurrying along the corridor and up the steps with her in his arms, followed by a chuckling Cullen.

"Now I understand her reputation," Cullen said.

"You don't know the half of it," Burke said with pride and hurried out into the night where Malcolm and Tanin waited for them.

There was no time to stop and discuss the particulars of the escape. Time was of the essence. They needed to get as far away from the prison as possible. Once the escape was discovered, soldiers would cover the land like locusts. There would be no safe place to hide.

Burke refused to put Storm down. He kept her firm in his arms and carried her without difficulty. There was no way he would chance losing her again. It would take nearly a full day to reach the ship, and then under cover of the night, they would sail away and finally—finally be safe.

"I can walk," Storm argued.

"Your neck is bruised."

"My feet are fine."

"Perhaps, but I feel safer with you in my arms," Burke said adamantly.

"You need to speak with your brother," she urged.

"It can wait until we reach the ship."

"No, it can't. You have waited a long time for this moment. Talk with him. I can walk on my own."

"I almost lost you," he growled beneath his breath.

"I, however, had no doubt you would rescue me. I called out for you and you came for me."

Burke near stumbled over his own feet. "I heard you. In my head I heard you."

Storm smiled and pressed her cheek to his, her arms wrapped snugly around his neck. "I knew you would. I knew you would not let me die."

He rubbed his cheek hard against hers. "You frightened the hell out of me."

"It's a good way to keep you on your toes."

Burke laughed. "I see you have adopted my sense of humor."

"It is a part of you I love. Why wouldn't I want to emulate it?"

Burke stole a quick kiss. "Damn, but I love you so very much."

"And I love you just as much, but now you need to see to your brother."

Burke stopped and lowered Storm to her feet. He didn't want to let her go but Storm was right. Not only did he need to speak with Cullen, he was eager to speak with him. He had waited many years for this and it was finally here. "Stay in front of me where I can keep an eye on you."

"Of course," she said with a smile and took off to catch up with Tanin, who led the group.

Burke shook his head.

"I admire that woman," Cullen said, coming up beside him.

"So do I," Burke agreed as they kept pace with each other and the group.

"She says you are my brother and that your ship

waits to take Alaina and me to America with you."

"Storm speaks the truth. We should be meeting up with the others shortly. Alaina is with them."

He heard his brother gasp and felt and understood his relief.

"I never thought this possible," Cullen said. "But then I never thought I had a brother."

"You do," Burke confirmed. "Shall I tell you the story?"

"Please, I am anxious to hear it."

Burke started from the beginning when their father left Scotland, leaving his young son behind with his sister-in-law, the child's only relative since his mother had passed. With no chance of owning land in Scotland, his father had decided to journey to America to build a life for him and his son.

Burke went on to explain how their father had returned, only to discover that his sister-in-law had died, leaving no sign of the child. He spent years searching for Cullen, but was never able to find him.

"Father's heart broke a little more with each unsuccessful trip," Burke said. "He'd leave America with such hope of finding you, but he never did."

"Yet you found me," Cullen said.

"Luck and Storm. Without either of them, I would have never located you. I also had hired men to track you down and one had given me a good place to start. Storm took it from there."

"I don't know what to say," Cullen admitted with a shake of his head.

" 'Hello, brother' would be a start."

Cullen stopped walking and held out his hand. "Thank you, brother. You have saved my life."

Burke reached out and gave Cullen a huge bear hug. "Damn, I've waited a long time to do that."

They were quick to keep going, both realizing the importance of time and both anxious to reach safe port as soon as possible.

Burke continued to tell him about their father and the wealth that awaited him.

"I'm wealthy?" Cullen asked incredulously.

"Extremely," Burke said with a satisfied grin.

"The news just keeps getting better."

Burke explained more about what awaited him in America and then finally asked the question that had haunted him all these years.

"What of your life?"

"Not much to tell," Cullen said. "I remember being passed from family to family until an old man took me in. He was a bow maker and an excellent archer. I lived with him from the time I was ten and he taught me his skills. His home was high in the Highlands, which is why Father probably had difficulty finding me. It's a land unto itself."

"Lady Alaina had mentioned your skills with a bow."

Cullen's face brightened. "How is she?"

"As eager to see you as you are to see her. She really does love you, you know."

Cullen shook his head. "I've wondered time and again how a lady such as herself could love a man like me."

"Why wouldn't she?"

Cullen stared at him as if he were daft. "She is a lady. I am but a peasant."

"Not in America. Besides, you're probably wealthier than her father."

"Truly?" Cullen asked in disbelief.

"Without a doubt. I offered the earl one of our gold mines in exchange for your release."

Cullen shook his head. "One of *our* gold mines?"

"Yes, and the fool thought he'd get the gold mine, you, and me. Now not only does he lose all three but his daughter as well."

"That makes me happy," Cullen said with a grin that turned to a wince.

"That lip looks painful."

"My heart feels too much joy to acknowledge pain."

The brothers smiled and continued walking. There'd be time to talk more of their past, but for now they hurried their steps toward the future.

In an hour's time, they reached the area where Alaina waited along with the others from camp. They would all travel from there to Burke's ship, and by nightfall tomorrow they'd be on board and setting sail.

The problem was, they wouldn't be safe until they were on the ship. Soldiers probably were already beginning to prowl the woods in search of them, and being they had a good head start, they had to keep it that way.

Everyone was advised to keep their voices hushed while Burke and Storm saw to organizing the group in sections and placing one of Storm's men in charge of each section.

"Where's Alaina?" Cullen asked, anxiously searching the sea of faces.

"Can't find her?" Burke asked with a grin.

Cullen gave a frustrated shake of his head, while glancing from person to person until . . .

"That's my Alaina," he said softly when what appeared to be a young lad removed a stocking cap and her long red waves fell free.

He rushed to her side, scooping her up in his arms and hugging her tightly to him. Alaina buried her face in his chest and when she lifted her face, tears stained her cheeks. Cullen kissed them away and they held on to each other as if they never intended to part.

Burke watched them, his smile wide.

"It must feel good to have found your brother and to reunite him with the woman he loves," Storm said, taking Burke's hand.

He grasped on to her. "I only wish my father could be here. He had searched so long and hard for Cullen."

"I think he knew that you would not fail him and died with a peaceful heart."

Burke leaned down and kissed her. "Did I tell you I love you today?"

She nodded. "While you carried me."

"Well, I'm telling you again. I love you."

She poked him. "I think the Longton brothers love—"

"For life," Burke finished, stealing another kiss.

"You mean I'm stuck with you until I die?"

"Longer," he said. "You're never getting rid of me."

She tapped her chin. "Maybe I should reconsider?"

Burke laughed heartily. "The deal is sealed, sweetheart, you're all mine."

"Really?" Storm said and moved to step away from him.

Her hand still in his, he yanked her back to him. "You're mine—" He kissed her forehead. "Mine—" He kissed her nose. "Mine!" He kissed her lips slowly and easily until her arms wrapped around his neck and the kiss turned deep and intoxicating.

"Soldiers have been spotted."

Tanin's warning tore them apart.

"How far?" Storm asked.

"An hour or less. We need to get moving," Tanin advised.

"We'll move out in groups, dividing and meeting up just outside of St. Andrew," Burke instructed.

Cullen and Alaina joined them.

"Once my father learns of the escape, he will send men to St. Andrew to make certain your ship doesn't leave port," Alaina said.

"The earl knows Burke's ship is docked at St. Andrew?" Storm asked.

Alaina nodded. "He questioned me about the American and I answered." She shook her head. "I am sorry. I shouldn't have told him."

"It isn't your fault," Cullen said, holding her close

to him. "Your father has his ways of getting information."

"Our best bet is to get moving and keep moving," Burke advised. "We have to get to my ship. We're going to go in groups."

"Alaina and I will stay with you and Storm," Cullen said.

"Wouldn't have it any other way, brother," Burke said and slapped him on the back. "Let's get going."

They left, spreading out, and kept a hectic pace. They had to make certain to keep the soldiers a good distance away from them. From what Tanin had told Burke there were more than a few soldiers, and that meant it would be more than a mere skirmish.

They would have a battle on their hands, and Burke wouldn't take the chance of possibly losing Storm again. Now there were his brother and Alaina to worry about.

It wasn't difficult for Burke to maneuver in the dark, but he knew the others weren't finding it easy, especially Lady Alaina.

She had slowed them down considerably.

"Go ahead," Cullen said at one point. "We'll catch up."

"No," Burke and Storm had said in unison.

As far as they were both concerned, they all would remain together.

"I'll do better when dawn breaks," Alaina said. "I'll be able to see where I walk then."

Burke smiled. "You're doing fine, don't worry."

His brother, however, sent him a look that he

understood. Daybreak brought light, which meant the group would be more visible, making tracking them easier.

Several hours after sunlight, Cullen informed Burke that they needed to rest.

"Alaina cannot keep up this pace," Cullen said.

"She doesn't have a choice," Storm said, sounding harsh.

"She's not like you," Cullen argued. "Used to endless treks through the woods day or night."

"Storm is right" Alaina said, coming up behind Cullen. "I don't have a choice. Now let's go."

Cullen grinned. "That's my woman." And hurried after her.

They kept going long into the afternoon and Burke was near ready to breathe a sigh of relief. They were getting closer and closer to St. Andrew and his ship. They were going to make it.

The yell pierced the air like a sharp knife and brought everyone to an abrupt halt.

"Malcolm's group," Storm said and drew her sword before charging forward through the woods.

The melee was a clash of swords and fists, and chaos reigned for some time.

Burke had no time to worry about Storm. It seemed he fought off soldier after soldier. Sweat and blood soon tainted the chilled air along with moans of the wounded and dying.

When it finally ended, Burke stood looking around at the carnage, searching and praying that Storm wasn't among the wounded or dead. Relief flooded him when he saw her bending over a body.

It was with a smile that she helped Malcolm up.

She was all right and so was Malcolm.

Burke headed toward her, and her bright smile registered her own relief that he was all right. He, however, didn't like how quickly it had faded, and he halted in his tracks, not wanting to turn around and see what had caused Storm to lose her smile and turn pale white.

He feared it was his brother, Cullen, and he silently prayed and swore and damned the powers that be that they had better not have taken Cullen away from him. He would never forgive them, never forgive himself for not having protected his brother after finally having found him.

Burke gathered his strength and swerved around.

He froze and his heart near stilled.

Cullen knelt on the ground, Alaina in his arms, and blood covering her chest.

Chapter 37

Storm followed Burke to his brother's side. As soon as she got a look at Alaina's wound, she knew death was imminent. She grabbed hold of Burke's arm and felt his muscles tense beneath his shirt and looked at his face.

His pain tore at her heart, and she was reluctant to glance down at Cullen, for she knew his pain would doubly stab at her heart.

Cullen's anguished voice drew her glance to him. "God, Alaina, you should have stayed where I told you."

She tried to shake her head but could only manage to turn it to one side.

"It should have been me. It should have been me," Cullen cried, and as gently as he could slipped his arm beneath her head and leaned down to press his cheek to hers.

Storm gently eased Burke away from the couple, knowing they needed these last moments alone together.

"Don't try to speak," Cullen urged.

"I must." Alaina struggled with her words. "You must listen."

Storm heard no more since she and Burke moved a distance from the couple.

He suddenly grabbed her and wrapped her tightly in his embrace. "God, I'm so grateful you're alive."

Tears quickly stained her cheeks. She not only cried for Cullen's loss but she cried in relief that she and Burke had survived. She knew Cullen's pain, had lived it herself, and she ached for his suffering, but she also rejoiced in good fortune, for in death there was also life.

"We need to get out here," Storm said, shoving her husband away from her and wiping her tears away.

"She's right. More soldiers will be coming," Cullen said.

Burke and Storm turned. Cullen stood, his shirt stained with Alaina's blood and his cheeks stained with the last of his tears.

"We will bury Alaina first," Burke said.

"No!" Cullen near shouted.

Storm looked past him to see Alaina lying on the ground, her arms crossed over her chest as if she lay in peaceful repose. "We can't just leave her."

"That was what she wanted," Cullen said.

Storm knew he presently held himself together with the anger and pain of her death, but soon, very soon, the pain would be beyond bearing and he would break.

"Why?" Burke asked.

Cullen looked to Storm. "You understand, don't you?"

Storm nodded. "Alaina wants her father to see her, to know that it was her choice to join you, to know that she was finally free of him."

"She stays as she is," Cullen said and walked off, not looking back.

They were soon on their way again, the wounded being helped and their pace hurried. They would never withstand another attack. They had to reach St. Andrew by dark and board the ship. It was their only chance.

Cullen remained silent for the remainder of the journey. Storm had cautioned Burke to leave his brother be, that once on the ship he could talk with him, that Cullen would probably want to talk and that Burke should be there when he did.

She told him not to worry about anything else but Cullen. She would see to settling her people. He was not to give them or her a second thought.

He had hugged and kissed her and kept walking, his steps anxious as all the others to reach port and have this done.

The last leg of the journey was the most difficult. Everyone was exhausted and could barely take another step, but they prevailed. It was the promise of freedom and a new life that kept them determined, and with the cover of darkness shielding them little by little, they boarded the ship.

"We'll be setting sail in a few minutes," Burke said.

Storm nodded. "We'll be ready. How is Cullen?"

Burke looked to the railing where his brother stood staring out at the sea. "He wishes to speak with me."

Storm placed a gentle hand on his arm. "Go, he needs you."

Burke leaned down and kissed her softly. "I am so relieved you are here beside me."

She pressed her cheek to his. "So am I."

Storm watched him walk over to his brother and place a comforting hand on his shoulder. Only time would heal his wounds, but having someone there would help him.

Burke wasn't certain what to say to his brother. He knew he would be inconsolable if he had lost Storm. He wasn't even sure if he should mention Alaina. He was at a loss as to how to help his brother.

"You will like America," Burke said, hoping it would help to speak to him of his new home.

"I am not going with you."

Burke's hand slipped off his brother's back. "Of course you are. You can't stay here. The earl's men will find you."

"They will think I sailed with you."

Burke spoke bluntly. "Alaina is gone. There is nothing here for you."

Cullen's knuckles turned white from how hard he grasped hold of the railing. "My son is here."

Burke was struck speechless for a moment. "Your son?"

Cullen nodded slowly and looked at his brother. "Before Alaina died she told me of him."

"But she planned on leaving with you for America."

Cullen shook his head. "No. She thought my new wealth would help us to locate our son. She planned to tell me when we reached the ship. She figured you would agree to help us and supply us with what we needed. Once we found our son we could then join you and Storm in America."

"Why didn't she just bring the child with her?"

"She doesn't know where he is."

Burke shook his head. "How can that be?'

Cullen's hands fisted at his sides. "Her father took the lad from her at birth."

"The bastard," Burke spit out.

"You know I'm going to kill him, don't you?"

"I can stay and help," Burke offered.

"No," Cullen said. "While I appreciate your offer, this is something I must do. Besides, if you stayed Storm would insist on staying with you, and she needs to be taken away from here if she is to be kept safe."

"You understand my apprehension in leaving you behind?"

"I know, but I also know that you above anyone understands why I must do this."

"I do," Burke said. "It is an awful thing for a father to know he has a son out there somewhere but is unable to find him. I will give you all the money you need and any help you want."

"The money will be the greatest help to me. It will buy me information."

"You shall have whatever you need," Burke said adamantly.

Cullen hesitated, then spoke. "I wish there had been time for us to talk more."

"We will," Burke assured him. "There will be time when you return home with your son."

"Home." Cullen shook his head. "I have never truly had a home."

"You do now. It waits for you along with your family."

The brothers hugged and Burke let go of Cullen reluctantly, fearful that he might never see him again.

"Give me your word you will come home," Burke said, holding out his hand to him.

Cullen grasped his hand firmly. "I and my son will come home, this I promise you."

The two men turned at the sound of harried voices.

Burke saw Storm speaking with the white-haired man she had freed from the prison. The older man looked agitated.

"I best see what's going on," Burke said, and Cullen followed him.

"I must leave," the older man said.

"What's the problem?" Burke asked walking up to them.

"I cannot sail to America. I must stay here," the older man said.

371

"I thought you had agreed to go with us?" Burke asked.

"I've changed my mind," the man said. "I want to get off the ship now."

"I'll help him off," Cullen offered and looked to Burke.

Burke understood. Cullen didn't want Storm to know that he wouldn't be sailing with them. She would certainly disagree and then insist on staying to help him, and Cullen was right. Storm needed to get far away from Scotland if she was ever to be safe.

"Let me get some coins for you," Burke offered the man.

"How generous. Thank you," the man said.

"Cullen, come with me," Burke said, and the brothers walked off together.

When they entered the cabin, Burke said, "I want to make certain you have sufficient funds to find your son."

Cullen stared wide-eyed at the coins he handed him.

"Enough?" Burke asked, ready to reach for more.

"I believe this will suffice," Cullen said and tucked the purse in his kilt.

"I also want you to have this," Burke said, slipping their father's ring off his finger and holding it out to Cullen. "It belonged to our father and he had hoped to give it to you."

Cullen looked at it but didn't take it from Burke. "Keep it for now. Give it to me when I join you in America."

Burke realized what his brother was saying without saying it. If by chance he didn't make it to America, Burke would still have their father's ring.

"I'll keep it safe for you," Burke said.

"I'll be looking forward to getting it from you."

The brothers stared for a moment at each other and then left the cabin.

"Hurry, Cullen, we leave soon," Storm said.

"I won't be gone long," Cullen said with a smile, and helped the older man down the gangplank.

"I need help with something," Burke said to Storm, drawing her attention away from Cullen and keeping her busy until the ship had set sail away from the dock.

Burke stood on the deck watching Scotland fade from view when Storm joined him.

"I can't find Cullen," she said, sneaking beneath his arm to snuggle against him.

Burke held her tight, knowing her reaction once he told her about his brother. "He's not coming with us."

"What?" she shouted and tried to slip out of his arms.

He wouldn't have it. He held her firm.

"I can't believe you let him stay behind. Why?"

"He has good reason," Burke said and explained.

A tear trickled down Storm's cheek. "Cullen was right. I would have insisted on remaining behind to help."

"Cullen will come home," Burke said, hugging her close.

"He'd better or we'll be returning to Scotland."

"You'll not be returning to Scotland," Burke insisted.

Storm slipped out of his arms and stood with her hands on her hips. "Is that so?"

Burke glanced around him, and with a glint in his dark eyes said, "From what I can see, this is my ship, therefore my command."

"Then it's the ship's commander who orders me, not the man who loves me?"

Burke grinned and reached out to slip his arm around her waist and tug her toward him, though she proved hesitant. "The man who loves you speaks out of love for you."

"Then the man who loves me will not order me about?" she asked.

"Let me think about that." He laughed and yanked her into his arms, and she braced her hands against his chest. "Just as I thought, the woman I love could never be ordered about. Besides, I admire and respect her courage. She is my equal in all things and I love her with all my heart."

Storm melted against him. "Don't think I'll always be taken by your sweet words."

"Maybe not, but you will be taken by this." He claimed her lips in a searing kiss.

She smiled softly once their lips parted. "Perhaps, Burke, but never forget that *you* were *taken by Storm* from the very beginning."

Next month, don't miss these exciting new love stories only from Avon Books

A Duke of Her Own by Lorraine Heath

An Avon Romantic Treasure

The Duke of Hawkhurst is proud—and really rather, well, poor! To save his estate, Hawkhurst finds an American heiress to marry and hires Lady Louisa Wentworth to teach his betrothed about London society. Trouble is, Louisa is in love with the duke and now Hawkhurst has to make a big decision—before it's too late.

Finding Your Mojo by Stephanie Bond

An Avon Contemporary Romance

Gloria Dalton is beginning to regret her plan to move to Mojo, Louisiana. The town's residents definitely don't want her around. And to make matters worse, she runs into her first love, Zane Riley. Zane doesn't recognize the person Gloria has become, and she's determined to keep it that way. But the best laid plans . . .

The Earl of Her Dreams by Anne Mallory

An Avon Romance

After her father's death, Kate Simon disguises herself as a boy and hides at an inn on the way to London. Of course, she hadn't anticipated sharing her room with Christian Black, Earl of Canley. When circumstances force the two to join forces to uncover a killer, they both discover more than they ever dreamed.

Too Great a Temptation by Alexandra Benedict

An Avon Romance

Damian Westmore, the "Duke of Rogues," has more than earned his nickname. But when tragedy strikes, Damian abandons his carefree lifestyle to seek vengeance. He never expected to encounter Mirabelle Hawkins, the one woman who could thwart his plans . . . and heal his heart.

Avon Romantic Treasures

Unforgettable, enthralling love stories, sparkling with passion and adventure from Romance's bestselling authors

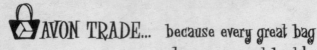